Legacy

Legacy

Book 7 in the Sir John Hawkwood Series

By

Griff Hosker

Legacy

SWORD BOOKS

Published by Sword Books Ltd 2024

Copyright ©Griff Hosker First Edition

The author has asserted their moral right under the Copyright, Designs and Patents Act, 1988, to be identified as the author of this work.
All Rights reserved. No part of this publication may be reproduced, copied, stored in a retrieval system, or transmitted, in any form or by any means, without the prior written consent of the copyright holder, nor be otherwise circulated in any form of binding or cover other than that in which it is published and without a similar condition being imposed on the subsequent purchaser.
A CIP catalogue record for this title is available from the British Library.

Cover by Design for Writers

Contents

Legacy i
Prologue 5
Chapter 1 11
Chapter 2 25
Chapter 3 36
Chapter 4 50
Chapter 5 60
Chapter 6 70
Chapter 7 81
Chapter 8 92
Chapter 9 103
Chapter 10 118
Chapter 11 130
Chapter 12 139
Chapter 13 149
Chapter 14 159
Chapter 15 170
Chapter 16 181
Chapter 17 193
Chapter 18 202
Chapter 19 212
Chapter 20 221
Chapter 21 230
Epilogue 239
Glossary 241
Historical note 244
Other books by Griff Hosker 249

Legacy

Real People Used in The Book

Sir John Hawkwood - Captain of the White Company
Giovanni d'Azzo degli Ubaldini - Italian warrior and condottiero
King Richard II of England
Robert de Vere, Duke of Ireland - an exile from England
King Charles VIth of France
Pope Urban Vth
Pope Urban VIth - Bartolomeo Prignano Cardinal Gil Álvarez
Carrillo de Albornoz - Papal envoy and general
Robert de Genève - Cardinal, papal legate and general, later Pope Clement VIIth, an anti-pope
Alberico da Barbiano - Captain of the Company of St George
Queen Joan (Joanna) I - Queen of Naples, and Countess of Provence and Forcalquier
Louis of Anjou - heir to the throne of Naples
John II - Marquis of Montferrat
Amadeus - Count of Savoy, known as the Green Count
Bernabò Visconti - Lord of Milan and Duke of Milan
Ambrogio Visconti - his son and leader of the Company of Ambrogio
Ettore Visconti - an illegitimate son
Rodolfo Visconti - a legitimate son
Donnina Visconti - an illegitimate daughter and later wife of Sir John Hawkwood
Carlo Visconti - Lord of Cremona, Borgo San Donnino and Parma, Donnina's half-brother
Gian Galeazzo Visconti - son of Galeazzo Visconti and Duke of Milan
Francesco 'Il Vecchio' da Carrara - the leader of the Paduan council
Francesco 'Il Novello' da Carrara - his son
Bartolomeo Cermisone da Parma - the commander of the Paduan infantry
Pellario Griffo - Chamberlain of Pisa
Lutz von Landau - Austro-Hungarian Condottiero
Luca di Totti de'Firidolfi da Panzano - Florentine warrior
Ranuccio Farnese - Florentine leader
Corrado Lando - German condottiero also known as Konrad von Landau and Konrad von Weitengham

Legacy

Giovanni Agnello - Merchant and doge of Pisa
Albert Sterz - one-time captain of the White Company
Annechin Baumgarten - Leader of the Star Company
Astorre Manfredi - condottiero
Sir John Thornbury - English condottiero
Sir Edward de Berkley - English knight and diplomat
Geoffrey Chaucer - poet and diplomat
Ivan Horvat - Ban of Macsó
Facino and Filippino Cane - Veronese nobles
Jacopo dal Verme - Milanese condottiero
John Count of Armagnac
Giovanni Bentivoglio - Head of the Bentivoglio family in Bologna
Jacopo d'Appiano - Head of the Appiano family in Pisa
Alessio Nicolai - Astrologer
Corrado Prospero - Swabian mercenary also known as Konrad Passberg

Sir John's family and retainers
Donnina Visconti - his wife
Ginnetta (Born 1378) - his daughter
Caterina (Born 1379) - his daughter
Anna (Born 1381) - his daughter
Michael - former squire and commander of the Florentine Army
Robin - former captain of archers and trainer of Sir John's bowmen
Zuzzo - Trumpeter and bodyguard
Gianluca - Bodyguard
John Coe - English lance
Peter - English lance
Robert Saxlingham - English lance
John Edingham - English lance
Robert Daring - English axman
John Balzan - English condottiero
John Beltoft - English condottiero
Ned - former member of the White Company
Edgar - former member of the White Company

Legacy

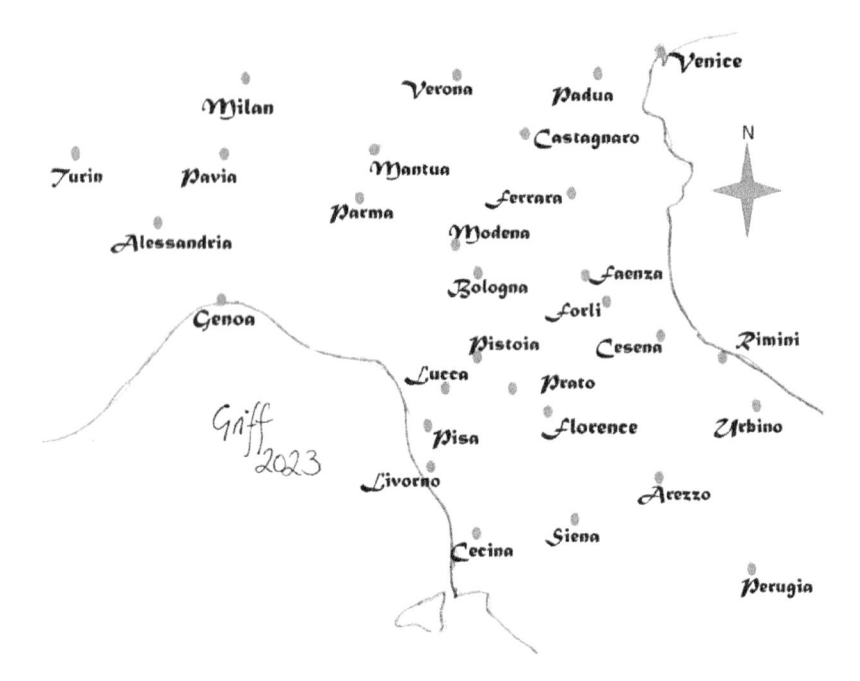

Northern Italy 1379

Prologue

June 1387 Casa Donnina

After the Battle of Castagnaro and the mopping up that always follows such an immense victory, it took some time for me to reach my home, close to Florence. In fact, it was months after the battle when I finally saw my home. There were complications that, for me, took some of the shine from the victory. I arrived at my estate just outside Florence to a welcome from both my family and the city itself. Although I had been fighting for the Paduans and not Florence, I had ended the threat from Verona and Venice. I was a hero in their eyes. They were still wary of allowing me to live in their city. I did not resent their fears for my huge estate, some miles outside of the city, meant I had more privacy and yet I had easy access to both the podestà and the council. I had been paid well and, once more, we were rich. I would still have been fighting for the Paduans but for Il Novello, the son of the head of the da Carrara family. The father, Il Vecchio, held me in high esteem but his son would not take orders or advice. He had almost cost us the battle of Castagnaro. Indeed, in the middle of the battle, I had hurled the marshal's baton, my token of authority, into a ditch. I was too good a soldier to lose the battle and it had been my sudden attack on the Veronese rear that had won the day. One would have thought that might have shown Il Novello that my words were worth listening to. Nothing could be further from the truth. He constantly did the opposite of what I had advised. When he tried to have me imprisoned it was the last straw. Fortunately, his father intervened and I left Padua. It would be the beginning of the end for the Carrara family. Il Novello would lose the war for them. Even worse was that my friend, Giovanni d'Azzo degli Ubaldini, who had been the mercenary who led Padua's armies, had also been dismissed by Il Vecchio and the worst of all events had happened. He had joined Galeazzo Visconti, Donnina's uncle and the man who had ordered the murder of her father. Milan was like its emblem, a snake that was trying to consume the whole of Italy. Giovanni had become Milan's Captain General. He was the only condottiero who could begin to rival me. I wondered if one day I might have to face him in battle. If we did, I was sure that I would win but it would be close. He had fought alongside me for many years and knew my mind better than any. My advantage was that my mind worked so quickly that I could conceive a new plan quickly. It was the reason the Italians called me Giovanni Acuto, Sharp John.

My three daughters, Ginnetta, Caterina and my youngest, Anna, all made a fuss of me when I returned. I was never sure if it was because of the presents I brought them but I was now at the age where such things mattered. Most men my age were grandparents and yet I had a six-year-old daughter and I had not yet given up on siring another son. I had other children but my firstborn, my daughter, lived in England, the wife of William Coggeshall. I had not seen my sons for many years. My eldest, John, was also a soldier whilst Thomas was a man of the cloth. I knew that comrades in arms like Robin and Giovanni had never married. They enjoyed the lives of bachelors. I suppose, when I was younger, I enjoyed the freedom of such a life. Now, in the latter years of my life, I took delight in not only seeing my children but speaking to them. It goes without saying that my greatest joy, when I reached my home, was the embrace of my wife, Donnina.

Donnina was a good mother but she ruled the house with a rod of iron. When the three girls had finished their food, they were dismissed so that we could talk. She ran the business side of the White Company. She had inherited those skills from her father, the legendary Bernabò Visconti. My wife had a financial mind that was like a steel trap. When William Turner was the one to run my finances, I was not as well off as I am with the financial success I enjoy now. When William Turner had first come to me, he had been grateful for the position and worked well. The change had come when he married into a Pisan family. He began to look out for himself more than the company. The company funds were still housed in Pisa but Donnina had taken charge of my personal affairs and since I had married her I had seen a growth in both our lands and our gold.

"So, husband, how do you see the war going now that you have been dismissed?" She was the cleverest woman I had ever known and was very well-read. She understood the politics of Italy better than most men. She listened to visitors when they passed through my lands and she had others who sought information for her. She believed, as her father did, that knowledge was power and she was a source of important knowledge.

I wiped the wine from my lips, "You know the fable of the frog and the mouse?"

She nodded, "I read all of Aesop's fables when I was a child. Is that not the one where a frog offers to give a mouse a ride across the pond and then drowns the mouse?"

"It is but do you remember the end?" She frowned as she tried to recall it. I put her out of her misery, "A hawk descends and eats them both."

"Of course."

"The Lord of Milan is the hawk and he is waiting for his moment to pounce. Verona and Padua are the mouse and the frog and Visconti will have them both, eventually. He will let them squabble a while longer to weaken themselves further and then he will devour them. From Bellinzona in the north to Reggio Emilia he has taken all the cities and counties that opposed him. With Giovanni as his general, he now has a leader to take cities by war instead of treachery. He will continue to do both."

She knew me well, "And will you oppose him? I know that you think well of Giovanni." She knew I shared her opinion of her treacherous uncle.

"What you really ask is, will others hire me to fight against him?" She nodded, "Probably."

"Then we should begin to sell some of the estates that lie beyond Florence's borders. They are hostages to fortune and I would rather have the florins and ducats here." She was right. I had been lucky over the years and acquired many estates. They brought a healthy income, but they were beyond my protection. Visconti could apply pressure to some of the places where I held lands and make life difficult for me.

"There is always England." I brought up the land of my birth for I yearned to return there. I had a daughter and grandchildren who lived there and my son-in-law had been a member of the White Company, albeit briefly. There were also old soldiers, like Dai, who had fought for me. I was getting old and I wanted to see them before death took me.

"England? Why? It is cold and wet. They eat grain like horses and I know it not." Her voice, not to mention her face, told me that she did not want to go.

I laughed, "Well, there is my homeland dismissed in a handful of words. I have estates in England. I have friends in England, not least of which is the king. I served his father and I am well thought of. When Geoffrey Chaucer last visited, he told me that King Richard would happily give me a grand title if I moved back to my home."

She put her hand on mine and, gently squeezing my fingers, shook her head, "Firstly, you have never been interested in titles and secondly, one reason you are so well thought of is because you are here, in Italy. If you moved back to England, then you might be seen as a threat."

She was wise and I nodded, "Perhaps I should retire and then I would not be a threat to anyone."

She laughed, "Retire? You are the greatest of the condottiero and you have no peer."

"But I am old. I have outlived all those alongside whom I fought: Baumgarten, Sterz, Thornbury, Paer, and even your half-brother, Ambrogio Visconti. Giovanni is ten years my junior. I do not feel old but I know that I am and while my faculties may be sharp who knows when my body will simply give up?"

"And if you did retire then I could guarantee that would be the outcome. It is because your body and mind are so active that you continue to be as successful as you are. Enjoy a brief time of peace. Let the other dogs of war wrestle over the bones that are Padua and Verona. Choose your moment and return to the game. Meanwhile, I will try to make your time here at Casa Donnina pleasant. You deserve it."

Legacy

She pulled me to my feet and led me from the dining hall to our bed chamber. I smiled; I had missed her.

Legacy

The campaign against the Malatesta family

Chapter 1

September 1387 Mondavio

I was not unemployed for long and did not enjoy as long with my family as we had hoped. Bartolemo Petrucci sent a messenger who arrived at my home a week after my return. As was usual my wife sat in on the meeting. "Captain Acuto, my master needs to hire your company for the Malatesta family and their allies are attempting to steal land that is ours."

The land ruled by the Petrucci was to the east of Florence while the Malatesta family ruled the east coast. The Petrucci family were allies of Florence and as I was paid a stipend to defend Florence then an offer of work for them did not cause a conflict of interests. I would be doing the work of Florence. The Malatesta family were the enemies of Florence and always had been. The Malatesta family was not as strong as it had once been but they were still a threat to Florence's eastern borderlands.

"And what is the length of the contract?"

"We need you to discourage them, my lord. My master has already hired another Englishman, Giovanni Beltoft and he is headed there now. You will be paid twenty thousand florins."

"For that sum, you may have my company for a month."

"A month? Will that be long enough?"

I smiled, "The Malatesta family is not what it once was. It will be long enough." Men did not argue with Sir John Hawkwood and he nodded.

The contract was agreed and the money would be waiting for me when I reached the Petrucci land. We would meet the others at Mondavio. I still had five hundred lances and the money would stop me from losing men. I summoned my lieutenants. John Coe, John Edingham and Robert Saxlingham were paid more than my other leaders. They were loyal and had proved that they could lead men into battle. Donnina had commented that every Englishman who came to me was called John. She may have been right. My leading lances were all English: John Wanlock, John Vale, Johnny Butler, John Colpepper, Johnny Svim, John Liverpool, John Lye, and John Balzan. David Falcan, Richard Swinfort, Roger Baker, and Richard Norlant were also part of the company. I was never confused but the Italians seemed to think that every English lance was christened Giovanni. John Balzan had brought with him more than a dozen lances and I knew that he had ambitions to be a condottiero. I was under no illusions. Many Englishmen came to work for the White Company as a sort of apprenticeship, to see how the great John Hawkwood did what he did. I took it as a compliment. I was happy to use English lances for they were reliable and I felt I could trust them. The language helped. I could speak other languages but I was most comfortable with English. Germans and Hungarians were untrustworthy and Italians were less predictable. As Giovanni had shown, even Italians whom I thought I could trust might let me down and, when I had been betrayed in the past, then Germans and Hungarians had been the reason.

"We ride on the morrow. It is eighty miles to the land of the Petrucci and I would do it in two days."

John Balzan nodded, he had shown that he wished to be a lieutenant and took charge of the others whenever he could. He had brought many lances when he had come and it made sense, "Then we take no wagons and the men can carry their own supplies. If this is a short campaign then there should not be a problem."

The contract delighted Donnina and I knew that she would have plans for its investment. It would not be a long one and it would be lucrative. She also knew that I could handle a general like Malatesta. I had fought and defeated him before.

As we headed east, I spoke with my leaders about our allies and our opposition. "What do you know of this John Beltoft?"

John Balzan had arrived the most recently. He had not been at Castagnaro, and he had served in other parts of Italy. The world of the condottiere was a close one, "He is a papal mercenary, lord. He is not the best leader but he has a large number of lances." I looked at him. He added, "My men and I served with him briefly." He went on to describe the Englishman.

As he spoke, I began to form a picture of the man and he seemed familiar, "I think he may have fought in the company, many years ago, when we fought the company of St George. If so, he was a solid enough warrior but I would not have thought that he had what it takes to be a condottiero." The John Beltoft I had known was a little dull.

"You may be right, my lord, but he is like a sailor. He knows how to use the wind. He seems to sense when is the right time to, shall we say, change sides?"

He was not to be totally trusted was what John Balzan was telling me. I would bear that in mind.

John Coe said, "And the Malatesta, lord, what of them?"

"I knew the father of Carlos Malatesta, Galeotto. I fought with him and against him as well as his son. He was predictable and I am guessing that his son will be cut from the same cloth. If we can act quickly then a swift defeat will mean we can be back home before the month is out."

We were still riding high on the success that had been Castagnaro. Confidence in an army can make it seem as though it has almost double the true numbers. I rode in my shining armour that was polished so that it looked white. Riding my white horse, Ajax, taken at the Battle of Brentelle, wearing a fine white hat and carrying a baton I knew the effect I had. It was deliberate. When men saw the white horse, shining armour, and white surcoat with the three shells on the inverted chevron then they knew what that meant. I wanted the Malatesta to know that Sir John Hawkwood, Giovanni Acuto, was coming. They would fear me. Gianluca, one of my bodyguards, carried the huge white banner with my coat of arms upon it. It had cost a great deal of money and I rarely carried it into battle. It was too precious and too unwieldy. When we rode into battle Gianluca had a smaller banner that allowed him to defend me and yet still acted as a rallying point for my army.

Mondavio was not the place where the Petrucci family lived. It was a village with a small castle. Most lords who hired a condottiero company did not want them where they lived. An army of condottieri could turn on their employers in a flash. It had happened before. Mondavio was large enough to feed us and close enough to Malatesta land to enable us to engage them and keep their homes safe. We were to be paid well and I did not mind.

The emissary who had commissioned the contract was waiting for us at Mondavio. He had with him the florins we would be paid and, almost as useful, twenty light horsemen from the region. They were young and keen to fight the oppressor. I could use them as scouts and I would not have to pay them.

I sent them out immediately to find Carlos Malatesta. If he intended to ravage the land of the Petrucci family then he would need a large army and it could not be easily hidden. I intended to move only when I knew where they were and when we did move it would be like lightning. My company was largely mounted. I had left my infantrymen at Casa Donnina.

John Beltoft arrived the next day and I recognised him. His armour was better and his horse was now an expensive warhorse. He still had the lean look of a predator and that was good. I hoped that his skills had been sharpened since we had last fought together and that he would not be treacherous. If he was then he would rue the day for Giovanni Acuto punished such acts.

I was happy when he readily deferred to me. He gave a half bow. It made life easier. Il Novello had constantly questioned my decisions and had tried to usurp me at the Battle of Castagnaro. It had almost cost us the day. John Beltoft was more than happy for me to make the decisions even though his company outnumbered mine. It showed he was clever. He served with me and as I normally won he would guarantee victory and his reputation would be enhanced. He would find more work and with every victory, a condottiero was able to demand a greater payment. Neither of us asked the other what our fees had been. Such questions always resulted in dissent. If we were paid the same then I would be insulted and if he was paid less, which was highly likely, then he would be insulted. In such matters, ignorance was bliss.

"So, Sir John, what is the plan?"

"Where is the enemy?"

"He has raided and taken Ponte Metauro." I looked at the map and saw that it was on the coast just twelve miles away. I did not want to risk a battle where the enemy could use ships to aid them. I needed them to be off balance. I wanted to make them move. Rimini and Ravenna were to the north. As soon as I knew where the enemy soldiers were to be found then my plans formulated quickly in my mind.

"My plan is to make Carlos Malatesta move in a direction he does not want to." I pointed at the map and I jabbed my finger at Rimini. "That is their stronghold and the one place we need him to defend. San Marino is papal but Ravenna is now ruled by a member of the da Polenta family, Guido da Polenta I believe, and they are allies of the Malatesta. I will let it be known that I intend to raid Ravenna and, perhaps, San Marino. They will have to leave Ponte Metauro and stop us." I smiled, "It is the sort of thing Giovanni Acuto would do. After all, I am a warlord and a bandit, am I not?" John Beltoft grinned. He knew my reputation as well as any. "Carlos Malatesta will try to get ahead of me. How many archers do you have?"

"Just fifty. Most English archers choose to follow you, Sir John."

"I have one hundred. It is not enough but it never is. I will detach them and send them north. Ned of Mansfield is a good archer. Sir Robin trained him well. He will find somewhere to ambush them and with our two companies hard on his heels he will be trapped."

I could see the condottiero was not convinced, "There are many ifs, buts and maybes there, Sir John."

Sometimes I felt like a teacher in school. I explained slowly, "Rimini is a powerful fortress?" He nodded. "Do we have the men to force the gates?"

"No, Sir John, not without heavy loss of men."

"Then we need to draw him away from the lands of the Petrucci family. That must be north. We threaten his heartland. He will not know that we have no intention of taking his town. If he does not take the bait and head north, he will continue to raid the Petrucci lands and we will be forced to shift him from a defensive position. My strategy will do two things, one it will give me time to come up with another strategy and two, it will keep Petrucci land safe. That is why we are here are we not?"

"You are happy not to give battle?"

"I want a battle but on my terms, and I am a patient man." In truth, I was not but I was convinced that my plan would work and that Carlos Malatesta would be like his father and bold enough to try to rid his land of condottiere.

Legacy

The scouts returned that day and reported, as I had expected, that the enemy were camped around Rimini but ready to march. It was evening and I said to John Beltoft, "Let us find the best tavern in the village and dine."

It was in the square and there was but one. In truth, it was the house of a widow who had taken advantage of our arrival and placed some barrels and tree stumps outside. She and her daughters brought us wine. It was poor wine and we were overcharged but I did not care. Being outside we had an audience. The village was not used to such arrivals and Giovanni Acuto had a reputation. As I had expected our arrival drew a large crowd and I was all smiles. I pretended to drink too much and became louder and louder. John Beltoft became concerned but he had not seen the smiles on the faces of my two bodyguards who knew my capacity for drink. I winked as I said, loudly and in a somewhat slurred manner, "So tomorrow, my friend, we will ride and raid the lands around Ravenna. If the Malatesta are too afeard to fight then we shall make money somehow, eh? We will make money from the Malatesta family. Let him enjoy what he has taken. We can enjoy victory for there will be no army to oppose us."

It was only when we were back at our camp and I had shed my drunken act that I explained what I had done. "There will be spies in the village. Even now, they will be riding as hard as they can for Rimini. Send your captain of archers to me."

"Yes, Sir John."

"Gianluca, find Captain Ned." When Ned and Beltoft's captain arrived, I said, "I want you to leave before dawn and ride north. I need somewhere between here and Ravenna where you can ambush the Malatestan army."

Will, Beltoft's captain frowned, "But how..."

Ned had served me since well before Robin had left. He was an older archer but he knew my mind. He was not Robin but he was as close to my Yorkshire friend as I had found yet. He would make a good captain of archers. He grinned, "Leave that to me, Sir John. I will explain to this youngster what must be done. You wish us to hold them until you can close the back door?"

"Exactly. Do not risk either your horses or your men. The flights from one hundred and fifty archers should hurt them and, at the very least, make them dismount and take shelter."

"Then a village would be best. Give them the illusion of safety. I will send a rider back to you when we have found such a place. If you would give me a squire…"

"Better, I will give you a lance. Robert."

Robert Saxlingham came over, "My lord?"

"Go with Ned and when he finds a place to ambush then ride back and tell me."

"My lord." He turned to fetch his horse.

"When we attack, you shall hear Zuzzo's horn. That will be the signal for you to launch your arrows."

"I will await the call. Come, my young friend, let me explain how Sir John works."

Left with John Beltoft the condottiero shook his head, "When I served with you, you made the task seem easy and yet now, as a condottiero myself I cannot fathom how you do what you do."

"I have seen well over sixty summers and for more than forty-odd I have been a warrior. Every battle I have fought has added to what is in here," I tapped my head. "God gave me skill and I have honed it."

We began to move as soon as it was dawn. My archers had left already and we had to move quickly but not so quickly as to get ahead of what I assumed would be the Malatesta response to my ruse. The enemy would try to reach their city and make an ambush. I used four of the Petrucci riders to keep an eye on the enemy. I wore not my hat but my helmet. We were going to war. The large banner was furled and in the wagon and I was flanked by my two bodyguards who were plated and helmed. We had further to ride than the Malatesta troops. However, I gambled on a slower start from the Malatesta troops. September was a hot month in Italy and we stopped whenever we passed water. We were all mounted and our horses were as valuable to us as a sword or a lance.

The young warriors from the area were still my scouts and it was they who reported that the Malatesta army was lumbering up the road. They had taken the bait. Robert appeared from nowhere and told us that there was a small village called Cattolica where Ned and the archers waited.

"It is perfect, my lord. There is no castle and it is a big place. There are houses we can use and the horses will be hidden. There are no soldiers there. We arrived in the dark and secured the place without anyone leaving."

"Excellent." Our scouts were still in contact with the rear of the enemy and we kept pace with them without letting them know where we were. It was easy. Their baggage, complete with their plunder was not guarded by soldiers. The carters thought that we were ahead of them.

We were just a couple of miles from the ambush when the scouts said that we were closing with the baggage train of the Malatesta soldiers. The young men were keen to attack. The village was a resting place on the pilgrim path from Bologna to Ancona and, ultimately, Rome. Malatesta must have left it untouched on his raid south for that reason. Ned would not bother with such niceties.

"You have done well but now is not the time to attack. Stay close to my lances and you will see the beauty of my trap. Watch and learn my young hotheads." My words were also aimed at John Beltoft who rode next to me. "We will let them get a mile closer to our archers before we attack." Beltoft looked as though he was going to ask a question. I knew the question and gave him the answer. "This column of men is almost two miles long. We need the head of it to be in the village before we attack." He nodded his understanding.

I gave my lieutenants their orders. Not all of my men would remain mounted. The men at arms would charge with lances and spears but the squires and the spearmen would dismount. It was a tactic I had used before. If the attack by our horsemen failed then there was a defensive wall of spears behind which they could shelter.

"Captain Beltoft, when I have Zuzzo sound the charge then we shall lead our men at arms to attack the rear of the enemy. Your squires and other warriors will dismount and form a defensive line. We make a hedgehog through which only our friends can pass."

"Yes, my lord. Antonio, you heard Sir John, pass the word."

Legacy

I was almost as eager as the warriors from Mondavio but I knew that I had to be patient. I would not use a lance but I would follow the leading lances into battle. I needed to use my eyes to react to any changes I saw ahead. It had won me the Battle of Castagnaro.

I saw the village spreading towards the sea. It was almost a town. There was no castle and that would be why Ned had chosen it. I saw the metal snake of the Malatestan army as it entered the village and when I saw what looked like a flock of starlings taking to the air, I knew that Ned had launched his attack. They were not birds but goose-fletched arrows, the harbingers of death. He had taken matters into his own hands. He knew that he could not allow the enemy to pass beyond his arrows. I had miscalculated how long the enemy army was.

"Zuzzo, sound the horn. Form lines." The horn would tell Ned that we were coming and would alarm our enemies.

The horn sounded and it was like a well-oiled trebuchet as the squires and spearmen calmly dismounted. Even as I was walking Ajax to take a position behind Richard Swinfort, Roger Baker, and Richard Norlant, the horses of those who would be dismounted were being led to the rear. The land was only wide enough for forty men and as soon as I saw the front two ranks were complete, I said, "Zuzzo, sound the charge!"

The men at arms who charged were all plated and heavy. The charge began at a walk. I saw the men at the rear of the Malatestan army turn in fear. They were the men with the baggage. They were carters and had no armour. They were not expecting to fight. Malatesta had not even bothered with a strong rearguard. The soldiers at the rear had heard the horn sound twice and now they could not only hear but feel the hooves of our horses as they pounded the ground. As we came to the canter, I saw men fleeing before us. The ones at the rear of the column had the baggage but without armour were swept away like the dust before a broom. At best, they wore a jack and a helmet. None would stand a chance against horsemen of any kind. Even though they fled I saw some were skewered by the leading lances. By the time we were at full speed, we were close to men who wore helmets and, in some cases mail. They had begun to turn but it did not matter for the speed of the horses, the thrusting of the spears and the sharpened tips meant that the lances tore through mail links as though they were not there. The crash of the collision and the screams of those struck filled the air. From ahead I heard the cries of men as they were hit by arrows from archers using the cover of the village. The narrow streets confined them and down the main thoroughfare my men at arms were coming. Soldiers like an exit, an escape route and there appeared to be none.

It was at that moment that I heard a horn and it was not Zuzzo. Malatesta had ordered the retreat. The enemy soldiers were fleeing north. They chose the line of least resistance and headed towards Rimini and the safety of their walls. The arrows still showered them as they ran. I recognised the banner of Carlos Malatesta as he led the flight. I halted and said to John Beltoft, "Continue the pursuit. Keep your lances in their backs. The horses and weapons we take will be useful."

"Yes, Sir John, a great victory."

I smiled, "An easy one and those I will take every day of the week." The villagers had barred themselves in the churches when my archers had arrived while others had stayed within their homes and hoped that they would be overlooked. When my bodyguards reached the centre, we walked into what seemed like a deserted settlement. "Gianluca, fetch the rest of the men. Let us see what this place has to offer."

"Yes, Sir John."

"Zuzzo, summon the archers."

I dismounted in the square. It was devoid of the living but the arrows in the many bodies told me to whom I owed this victory, my archers. The lances had not been asked to do too much. Chasing fleeing men was an easy task with little risk to the rider. My archers walked towards me. It was when I saw the bodies draped over the backs of horses that I realised the price we had paid. To my mind, my archers were the most valuable part of my army and English archers were hard to come by. There were ten bodies and when I saw Peter of Wye leading one and recognised the archer I knew that the price had been too high. Ned of Mansfield was dead. Robin had been my captain of archers and Ned had shown himself to have the potential to be as good. Now

I would never know. It soured what had been, up to that moment, an almost perfect victory.

Before the lances had returned, we had dug graves in the small churchyard and buried my men. They deserved the honour. I let the archers sack the village. We were condottiere and did not worry that pilgrims used this place to rest. What little there was, the archers could have; they deserved the reward. By the time my weary lances returned it was dark and we commandeered houses. It was too late to return to Mondavio and we would spend the night under rooves.

It was John Balzan who came to fetch me. I had eaten a passable stew and consumed a good half a jug of wine and I was ready for bed. "Sir John."

"What is it, John? I need a piss and then my bed."

"There is a visitor to see you."

Zuzzo and Gianluca had heard his words and they rose. "Where?"

"He is at the edge of the village. I was checking that the sentries were vigilant. It is one that you know."

He said no more but as John Beltoft and his lieutenants were within earshot I understood. Zuzzo and Gianluca took no chances and they drew their swords when we saw the hooded figure standing in the stable at the end of the village. As the man slipped his hood down to reveal his face I heard a familiar voice, "Is that any way to greet an old friend, Sir John?"

I smiled when I saw that it was Giovanni d'Azzo degli Ubaldini, "Giovanni, what are you doing here?" He glanced at John Balzan and I said, "You three wait without." I could trust my old friend and my bodyguards would not be needed. I knew that he had something secret to impart, hence his clandestine arrival. Left alone I said, "Well? What brings Galeazzo Visconti's man to see me?"

"I am here doing as you are doing although, clearly, not as successfully. I took some castles from the Malatesta family. They were not so keen to buy them back." He smiled, "Perhaps now they will do so."

"I wondered why my ruse to lure them north worked so well. They feared that we were in collusion. We will only stay a few more days, old friend. As soon as Malatesta sues for peace and buys us off then we shall leave."

"I need to act quickly. I will not make as much as I had hoped but perhaps I can keep together more of my company. They are deserting me." He sighed, "Visconti and I have parted company. He forgot to pay me or, perhaps, it was deliberate. If I am here then I cannot defend Padua and he still seeks that particular pearl."

A condottiero who was losing men would not last long, "Men who are not paid will do that. And where will you go then?"

"I think there may be work north of here. Pandolfo Malatesta and Bartolomeo da Pietramala have contacted me."

"Pandolfo Malatesta?"

"He has fallen out with his family."

"My work here will be finished soon and I might join you."

He spoke quickly and his answer told me that he did not want me with him, "The contract is not a big one. It is too small for you."

My friend was being evasive and less than truthful. I did not need the contract but I was interested, "When you are not at war come and visit. Donnina would love to see you and the girls ask after you."

He held out his hand, "Then when this is done and I have a little time of peace, I shall join you there." He clasped my arm. He slipped his hood up and disappeared. My three men had remained out of earshot but had drawn weapons and were close enough to protect me if I needed them.

"What did he want, Sir John?"

"I don't know, Zuzzo, but my friend has changed and I shall be wary of him in future." I added, as we left, "Now I know, at least, why Visconti hired him. It was to draw him and, perhaps us, away from Padua. If Hawkwood and the White Company are in Rimini then they cannot stop his advances in the north."

Emissaries came from Carlos Malatesta a couple of days later. He wanted to rid his land of condottiere. I was flattered that he chose not to fight us but to buy me off. We were paid ten thousand florins to leave his land. I said to the emissary, as I accepted the gold, "If we are hired again by the Petrucci family, we will return. Your master knows that?"

"We have taught the Petrucci family enough of a lesson. My master will now deal with the other condottiere." Giovanni would have to fight. Carlos Malatesta had been defeated by Hawkwood but my friend was another matter. I had a full company and he did not.

We left four days later. We had horses, plate and weapons taken from the dead. We had stripped the food from the village and we headed back to Casa Donnina. Captain Beltoft said that he had another contract in the Ovieto area on the other side of the Apennines. I did not believe him but it was far enough from Florence for me not to worry too much. We reached my home at the end of September. I sent word to Robin at Montecchio Vesponi that I needed archers to be replaced and I paid my men. Some left. It was nothing to do with our work but some men had goals and aims that were different to mine. Many had made enough in my service to head back to their homeland and retire. Some might return in the future and others I would never see again. Such was the world of the condottiere.

Legacy

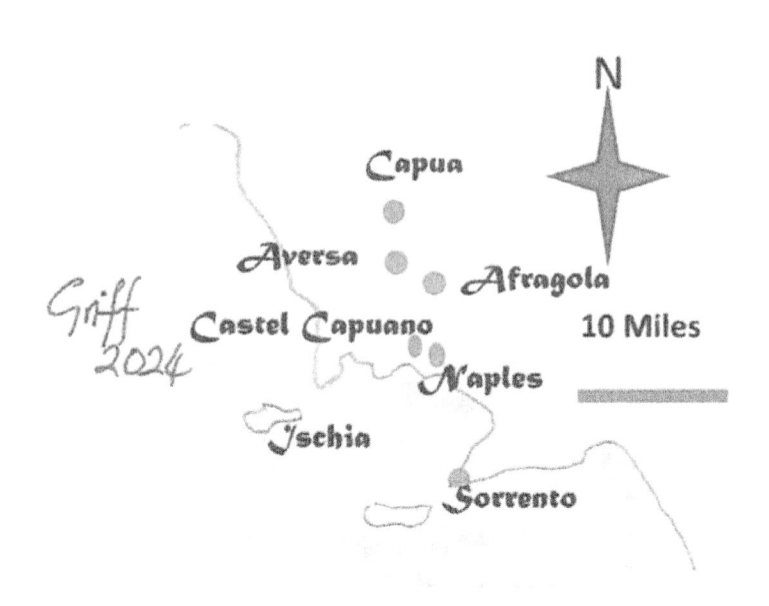

Naples 1388

Chapter 2

January 1388 Siena and Naples

We returned home richer and I was in a better position to plan for the future. I had seen my new men and knew their worth. They had all impressed me. I still had a problem with my captain of archers and I would have to find a solution soon. Ned was a serious loss. Robin now enjoyed a pleasant life pleasuring women and training archers at my estate in Perugia, Montecchio Vesponi. The plate, mail, helmets, and horses we had taken meant that we were able to equip more of the men at arms and older squires who were less well protected in the time we had at home.

Before the year was out, we were given another contract albeit a short one. Bernardo della Sala was an old French bandit. He had left France where he was a wanted man and had come to Northern Italy. He rarely worked for direct pay but he robbed and raided. He even took hostages for ransom. This was not unusual but the number of captives he had taken was high. He had defeated John Beltoft at Viterbo and then, after heading north, raided Padua. The Sienese feared he might raid them on his way to further raids. I was offered four thousand florins to deter him. For me, it was an easy contract to accept. I could have defeated him with my archers alone but I counted on my reputation. He might have defeated John Beltoft but I was a different matter. As soon as I barred his way and he saw my white standard and surcoat, he took a different route to reach Perugia, his chosen target. I steered him towards the land of the Malatesta. We followed him through the mountains and when he could no longer cause harm in Siena we halted. The chase ended close to my estate and afforded me the chance to visit Robin at Montecchio Vesponi. Whilst there, I told him of my need for more archers and a captain. He said that he would find me some. Robin was a perfectionist. He wanted to test every archer to his breaking point before he sent them to me. I could wait for we had not needed the archers to thwart the French condottiero.

By Christmas, I was home once more. My men were a little richer and we had not been required to draw a sword. We had used not a single arrow. Of course, that meant no plunder but you could not have everything. We enjoyed a quiet Christmas. The men sought the company of women and frequented the taverns and inns that were close to my home. Since I had been in residence more of them had sprung up close to the place where I trained warriors. They were eager to make money.

    I was somewhat surprised when, at the start of January, the representatives of two old comrades and condottiero, Alberico da Barbiano and Otto of Brunswick, asked me to join them in Naples where the war between two French families was still ongoing. The representatives were with a cardinal, for the pay for this contract would be coming from Rome. The situation there was a complex one. The Queen of Naples had promised the crown to Louis of Anjou before Charles of Durazzo had her murdered. Both Charles and Louis were Frenchmen and they wrestled for control of the rich kingdom of Naples. I knew why Otto would be fighting against the Angevin. His wife, who had been the Queen of Naples, had been murdered on the orders, it was said, of Charles of Durazzo. Her named heir had claimed the throne and Otto was not happy about that. My steward Guccio brought them into my hall and Donnina and I sat to speak with them. I had fought in Naples before. I listened to their arguments and offers of florins. I only accepted when I learned that the forces we would be facing were those of the anti-pope. Pope Clement was an old enemy of mine. As Robert of Geneva, he had ordered the massacre of Cesena and many men blamed me for what he had ordered. I would also be serving the rightful pope, Urban VIth and that could do me no harm. In the past, I had been excommunicated. That meant nothing to a young warrior but an old man who knew that he might soon be meeting his maker was another matter. I knew that Otto of Brunswick had more reason than most to wish to fight Louis of Anjou for he felt that he had the right to be king having been married to the queen. Alberico da Barbiano had lands in Puglia. It was in his interests to have some control over who ruled in Naples. I would be the professional who would command them both.

    The contract was a simple one. We were to relieve the siege of Castel Capuano. It was not our usual work but I was quite happy to earn the ten thousand florins and to spite my old adversary. Once more I was the senior condottiero and the representatives of the other two told me that the condottieri were happy to follow my banner. I knew Alberico da Barbiano for we had served together before and like John Beltoft, I had mentored him. My company and I had fought both for and against Charles of Durazzo. I did not like the man and I had parted with him on bad terms when he failed to pay me. I made sure, before he left, that the cardinal knew we expected prompt payment. Sometimes popes tried to save their gold. As a young condottiero that had happened in France. Then I had raided papal lands until I was paid. Such things are remembered.

As I headed south with my men, I reflected that the days of serving the real pope had been lucrative ones. The last papal contract had been for forty thousand florins. Of course, I was not paid that whole amount. The papacy was not averse to finding reasons not to pay mercenaries but now I led my company to war for ten thousand florins and I would ensure we had the coins before we drew our swords.

I took the contract because it was winter and my men would be paid for six months but I was less than happy with the arrangements. Otto of Brunswick and Alberico da Barbiano had both been expelled from Naples by Louis de Montjoie. He was not to be underestimated for although he was a condottiero he had close connections with the would-be King of Naples, Louis of Anjou. He would fight without pay for his countryman. This was a fight between Angevin Frenchmen. Brunswick and da Barbiano were also fighting for pride. They had been hired by the Prince of Durazzo, Charles of Naples, and given positions and titles in the Neapolitan government. That they had been expelled so easily gave me no confidence at all in the companies that they led. My White Company were the only men I could truly trust and rely upon.

It was a long ride to Capua. This was another reason I did not relish a Neapolitan contract. It was far from home. If it had not been winter then, lucrative contract or not, I would have not taken it. Summer in Naples was like fighting in a furnace. The contract was until May. We would be able to return to our home before the days became unbearably hot.

Alberico da Barbiano and Otto Brunswick were at Capua and licking their wounds when I arrived. I wasted no time in pleasantries and took charge. "So, how many men do I lead?"

"You, Sir John?"

"Your representatives told me that was acceptable. Were they misleading me?" I allowed an uncomfortable silence to descend before I continued, "Let me be blunt, Otto, you have been ousted from Naples. Are you able to defeat Louis de Montjoie without my help?"

"We were unlucky, that is all." He was evasive but his shamefaced look told me all that I needed to know.

"Then let us hope that I bring you more luck. Give me an answer. How many men do I lead?"

They were cowed. "With the men you bring, we have four thousand horsemen and five hundred infantrymen." Alberico pointed to the west and the island of Ischia, "We have some galleys in the harbour at Ischia. De Montjoie has his fleet in Naples itself."

"And our employers are besieged in Castel Capuano?"

This time Alberico tried to take control of the conversation, "The contract you have been given, Sir John, is paid for by the pope. Your pay is safe."

"Alberico, you of all people should know that promises of gold from the pope are just that, promises. I shall send to Rome to ensure that we are paid promptly. This vicious family fight will still be going on long after you and I are in our tombs. Is Louis de Montjoie with those besieging Castel Capuano?"

"No, he is in Naples. The men who surround the castle are happy to play a waiting game."

"Good, then we shall show them that the Englishmen we have brought are stronger than the ones they chased north."

"Sir John, you insult us."

"Alberico, you have been a condottiero for a long time, not as long as me but long enough to know the way the wind blows. Was Naples your retirement?" He flushed and I knew it was true. "My men and I are still lean and hungry. We have come from Rimini and Castagnaro where we were victorious. Do you dispute my words?"

"No, but we have our honour."

I laughed, "We are condottieri and honour does not enter into it. We fight for pay and not glory or strange ideals of chivalry. I will ride to view the enemy dispositions while my emissary rides to Rome." I smiled, "We will attack when we are paid. Until then we take food from this land so that those who besiege it are hungry too. And who commands the defenders of Castel Capuano?"

"Ugolino dalle Grotte." I knew him. He was also a condottiero and not to be underestimated.

I sent John Edingham and Robert Saxlingham along with ten men at arms to Rome for the payment and went with just my bodyguards and lieutenants to view the enemy. We were able to view the castle which guarded the western side of Naples from a safe distance. We were beyond the range of the besiegers' crossbows. The castle was Norman in construction and was part of the city walls of Naples. The city side was held by the enemy and I could do nothing to shift them but on the Capua side, they had dug entrenchments and were making mines to get closer to the walls. Their progress was not impressive. I concurred with the two men who had been ousted from Naples. They were hoping to starve out the defenders.

We sat on our horses overlooking the castle and bay. Vesuvius, the ancient volcano dominated this land and rose behind us. John Coe said, "I can see how we can shift those men to the northwest of the castle but Naples itself would need a fleet."

"There are ships but I am not as confident fighting on water as I am on land. However, an attack from land and sea might well succeed. I have seen enough. We will return to Capua and await the news from Rome. If there is no pay forthcoming then we shall march home."

"Without pay, my lord?"

I smiled, "John, to reach home we have to pass through the Papal States. If the pope does not pay us for the contract directly then we will take it indirectly."

Neither Brunswick nor Barbiano were happy at the delay. "The enemy grows stronger and those inside the castle grow weaker."

"I have a plan. Alberico, I need you to take command of the fleet and be ready to launch an attack on the port. Otto, we will attack those besieging the castle at the same time. This will take time so let us proceed cautiously. If the pope is determined to restore Charles to the throne then he will pay promptly."

It took almost two weeks for John Edingham and Robert Saxlingham and the men at arms to return. When they did there was not only the welcome payment of florins but there was also a letter from Donnina. I read it and called a meeting of my men. I was smiling as I held up the letter and announced, "This is from my wife. We have another commission. John Balzan, take one hundred lances and ride to Siena. The Pisans are being threatened and William Turner has secured us a contract of four thousand florins to end the threat."

John nodded and asked, "And who leads the threat?"

I smiled, "Our former comrade in arms, John Beltoft. It seems he was less than honest about his intentions when he left us at Cattolica. One hundred lances and the attendant squires, spears and archers should end the threat."

Roger Baker said, "That depletes our numbers, my lord."

Sometimes my arrogance gets the better of me and that day was one. "We use the men of Brunswick and Barbiano. Our soldiers will be the core of the army but we let them bear the brunt of the fighting."

John Balzan left to choose his men. I knew he would pick the best but as I still retained all my archers, I was content. John had his own archers whom he had brought from England. They were as loyal to him as mine were to me. Zuzzo asked, as my food was fetched, "And how is Lady Donnina?"

The bodyguards were like friends and I could speak with them. I smiled, "I am to be a father once more. My seed is strong and this time I hope for a son. I love my daughters, but a son would be a gift from God."

They were genuinely pleased for me and when the word spread around the White Company that John Hawkwood was to be a father again, even though he was an old man, it put a spring in their step and there was more purpose to my men than the rest of the army.

Legacy

I organised my men and we moved our camp to Aversa. With Barbiano and his men with the fleet, we had just two thousand lances. I deemed it enough. Otto Brunswick knew the area and I allowed him to choose the site for the camp. I made sure that my men were together and that we made our camp defensive in nature. We dug a ditch around it and embedded stakes. The people of Aversa had endured mercenaries and warlords for many years. Two of their leaders had been murdered and they simply wanted us to be gone. What food there was we had to take with us and so we camped. Otto of Brunswick and the bulk of the army felt that they had a right to be fed and housed. They commandeered houses and did not bother with a camp.

Louis de Montjoie had one advantage over me, he believed in the cause of Louis of Anjou. He wanted to be rid of us. I did not care who ruled Naples. He came early one morning with less than fifteen hundred lances to attack us. The first I knew was when my horns sounded. My defences and my sentries meant that we were not taken by surprise. When I heard the alarm and the clash of weapons, I was out of my tent as quickly as most of my men. I donned just a mail hauberk and grabbed my sword. Robert Saxlingham was plated and armed. He had been the captain of the night guard. He ran to me, "Sir John, there are enemy soldiers attacking us. They are French and Italian. The archers are holding them but see," he pointed. I could see that Otto of Brunswick and his men were being slaughtered as they poured from the houses. There were no defences there. The men of Aversa were joining with de Montjoie and his men. My island of men would soon become surrounded. While our total force outnumbered de Montjoie, the White Company did not. Robert's words echoed my thoughts, "We must flee, my lord."

Zuzzo and Gianluca had brought my plate and even as they spoke, they were dressing me as well as my horse, "He is right, Sir John. Once the enemy brings crossbows up then our archers will start to fall."

I nodded. He was right, as was Robert. My archers were too valuable to lose and this battle which had just begun was lost already. "Sound the retreat but I want an orderly one. We fall back to Capua. There, at least, we have support." I was soon ready to mount and I clambered onto the back of Ajax. My bodyguards and lieutenants flanked me and my archers unleashed an arrow storm on the Neapolitans who, having defeated the rest of our army turned their attention to us. If they thought we would be as easy a piece of meat to digest we would prove them wrong.

Raising my sword I said, "Zuzzo, sound the charge!" We would not charge in a line but a column, almost a wedge and my protectors would be the diamond that tipped the charge.

We rode towards men who thought they had won already. What they failed to realise was that our horses were fresh and they had endured a night march and a charge. John Coe and John Edingham, along with Robert Saxlingham, had men at arms wielding lances and they cleared a path, unhorsing the men of de Montjoie. I slashed and hacked at the men on foot who raced to unhorse Giovanni Acuto. My armour was expensive and that morning proved its worth. I did not deflect every spear that came at me but I stopped enough and my armour did the rest. The most serious threat was to Ajax but he had a mail coat too. Zuzzo and Gianluca were in their element in such a fight. Both were more like street fighters than knights and none survived their blows. By the time the sun had fully risen and bathed the scene in light, we were north of Aversa and the enemy had ceased to follow. I reined in. My white surcoat and shining mail were bespattered with blood and gore but I was whole. I was an old man yet I had fought the same way as I had at Poitiers. There was life in the old dog yet.

There were losses. Ten archers had died and we had lost fifteen men at arms. I was angry for I had relied too heavily on Otto of Brunswick. I would not do so again. His need for comfort had cost us dear.

We spent a week recuperating. Otto of Brunswick's men and those of Barbiano who were not with the fleet trickled in over those seven days. By the time the survivors had arrived, we discovered that we had lost one hundred mailed men as well as my ten archers and fifteen men at arms. It was too high a cost. I summoned Alberico from his ship and held a meeting with the two captains. "We will make our assault at the start of April. Our contract runs out in May and thanks to the disaster that was Aversa, this is our only opportunity to end this campaign successfully. We time our attacks to be at the same time. Alberico, your men on the ships have not been hurt yet. You destroy their ships and then land to attack the defences on the port side. Otto, you will lead your men to attack the besiegers on the west of the castle. My men will be in reserve. I intend to exploit the gaps you create." If either thought to argue, my tone left them in no doubt that I would not brook such arguments. "We take a leaf from de Montjoie's book and attack at dawn on the morning of April the 2nd."

That left us just three days. I know that I should have made it a shorter timescale, but Alberico had to get to his ships and move them into a position to launch their assault. Every day would see the defenders of the castle weakening. If the castle fell then all was lost and the contract would be over no matter what the other two condottiero or the pope thought. We left our camp on the night of the first and headed towards Aversa. I sent twenty lances to secure the town which we knew supported the enemy. I used my men as I wanted it done properly. We passed through the town as dawn was breaking. This time the enemy would have no warning of our attack. Any of the townsfolk who came to their doors were told that if they emerged, they would die. They barred their doors. The sea, to the west, was still in darkness but I had to hope that Alberico was on station and edging his way into the harbour. Surprise was everything. Before we could begin our attack, we needed de Montjoie and his men's attention on the sea. That was our only hope of success.

The sudden flaring of flames in the half-gloom before dawn was the sign that Alberico had begun his attack. The horns we heard in both Naples and from the besiegers were reassuring. I had told Otto that he was not to use his own horns when he attacked. Silence would allow him to get closer. It was a vain hope for moments later and to my dismay and disappointment he had his trumpets sounded. Even as the sunlight burst above Vesuvius, the enemy soldiers were turning to prepare spears to meet Otto's men. He was making, as I had ordered, an attack on foot. I deemed it had the greatest chance of success. There was no open plain over which his horses could gallop.

"Archers! Support the attack."

Legacy

I would not commit my lances until I was convinced that we had a breakthrough, but my archers could still hurt those besieging the castle. I was able to see, as light flooded the scene, that Otto's men were engaged closely with the besiegers. Despite his mistake, I wondered if he might succeed. He was a brave enough leader and I saw him at the fore of his men trying to make the enemy fall back. When I saw men flooding from the castle to help him, I ordered my lances into two wedges. I would wait for the right moment and use the extra weight of my superior soldiers to win the day. The horn of de Montjoie ended that hope. He charged into the flank of Otto and his men. Almost as soon as the first blades had slashed and hacked into their sides, Otto's men broke.

"Richard, have the men mounted. Archers, one last flight and then retire to your horses."

Otto's horns sounded the retreat. Half of his men had already fled by the time the horn sounded and the retreat was in danger of becoming a rout. As my archers mounted their horses I shouted, "Zuzzo, sound the charge!" The only thing that could stop Otto and his men from being massacred would be if I could hurt de Montjoie and his men. Our advantage, a slim one at best, was that we were mounted and de Montjoie's men were on foot. I confess that some of Otto's tardier men were trampled in our charge but my charge saved the bulk of Otto's men. I was in the third rank where I could see the action better and time our own retreat. My men were well disciplined and hit the enemy as one. Some lances cracked and broke but every tip found flesh. The front rank wheeled and the second rank did the same, thrusting and stabbing in as professional a manner as I had ever seen. By the time I reached the enemy soldiers, they had halted and my men rode over the bodies of those that had been already slain.

"Zuzzo, sound the retreat." I spied my opposite number. Like me, he was mounted. I took off my hat and swept it in an elaborate salute. He raised his sword in response. We were both good condottieri. I had not beaten him but the reverses I had suffered were not of my doing. They were Otto of Brunswick's mistakes.

Alberico had managed to destroy most of the enemy ships but he had not enough men to force the walls. He retreated and

Legacy

joined Otto and me at Capua. There was little point in berating Otto for the mistake that had cost us the battle. For one thing, it was in the past and for another, we had just three weeks of our contract left. The army needed reinforcements and would not be in a position to fight another battle until June at the earliest. The men who would fight at Naples in the summer would soon arrive but they would not be the White Company. The Pope would hire other men. At the end of May, we mounted our horses and left a despondent pair of condottieri wondering what might have been.

Chapter 3

June 1388 Ducato

Donnina was a petite woman and when she was pregnant it showed sooner than with other women. Even without the letter she had sent, I would have known that she was with child. She looked healthy and that pleased me. Our embrace was a long one and she whispered in my ear, "I am glad that you are home and whole."

"And I am pleased that you are well." I put my hand on her bump and she smiled.

"This one feels like a boy, my love. Perhaps I will give you an heir." I had two sons but they were estranged from me, I had done what I could for them while they were young but they were not my heirs. My next son would be my heir.

I was just happy that I was home and that we had not suffered too much. Beltoft had retreated as soon as John Balzan and the White Company appeared and William Turner had paid us promptly. Of course, he had made gold by simply sitting in Pisa. No matter what happened to soldiers, agents always profited. He was our agent and a necessary expense. In one way it was why I had taken the Neapolitan contract. There was no fee for William Turner. With no contracts in the offing, I was able to rest and enjoy my home and good food for a short time. I grew a little fatter but I was not idle, far from it. Donnina, despite being pregnant, and I rarely rested. We sold most of the estates in the other parts of Italy: Pessano con Bornago, Carugate, Valera, and Santa Maria alla Molgora. The one I owned at Montecchio Vesponi, managed by Robin, was an exception, and Donnina consolidated our money in Casa Donnina. Many of my men left to either join other companies or retire. Had the last campaign been as successful as Castagnaro or Rimini then they would not have left in the numbers that they did. They did not blame me for our retreat but they knew that sometimes, increasingly so, we had to fight alongside other companies. They had all benefitted well from their association with me but they were condottiere and needed to be paid. I retained just a handful as familia: Zuzzo, Gianluca, John Edingham, Robert Saxlingham, John Coe and

Legacy

Peter as well as John Wanlock, John Vale, Johnny Butler, John Colpepper, Johnny Svim, John Liverpool, John Lye, David Falcan, Richard Norlant, Richard Swinfort, Roger Baker, and, of course, the resourceful John Balzan who was rapidly becoming my captain of men at arms. They had served me well and I would use them as lieutenants on the battlefield. For their part, they were happy to stay. The two servants Ned and Edgar were also kept on. When I went to war again these men would be my core. I trusted them all and they had shown, especially at Castagnaro as well as Rimini, that they were not only highly skilled but loyal and reliable. They were worth the retainer I paid them.

When my old friend Giovanni rejoined the Visconti it did not bode well for northern Italy. Perhaps Visconti still wished to use my old comrade against me. He immediately took Verona and Padua began to look nervously to the west. Were they next? When his company headed south towards Bologna and began to raid the Modenese area with fifteen hundred lances it made all of Florence nervous. The news that Florence sent some men to help them made me wonder if they might employ my company to fight my old friend. I did not need the contract but I needed to be prepared in case it materialised. When I heard that Michael did not lead the Florentine soldiers, I knew that the troops sent were just a gesture, for Bologna were allies of Florence. Seeking more information, I invited Michael and his wife to come to dine with us. He commanded the Florentine army and if I spoke to him he would be able to confirm what I thought. His father-in-law was an important member of the Florentine council, he was the podestà, the titular head of the council. Michael came alone. Marriage had changed him for his wife thought herself above associating with condottieri. It did with most men. Of all my men, only Robin and Giovanni were still the same men I had known and they were both single.

Michael got on well with my daughters and Donnina and he was genuinely happy that she was pregnant once more. When the meal was over, the girls were sent away and I was able to question Michael. "Does Florence make war on Giovanni?"

Michael smiled, "Bluntly put, Sir John."

"I am too old to do the dance of words. Michael, you are a good leader and I have trained you well but you are not the man to fight Giovanni. He has one master and he is sitting opposite you now. If Florence wishes to use me to fight my old friend, then I will need time to hire men. Since my last victory, my men have spread to the wind."

He sighed, "I had thought you had given up the sword, Sir John. God knows you deserve some peace."

"Michael, you are being evasive."

He shook his head and sighed "There will be no war against Giovanni. The lances and crossbows that were sent are a token only. Giovanni will be paid not to raid. The council is debating the amount."

I smiled, "And that is why you do not lead the lances and I have not been asked. That is good. I am satisfied."

Michael studied me, "You would go to war again?"

I drank some of the heavy red wine from Lusitania I so enjoyed and tapped the side of my head, "Up here I am as sharp as ever."

"Giovanni Acuto." He raised his goblet to toast me.

"My husband is well named, Michael, as you know. His mind never stops working and he has yet to be bested by another."

I nodded my thanks at their words, "You are both kind. However, I am the only one who can stop the tentacles of the Visconti from strangling the whole of Northern Italy. Perhaps your uncle has designs on the whole of Italy. I hear he supported condottieri in the Neapolitan War. Galeazzo knows that I am his greatest threat and it is why he has employed Giovanni d'Azzo degli Ubaldini. He would like me as his warlord but there is too much bad blood. Hiring the second-best condottiero in Italy is a clear sign of his intentions. He has Verona and now he seeks to add Bologna and Florence to his growing empire."

"Then I will tell the podestà that you are not averse to taking the field again."

"As always, my sword can be hired…for a price."

Michael must have spoken to his father-in-law for, within a week, we were offered a contract. John Beltoft was to the south of us close to Siena and threatening to raid. He had become more of a bandit than a condottiero but I was happy to take the contract as I knew I had the measure of Beltoft. I spent July seeking out the English condottiero. It was tiresome as he would not face me in battle and I was weary of travelling around Ducato and Tuscany. I sent word to John Beltoft that I wished to hire him and his lances. I had sent word to Carlos Cialdini that if he provided me with extra funds, we might be able to buy off the condottiero and his company. I wanted to be home by Christmas.

Beltoft was in the land of Ducato to the east of us and so I pursued with my company. Sometimes just the presence of the White Company on the borders of a city-state had the burghers filling their breeks and so it proved. A representative of the council of Bologna came to speak to me. We were offered what amounted to fourteen thousand florins not to attack Bologna and, if the city was attacked, to defend it. It was all pure profit and I agreed. This was unexpected money. I had been chasing Beltoft and I had no intentions of attacking Bologna. When, in August, John Beltoft agreed to my request to be bought off, I had achieved all that I had hoped and more. I had been relentless in my chase and it had brought its rewards. We had not lost a man, we had made money and we had stopped John Beltoft from causing too much trouble. I did not part with any money, of course, until the lances, led by John Beltoft, arrived at my camp. We returned home passing fields where the grape harvest was being gathered.

That evening Donnina pecked at her food and looked uncomfortable. We had just finished the fish and she winced. I was concerned, "The baby?"

She nodded, "I am sure this one is a boy. It may be my age but the girls never kicked like this one."

I loved my wife and I knew that she was close to thirty summers. That was old to be bearing children. "You have doctors on hand and midwives?"

"Doctors are expensive and when it comes to babies women are better. Yes, there are three of my servants who can help with the delivery. Do not fear, my husband, like you, I am not too old yet. You fight your battles and I will do what I need to do here."

When the baby came it was a boy and he was healthy. We named him after me. That there was another child called John Hawkwood did not bother either of us. My firstborn son lived

Legacy

somewhere in England. My Florentine son would be Giovanni Hawkwood. He would be my heir.

Robin came to visit with me after my son was born. He was not a sentimental man but he was fond of both Donnina and me. When he arrived, with gifts for the girls, he brought eight archers with him. We had plenty of room, my home was palatial, and I would get to speak with them later. I was just pleased to see Robin. Now that Giovanni had deserted me and Michael was preoccupied with Florentine matters, I missed the archer who had been at my side for most of my life. He lived at my other estate close to Arezzo. I had thought of moving there myself but Donnina liked to be closer to Florence.

He looked a little older. He was losing his hair and he now had a stomach that bespoke fine food, good wine and less exercise. He still practised with a bow but I could see that he was not as well-toned as the men he had brought with him. The birth had taxed Donnina and she spent more time in bed with the baby. It allowed Robin and I the time to simply talk.

"The archers, is there a reason you brought them?"

"Aye, I think you might need archers sooner rather than later. These eight are all vintenars. I thought you should get to know them."

"What do you know, Robin?" Robin might be getter fatter but he was still my man and a soldier. He lived far enough from Florence that he spoke to visitors and travellers we did not.

He smiled, "Giovanni is losing his men once more. They are deserting him in droves. Some of the Tuscan castles he took are now reclaimed by Florence and Bologna. Visconti can simply take the loss or, more likely, seek to retake them. Giovanni has come to an agreement with the Malatesta family and was asked by Florence to fight against Pisa. He declined the contract. It is a sign. We both know that Giovanni would never fight against you. He would lose. However, another, younger leader might try to take your crown."

"I wonder if he is losing his touch."

"Perhaps."

"A younger condottiero who might challenge me, is there such a one?"

He nodded, "Jacopo dal Verme. He took Padua for Visconti."

"He is my equal?"

"I did not say that, but he is good. "

"You seem to hear more than I do."

"Since you and William became distant you do not have the intelligence that you once did. I am lucky. Montecchio Vesponi is far enough from Florence so that it is not seen as Florentine and men seem to think that you and I are estranged. The archers who come to me bring news of contracts and condottieri. Then there are others who pass through my land. I am a generous host and they speak to me."

"And?"

"Giovanni refused to attack Padua as he had been the Captain General. Visconti was not happy and gave him an ultimatum. The rumour is that he is heading to Florence."

"Interesting. He refuses to fight the Carrara family but seems happy to risk war with me. He has changed."

"We all change, Sir John. Personally, I do not think he will risk war with you. He will take easy targets and make as much money as he can. Now the Bolognese, they may suffer his sword. He has no ties there and also, as Bologna is an ally of Florence, he may well be seen by Visconti as fulfilling his contract."

I laughed, "Robin Goodfellow, the simple archer from Wakefield has now become embroiled in Italian politics."

He smiled, "It is a pastime, Sir John, and, for me as an outsider, less dangerous than war. I just enjoy the company of women and training archers." He patted his stomach, "And eating and drinking. It seems to me that the princes and dukes of Italy hurl themselves into beds with any who might give them a little more power. You and I are more honest. We take the pay and fight for our master. We are like whores with swords."

I could not help but like Robin. He had changed over the years but not in a bad way, he had just become slightly more Italian.

He took me to meet the archers. All were English and had come to Italy to make money while they could. He warned me before we met them that they had no intentions of living in Italy for any longer than was necessary. "They want to make as much money as they can. I know that you will need them sooner rather than later and thought it best to bring you together with them. I will continue to train the men that they will lead but the eight need to know your mind, my friend."

They were enjoying the autumn sun with my lances when we approached. They stood and the archers bowed. I knew that Robin would have added to their knowledge of me. The archer from Crécy who had been knighted by Poitiers was already a legend. I did not doubt that some of them harboured dreams of emulating me.

Robin said, "This is Sir John Hawkwood known in these parts as Giovanni Acuto." He walked along the line, "This is Jack of Derby, William Yew Bow, Edward of Tewkesbury, Walter of Cheltenham, Tom White Fletch, Robert Green, Edmund Williamson and Gurth of Chester."

"Welcome to my home and my service."

Gurth of Chester said, "Before a contract is signed, my lord, what are the terms?"

I frowned at Robin, I thought such matters were already sorted, "Terms?"

"Aye, Sir Robin has paid us as archers while we lived at Montecchio Vesponi but we were promised vintenar pay once we reached here."

"Aye, vintenar pay." Walter of Cheltenham had a face covered in bulbous pustules and an angry look. His words were almost spat at me.

Gurth nodded in agreement, "When we fight there will be a bonus for battle?"

Such things happened after a victory but normally no such promises could be made in advance. "When you draw your bow in anger and lead your twenty men then, aye, there will be extra payment."

He was like a dog with a bone, "And is there the prospect of drawing a bow in battle?"

I was becoming angry but I forced myself to stay calm, "I have no contract at the moment."

He shook his head, "Then, Sir John, I must decline the offer and I will seek employment elsewhere."

Walter of Cheltenham nodded, "And I too. I came to Italy to make as many coins as I could. We will take our pay and leave."

"There will be no pay. You have been paid by me while you were at Montecchio Vesponi. You have been fed and housed by Sir Robin. That is enough." The two looked angry but they could see that both Robin and I were in no mood for negotiation.

Robin snapped, "And you other six, have I misjudged you as I have these curs?"

Jack of Derby shook his head, "No, Sir Robin, for my part, I am happy to be in the White Company and serve Sir John Hawkwood. I know that if I am patient I will be rewarded."

The other five nodded their agreement.

It was Robin who roared at the two, "Leave!" They headed for the horses and their gardyvyans. Robin shouted, "The gardyvyans are yours but the horses are mine. Ingrates like you can walk."

The two made an obscene gesture and it was aimed at me. Zuzzo said, "Do you want them punished, Sir John?"

I laughed, "No, I have had greater insults. I am just glad that we found their true nature before battle. Such men are like inferior yew staves. They break under pressure." I turned to the other six. "You will be paid each month. There will be food and there will be a bed. Your clothes will be washed by my servants. You are now members of my company and the only people who will be closer than you are my family."

They all looked pleased. I left Robin and Zuzzo to see to their housing and returned to the house. Donnina had put John in his cot. He had fed and was asleep. She was eating when I entered. I told her of the incident and she smiled, "You are right, my husband, it is better to find out the flaws now. It is good that you have leaders for your bowmen. Will one be another Robin, I wonder."

"You can never tell until you are on the battlefield."

She dabbed her mouth with her napkin, "And Giovanni? Is he a threat?"

"I do not know but it seems to me that a visit to Bologna might be in order. If he is heading there, I can meet with him. It is better to speak face to face with him than through intermediaries and I can also speak to whoever controls Bologna."

She frowned, "I know not who that is. The papacy ruled the city until the War of the Eight Saints and the Pope has not managed to bring the city back into its grasp. It is why my uncle sees an opportunity to enlarge Milan. You did the hard work and he seeks to benefit."

"Then a visit seems overdue."

Robin was like a member of my family. The steward, Guccio, admitted him immediately without announcement. Robin bowed, "Lady Donnina you suit motherhood. I have never seen you glow as you do now."

She laughed and held out a hand for him to kiss, "Sir Robin, you are a silver-tongued liar. I know how I look. It is good to see you. Sit. Guccio, wine for our guest."

"Yes, my lady."

"Are the new archers settled?"

"They are and getting to know Zuzzo and the others."

Guccio left and closed the doors. We were alone. "Donnina and I were thinking of investigating Bologna."

"You would visit there?"

"If Giovanni is looking to take Bologna then, aye. I am bound to Florence and Bologna is an ally. What do you know of the city?"

"There is no one ruler, not yet, anyway. Just as in Florence, there are families who control the city. The leading family is the Bentivoglio clan. Their leader is Giovanni. He is, I believe, the podestà. He would be the man to speak to." He sipped some of the wine. "A good move, Sir John. Bologna has never hired the White Company and the city is close enough to our heartland to make life easier."

"I do not think that we will be hired, not unless Giovanni is ordered to take Bologna. I need to speak to my old friend."

"Be wary, my friend, times change and Giovanni, while he is also my friend, is now a Visconti man. Men can change."

I nodded. I knew what he meant but at the Battle of Castagnaro Giovanni had deferred to me. However, I was aware that Robin, alone out of every one of the leading warriors in Italy, did not have ulterior motives. He would always speak the truth to me. Was my arrogance leading me into danger?

Legacy

After he left I was unwell. It was nothing to worry about, I just had a runny nose and an annoying cough but I did not like it. I was old, by my reckoning I had seen more than sixty-five summers. I did not know anyone as old as I was. Certainly, there were no condottiero my age. The illness was a warning and a sign that my body was weakening and as soon as I felt better, I took to my old practice of joining my men to practise with weapons. It was some days until I felt ready to do so. Zuzzo, for one, was more than pleased. He hated the idle life and he was a superb swordsman.

We practised outside in the gyrus. A circular enclosure, with a low wooden wall, it was big enough for many men to spar and even to ride horses albeit in a more confined space than was normal. We found it helped to prepare riders for the confusion of battle. We wore padded jackets and just arming caps on our heads. We had blunted weapons but they could still hurt. I let Zuzzo take charge. He was more skilled with a weapon than I had ever been. I had the strength of an archer; I could no longer draw a war bow but you never lost all the strength you had used to draw a war bow. I was not deformed as Robin was but when I swung my sword and struck, an opponent felt the blow.

"My lord, I do not think that you will have to fight in battle but it is good that you maintain your skill."

"Zuzzo, who led the attack at Castagnaro? Who slew many men on the flight from Aversa? I will still need to use my sword. Preparation for war is never wasted."

"Then you need to be cleverer about how you fight. Let us see if we can remove some of the rust you have gathered during the winter."

I held a small buckler in my left hand as did Zuzzo. The sword was not the longest in my armoury but long enough. Zuzzo came at me with hands as fast as lightning. It was deliberate. He was trying to make a point. I should not need to fight. I was just as determined to show him that I was still a warrior. I blocked all the blows with sword and buckler but, despite my strength, Zuzzo's fast feet drove me back and I feared I might trip. When that happens in battle you are distracted and in distraction comes death. He smacked the flat of his sword against my stomach when I glanced behind me to see that there were no obstacles.

"And thus, Giovanni Acuto dies."

I smiled, "Then let us hope that I do not meet a swordsman as skilled as Zuzzo on the battlefield."

"Unlikely, my lord, as I have no peer." His words were not arrogant, merely a statement of fact. He was the best.

John Coe said, "And do not forget, Zuzzo, that we would not be standing idly by. We would be defending our captain."

I put him straight immediately. "No, you would not, John. You are not my bodyguards. You are my lieutenants. If the White Company is hired to fight then, Zuzzo and Gianluca apart, you would be leading lances. You and my other lieutenants are an extension of my mind. I did not just retain you for your pleasant company. You will know my plans and carry them out."

Gianluca asked, "And who will lead your archers?"

It was a good question. Robin had given up war. He trained men for me but he would not lead them into battle. His archers were an expense. I had learned that while lances were always available, English archers, and there were none better, were as rare as hen's teeth in Italy. Robin's estate was the flower that attracted the most powerful element of the White Company. Every six months he sent me a short letter with the numbers he had in training. Donnina viewed the accounts but I counted the men. We had just two hundred archers there at the moment. That was not enough but it was a core. If the White Company went to war again then they would be the core. Once I began to hire men then my ranks would be filled. Swords and bows for hire knew that Giovanni Acuto always paid.

"At the moment I do not know."

"Then, my lord, let us simulate what might happen in war. You will be mounted."

I shrugged, "Or on a wagon, as I was for part of the battle of Castagnaro."

"Horses we can plan for." He whistled, "Ned, Edgar, fetch horses."

Once mounted the world looked different for you had height and fighting on the back of a horse needed different skills. The small bucklers were replaced by the small, rectangular curved shield that afforded more protection. While the men I led would use lances I would have just my baton and sword as weapons. More often than not we did not even take shields into battle but Zuzzo was being careful. He did not want a loose blow to incapacitate the captain of the White Company. Edgar had brought out Caesar for me. He was too old for war but a little exercise would not hurt him and I still liked my old war horse.

Zuzzo shouted, "Let us try to replicate how it will be in battle. If we fight the Visconti snake then men will come to end the threat of Giovanni Acuto. John, Peter, Robert, and John, you outnumber the three of us. Try to get close to us."

They were keen to impress me and the four of them hurled their horses and swords at us. I might have seen too many summers but I still enjoyed the thrill of combat. I knew I was lucky to have my two Italian bodyguards but my four English lances were also skilled. Caesar showed that while he might have been rested for more than a year, he still had instincts and he bit and snapped at the horses he shared a stable with. None came close to striking my body but I took four hits to my shield. I resolved to take one with me when next I rode to battle.

By the time it was noon both we and the horses were tired. We led the animals to the stable. John Coe said, "It is good that you have Gianluca and Zuzzo, my lord. I think that we might have taken lesser men."

"Remember John, the purpose of the White Company is to defeat an enemy. We do not send assassins to kill the enemy leaders. You will not be trying to get to the enemy captain but winning the battle. As we showed at Castagnaro, it is not always the superior numbers that win."

Robert smiled, "It is the sharp mind of you, my lord, that saw the opportunity and exploited it."

"This was good. Let us do this three times a week." The fight had done me good and I felt twenty years younger. It was a good feeling.

Zuzzo said, "No, my lord, you can do this three times a week but we need to do this on six of the seven. I have seen how we can make your four English lances almost the equal of Zuzzo."

Whilst I had enjoyed the fight, I had felt the exercise. My buttocks ached and my muscles complained. Before we ate

Donnina had a hot bath run for me and had the masseuse we employed on hand. By the time my body was bathed, massaged and oiled then I felt better and I enjoyed my food all the more.

We sat and talked after we had eaten. "It is good that you prepare for war. I think that someone will need to oppose my uncle and the only man capable of such an undertaking, is you."

I nodded at the compliment. She was right. Until there was another Giovanni Acuto on the battlefield then I was confident I was the only one who could hold the enemy that threatened to wrap Italy in his coils. I had long ago worked out that victory was not always important. Not being defeated could be seen as a victory. Milan now had far more men than I could raise. I would not be looking to defeat Milan, merely not lose.

Legacy

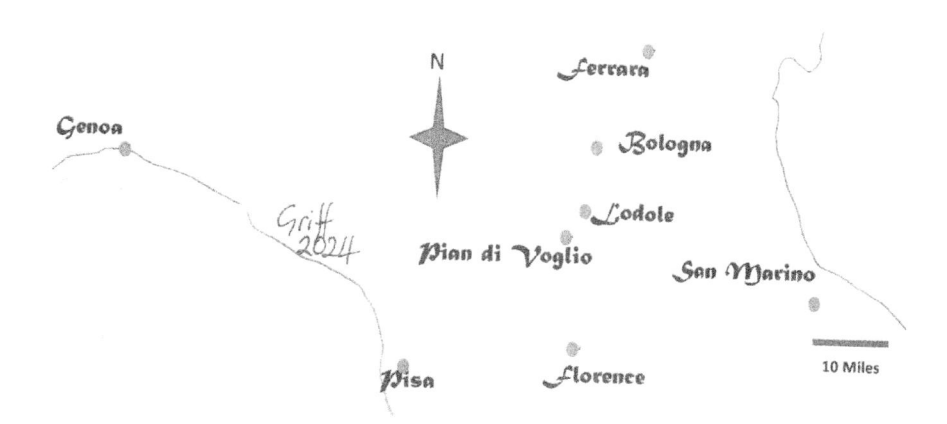

The Bologna campaign 1388

Chapter 4

1388 Bologna

Before preparations for my trip were complete, I was visited by Michael and his father-in-law. The visit did a number of things. It showed me that Michael was now lost to me and was Florentine but it also showed me that I had a spy in my home. The two knew things that were private. They knew what Robin had told me. Donnina had already fed the baby and she was with me when they entered. Carlos Cialdini was rich. He had many businesses and all of them made him money. I never underestimated him for although he had never drawn a sword in anger, he had enough money to hire a company five times the size of mine.

"It is an honour to see you in my home."

Donnina smiled, "And what brings this honour to us, my lord?"

"Word has come to me that you are considering meeting with Giovanni d'Azzo degli Ubaldini." As soon as those words were spoken then the presence of a spy in my home was confirmed.

"You have good information." I glanced at Donnina. The slightest of frowns was not seen by any but me. She would discover who the spy was.

Michael said, by way of appeasement, "I did not know it was that much of a secret, Sir John. It is well known that you and Captain Ubaldini are friends."

"I have many friends, Michael, and there are many more who purport to be friends." I fixed him with a stare. Michael was not as consummate a player as his father-in-law, and he hid from my gaze.

The would-be Master of Florence smiled, "All that the council wishes is that, if you are to visit with him then you offer Captain Ubaldini a contract. We would have him take his company and raid the lands of Pisa. Jacopo d'Appiano has begun to make moves to retake some of the land of Florence, land you won for us, Sir John."

"Yet you do not ask me or the White Company to do this. Nor do you use Michael and your Florentines. May I ask why?"

He sighed and I saw his eyes hooded and veiled as he hid his thoughts from me. "Your company is not yet ready and with the Visconti family seeking to enlarge their own lands it seems prudent to keep the Florentine army close to our city. I ask you to do this as a courtesy. Our retainer will continue to be paid and we ask little more from you. There will be five hundred florins added this month to your retainer. If you do intend to visit Bologna and seek words with Captain Ubaldini then this should not be an inconvenience." His words confirmed the spy for how else did he know that my company was not yet ready?

The retainer was not huge, just one hundred florins a month but it paid the wages of the staff and also ensured that we received a few crumbs from the Florentine table with commissions like this one. The slightest of nods from Donnina was sufficient and I said, "I am ever the servant of Florence. I will deliver your offer. The contract?"

He shook his head, "All you need is to offer the contract. If Captain Ubaldini is agreeable then he can come to Florence to complete the negotiations."

After they had gone, I said, "Your thoughts, my love?"

"This is a way of buying off Giovanni. Florence sees, as you do, the threat. Pisa is nothing and Giovanni can easily defeat their army. This way he stops Bologna and Florence from being attacked and uses Giovanni to betray his master. It is clever."

"Then we will leave by the end of the week. And the other matter?"

"The spy?" She said. I nodded. "I have my suspicions. When you have gone, I will investigate. Be careful, my sweet. You have enemies out there. This spy may work for more than just Florence. The council may not be the spy's only paymasters. There are many enemies out there who would like you dead."

"Your uncle being one of them."

"Exactly."

I met with Zuzzo and my lances. "We will take just two of the new archers. I do not wish to travel with a vast retinue. Zuzzo, you and Gianluca shall be my bodyguards. We will take Peter and John along with Ned and Edgar. John and Robert will stay here. We need to spread the word that we are hiring again and

Lady Donnina may well need them." I did not mention the spy to them.

We did not ride plated but I was not a fool. Beneath my surcoat, I wore a mail hauberk as did my men. We carried swords and shields but neither John nor Peter took their lances. I wore a cap but they had helmets hanging from their cantles. William Yew Bow and Tom White Fletch took their bows, carried in cases, as well as twenty arrows. They too wore helmets. All of my men wore my livery with the three shells and inverted chevron on the shield. I was too well known to go in disguise, I had been fighting battles in Italy for more than thirty years. There was no disguising Sir John Hawkwood.

I knew every eye was upon us as we left my home. There was at least one spy but were there others? Donnina would discover the identity of all of them and Robert and John could deal with them. As we passed farms and estates I wondered if they too would be passing word of our progress although, as the road we took led to Bologna, everyone would know our ultimate destination. It was a mountainous road and once we left Florence, we would be in a land filled with those who had one reason or another to wish me ill. As it was just sixty miles, I hoped we might make the ride in one day. Zuzzo was less certain.

"Sir John, you are no longer a young man. Let us rest overnight."

I shook my head, "Speed is our ally and we are well mounted. Our horses have done little for over a year. They are well fed and healthy. I would use that to our advantage."

As we rode, I took the opportunity to get to know my new archers. I discovered that Tom White Fletch was not just an archer but also a fletcher. "It is how I came by my name, my lord. I was always going to be an archer but I learned how to fletch before my body was that of an archer. My grandfather had been a fletcher and, before he died, he taught me to become one. I first made arrows just for me. I always used pure white feathers for the fletch. Call it an affectation. When others saw my skill with the arrows, more enemies fell to my flights than theirs, then they asked me to make arrows for them. It has given me a healthy income and I make good arrows. They are true and fly well."

It was many years since I had been an archer but I still appreciated the skills of the fletcher and the bowyer. They could make all the difference. I was pleased that Tom had joined me. Will Yew Bow was also a good archer. Whilst not a bowyer as such, he had made his own bow. It fitted him perfectly. Such a weapon would give him confidence and that could add a pace or two to the range of an archer.

We halted for lunch at the village of Pian di Voglio. It was not randomly chosen. Guiseppe Gucci had been one of my men until he retired after Castagnaro. Such had been the scale of that victory that it made rich men of all those who fought for the White Company. He had bought a small inn. The road was a busy one and being halfway between Bologna and Florence was popular with travellers. He also kept animals. He raised them for milk and for food. Rabbits were a good investment! We were not the only customers. There were merchants travelling from Bologna to Florence already in the small dining room. I saw one of them giving me close scrutiny. That was not surprising. I was well known.

"Sir John," even my Italian soldiers addressed me thus, I was still called Giovanni Acuto but the White Company was largely English and they all addressed me the same way, "it is good that you honour me with a visit. If you would allow me to choose your food, I promise that you will not be disappointed. My wife is a most excellent cook and her rabbit stew is superb."

It was always as well to take the advice of a tavern keeper and I nodded, "We are in your hands."

He scurried off and Zuzzo asked, "And how is the backside, Sir John?"

I gave him a wry smile, "It is asking me why I do not use a cushion beneath my rump."

They laughed. Wine was brought and as I had expected it was good. Guiseppe would want to impress me. I was still an important man and a recommendation from me would bring him a trade that had gold coins. When the food came it was every bit as good as I had been promised. A rustic stew with game, mainly rabbit, and spiced beans, it was filling and with warm bread to mop up the juices would keep us going until we reached Bologna.

When I had finished, I rose to make water. Guiseppe, like most people in the region, kept a large pot outside the back door for customers to use. They had done so in these parts since the time of the Romans. The contents would not be wasted. They would be used to kill the wildlife on bedding and clothes before they were washed. I had just finished when the merchant who had watched me closely came out.

"Signior Giovanni."

"Yes?" My hand was on my dagger but the overweight man did not look to be a threat.

"You will not remember me but I remember you. You saved us from the Florentines when I lived in Pisa. But for you, I would have lost all."

I nodded, "I am pleased to have been of service. Your name?"

He waved a hand, "It is unimportant, but I have a warning for you. When we left Bologna, I heard men plotting. They were in the yard when we packed our horses. Your name was mentioned. I cannot be sure but I think that there might be an ambush waiting for you. They were well-armed and looked like soldiers. They said that you were heading for Bologna. When I saw you dining it confirmed what I had heard."

"And you do not wish to give me your name in case the ambushers discover who spoiled their plan."

He looked relieved, "Just so. I am not a warrior and if I am to earn a crust for my family, I must stay alive."

"How many men were there?"

"Eight, at least. They wore no mail but had the brigandines such as the feditore wear. They had swords, shields and helmets. There were two crossbows."

"They were mounted?"

"They had horses but they were not the war horses you and your men ride." He smiled, "They saw a fat merchant who they thought was more interested in gold. They did not hide their words."

"Thank you. Your information is valued." I clasped his arm.

I re-entered the room and Zuzzo said, "That was either a gallon of water or you have the shits, my lord." He was smiling.

I smiled back at him, "At my age, Zuzzo, a man is careful when he makes water. Come, let us pay the bill and leave."

Guiseppe shook his head, "It is my treat, my lord."

Shaking my head I put a florin in his hand, "I pay my way, Guiseppe, I always have." I spoke a little louder, "And I will tell all that I meet that this tavern, the Leaping Hare, is well worth a visit for the fare is beyond compare." I saw the look of pride on his wife's face.

Once we reached our horses I became serious as I said, "There will be an ambush somewhere along this road. Eight men at least and they sound like men who have served in the wars. They had leather jacks, swords and helmets. They do not sound like bandits. They also had two crossbows."

"How do you know, Sir John?"

"I was told, Peter. As I suspected, there are spies in my home and my enemies have been forewarned. I do not doubt that Galeazzo Visconti has put a price on my head." I smiled as I donned my helmet, "I hope that it is worth the risk that these men will take."

Tom and Will took their bows from their cases and strung them. It would mean that the string could not be used in battle but an archer could not string a war bow quickly. All my men donned their helmets and, as we mounted, slid their swords in and out of their scabbards.

"Peter, you ride in the fore with Will and Tom behind you. Ned and Edgar, place your mounts behind my bodyguards. John, you are the rearguard. I want you ten paces behind Ned and Edgar. Peter, watch for an ambush ahead and John ensure that no one sneaks up behind us."

I did not think that the ambush would be close to the village. It would be somewhere along the road. I guessed that they would choose a remote place between villages. It added to the stress of the journey as we could not guarantee which direction the attack would come from. It would also slow us down. We studied every rock and tree. Each time the road turned or dipped Peter would slow down. Knowing that they had two crossbows gave them an edge. Whilst war bows were far superior to crossbows, in an ambush, a crossbowman could release one bolt quickly and from cover and that could prove deadly. We did not speak as we rode.

We listened and we sniffed the air. With the wind in our faces, we might smell horses or men before they could detect us. We watched the ears of our horses in case they sensed danger and, of course, we studied the land.

We passed Lodole where there was a bridge and a twisting road that climbed up to Monzuno. The road ran alongside the river, Torrente Savena. We watered our horses and they briefly grazed for there was a flat area close to the water. I asked the locals if they had seen riders. They spoke of the merchants we had met at Pian di Voglio but said that they were the only ones who had passed before our arrival. I believed them. It told us that the enemy warriors were ahead of us. The river passed through a gorge and the road began to climb, twisting and turning as it did so just a mile from the village. One side was thick with trees and the other tumbled down to the river.

Zuzzo said, "If I was a man wishing to attack us, I would choose the trees ahead, my lord. Our right sides are unprotected."

He was right and we needed to change my plans, "My horse has a stone."

We halted and I dismounted to examine the hoof. It was a ruse for my horse had no stone but I did not think that we could be seen from ahead as the road turned and I wanted to give orders. "Will, Tom, take your bows and slip through the trees. Ambush the ambushers. Ned and Edgar, lead their two horses."

The four obeyed me instantly and my two archers, an arrow held next to the bow, scurried up through the trees.

"Peter, ride closer to us and put your shield over your right leg."

We all did the same. You could not use a shield and a sword at the same time but the shield would afford some protection from the right. We began to move. I hoped I had given my two archers enough time to get ahead of us. We did not rush along the road which was still climbing. I did not want to overtax our horses. I also knew that the waiting would have an effect on the waiting men. Nerves would be stretched as they waited for their prey to arrive. Zuzzo had been right. The trees and the rocks were perfect places for an ambush and the rising road would tire horses.

We turned the corner and I saw something glinting in the woods. A shaft of sunlight had reflected off metal. It was little enough but when you are wary such warnings are handy. Peter saw it too and he had just pulled up his shield when we heard the distinctive crack of a crossbow.

"Now!"

Pulling up my shield, I spurred Ajax and he leapt forward. The bolt struck my shield but at an angle and skittered off behind us. Ned and Edgar had been soldiers and they did not panic. They slowed and parted to allow John Coe to take Gianluca and Zuzzo's place behind me. They had raised their shields and flanked me. I changed hands with my shield and drew my sword. Knowing that the crossbows were being reloaded Peter galloped off into the trees. We could now use our shields on our left and wield our swords. We would be able to turn to face the men now that we knew where they lay. I spurred Ajax and followed him. The four of us hurtled from the light into the dark. The spear that came up at me was from behind a tree and came perilously close to ending the life and career of Sir John Hawkwood. I was saved only by two things. My natural reactions and my mail hauberk. My sword struck the shaft of the spear which scraped along the mail rings. Zuzzo, riding close to me, slew the man by slashing down on his neck with his sword. There was a scream from my left as Peter slew one crossbowman and Gianluca ended the life of the other. In the darkness of the trees, I could not make out where the other ambushers were but when I heard the distinctive sounds of arrows, I knew that my archers could. There was a scream of pain and then the sound of a second arrow and a second cry of pain.

"We are undone! Flee, my brothers." As they turned to run, they revealed themselves. We moved as quickly as we could through the trees. I brought my sword down to crack into the helmet of one man and the blade ripped down the back of his jack. When we heard the sound of horses, we knew that the survivors had fled.

"Anyone hurt?"

There was a chorus of, "No, my lord."

"Peter, John collect the horses. Destroy the crossbows and see if any of the other weapons are worth salvaging." I dismounted and went to the man I had just slain. I turned him over. He had a beard, flecked with grey. He was a veteran. His sword was the short one favoured by spearmen. I saw his spear lying on the ground where it had fallen. I took his purse. Inside were twenty freshly minted soldo, Milanese currency. It confirmed that they had been paid by Milan for they had the image of Galeazzo Visconti upon them. "Check their purses. Look for soldo."

By the time we had collected the horses, coins and weapons, it was the middle of the afternoon. An examination of the purses confirmed that they had been sent by the Lord of Milan. I had another score to settle with Galeazzo Visconti.

"Let us push on. I want to be in Bologna before dark." I did not want to have to bang on the gates of the city. We would not be able to slip in unseen but a clamouring at the gates would draw even more attention to us.

Ned and Edgar led the six horses we had taken. The weapons hung from their saddles. The horses and weapons would be sold when we reached Bologna. We barely made it before the gates were closed for the night. Our late arrival prompted questions from the captain of the guard.

"You are late to arrive at the city, my lord."

"We would have arrived at a more civilised time had we not been ambushed after Lodole."

Suddenly he was more worried about the attack than the strangers in his city, "Ambushed? Who by?"

I shrugged, "I know not but as most of those who tried to take our animals and lives are dead it matters not."

"I will have to report this to the podestà."

"Good. Can you recommend an inn?"

I knew that the captain would have an arrangement so that he was paid for customers he sent to the nominated inn. His smile showed me that I was right, "The Red Grape, just off the main square is a good place. They have stables and you will not be rooked. Tell them I sent you and it will afford you a warm welcome."

I nodded. The mention of his name was to ensure that he received his cut. I knew that we would be overcharged. Having taken more than one hundred silver coins in the forest it would be the dead men who would be paying. The inn was clean and the stables adequate. The fawning tavern keeper made us welcome. He found three rooms for us. I was just relieved to have hot food, a bed and stables for our animals.

As we ate, Zuzzo smiled, "You can bet that the captain of the guard is even now speaking with Giovanni Bentivoglio, the podestà."

I nodded, "It saves us from having to seek an audience. I am betting that we will be summoned to the palace."

John Coe asked, "And how does this help us to get to Captain Giovanni?"

"The same way that our enemies knew we were heading here. Spies. There will be men paid by Milan who live in Bologna. As soon as the gates open in the morning a rider will head for Giovanni and he will find us. We will enjoy a second night here. The horses need the rest and then we head to Ferrara for that is where I believe Giovanni and his men will be found. If we make it five miles down the road before we are met then I will be surprised."

Zuzzo chuckled, "Men are foolish if they see your grey hairs, Sir John, and think you feeble-minded. You are still as sharp as ever."

"And the day that I am not I will know it is time to hang up my sword."

Chapter 5

1388 Bologna

The liveried young noble who arrived at the tavern was there not long after we had finished our breakfast. I was unsure if he had deliberately waited but the timing was impeccable. "Sir John, my master, the head of the council, would speak with you."

"Of course." I turned to my men, "Zuzzo, you come with me. The rest of you, enjoy Bologna." I stroked my right ear as I stood. They nodded, understanding the signal. They would find as much information as they could. "I will meet you in the main square," I looked at the young noble, "At noon?"

"You will be finished by then, Sir John."

I had not bothered with my mail and it was a relief to walk unencumbered by metal. The young man felt obliged to speak as we walked, "Your victory at Castagnaro was nothing short of miraculous, Sir John. How did you manage to turn defeat into victory?"

I shrugged, "I learned long ago that when things go against you in battle you must change your plans. I am lucky in the men I lead. They do not give up easily. In every battle, there is something you can do to influence the outcome. It is all to do with timing."

"I should have liked to have been there. The Veronese needed to be taught a lesson."

"And they have suffered a worse one now for they have a new master, the Lord of Milan. In trying to take little Padua, they have laid themselves open to be devoured by a much fiercer beast." I looked at the young man who had a fine sword. "And are you a warrior?"

"I am of the Bentivoglio family."

"That does not answer my question. Do you have a war horse and armour?"

"I do and it is a magnificent animal. My armour was made in Siena."

"Good and in how many battles have you fought?"

He stopped and looked at me quizzically, "Fought? Why none. I was too young for the war of the Eight Saints and Bologna has kept the peace since then."

I smiled, "Then I would seek service with a company. If you went to war now then you would not last long. A good war horse and Sienese plate are no guarantee that you will survive."

The young man was silent for the rest of the way to the palace. I realised that Bologna was ripe for plucking. They had escaped the clutches of the Papacy but done nothing to protect themselves from other predators and Visconti would like to take the wine-rich region of Bologna. It was no wonder that Captain Ubaldini was taking chunks of Bolognese territory.

Giovanni Bentivoglio was not even a duke let alone a prince or a king but he was doing his best to appear as one. In the palace, he sat on a throne-like chair that was on a raised dais so that he was above everyone. He wore no crown but his hands were adorned with jewelled rings and about his neck he wore a golden chain. There were just four other men in the room but there were guards at the doors. "Sir John, you may enter but your man should stay in the ante-chamber."

I was amused. I still had my sword and neither the guards nor the other men looked like a threat. "You may wait without, Zuzzo. I think I shall be safe."

He smiled at my tone, "Of course, Sir John."

There was a seat before the five men. "If you would sit. Wine?"

"I have just enjoyed a fine breakfast, thank you." The young man positioned himself behind my chair. I turned and stared at him until he moved a couple of paces away to the right. I did not like men to stand behind me.

"So, what brings the Captain of the White Company to Bologna? Is this a scouting mission? Are you seeking weaknesses in our defences?" I could almost hear the fear in his voice.

"No, my lord. My men and I are travelling north." Speaking quietly and softly, I deliberately gave him the least information I could.

"You have too many men with you for leisure. Who is your employer?"

I put my hand on my chest, "I can say, honestly, that, at this moment, I have no employer. I am retained by Florence, but they pay me to keep my sword sheathed."

"Then why are you here?"

"It has nothing to do with your city. This happens to be on the road I am taking." I did not mind lying but I was being honest.

The five men conferred. I heard the occasional word but that was all. The would-be king rose and said, "Sir John, walk with me. It is cooler in the cloisters." He nodded to the young noble. I rose and we headed to the door. The guards opened them and Zuzzo waited.

"I think, Zuzzo, that we are going to take a turn around the palace cloisters. If you would walk a few paces behind. I think that the men here think that an old man and his bodyguard are something of a fearful sight."

"No, no, no, Sir John," Giovanni Bentivoglio said, "but you are a mighty captain, the most renowned condottiero in Italy. You must understand your presence here is alarming."

I nodded, "You think that the fox is in the henhouse? Fear not, my lord, you should know that I have never broken my word and I can swear that I have no desire to fight against Bologna." That was not true, of course. I had used ruse de guerre and been somewhat loose with the truth many times but he did not need to know that.

He sighed, "Thank you." We reached the cloisters and, he was right, it was cooler there. He said, "You are a friend of Giovanni d'Azzo degli Ubaldini?"

"He served in my company and, yes, I would regard him as a friend."

"You know that he has taken some Bolognese castles?" I nodded. "Would you rid our land of him for us?"

I laughed, "With a handful of men? My company are dispersed to the four winds, my lord, it would take me time to gather them and during that time Captain Ubaldini grows stronger."

He nodded, "Then would you undertake a mission from us to broker a peace?"

"I can see no harm in trying but I may not be persuasive enough."

"Perhaps ten thousand florins might be enough to persuade him to find other pastures on which he can graze." He smiled, "And there would, of course, be a fee for you as a broker."

"I can try for now that I am an old man I seek for peace more than war." That was another lie, of course, but I think he knew that. "And where would I find my old friend?"

"He has just taken Castelfranco to the west of here. Certainly, his soldiers are to be found ravaging the region."

"Then I shall leave tomorrow and try to broker a peace." Things were working out well. I had permission to travel in these lands and I could deliver my message to Giovanni. Ten thousand florins was a good payment and he might accept.

"Will you dine with me this evening?"

"I would be delighted."

I waited until I met all my men before I told them my news. Zuzzo laughed, "So you are going to be paid to meet the man you would have met anyway? Sir John, I am in awe of you."

I shrugged, "I just use my mind to its best effect. I will dine with the Bolognese tonight." I handed a purse of the Milanese silver we had taken from the assassins to Zuzzo, "Enjoy food but keep your ears open. I think that Bologna is weak. Perhaps we might bring the White Company and make some serious money."

Donnina had packed my finest clothes and I wore them for the feast. I sat next to Giovanni Bentivoglio and his wife. She was as dull as ditchwater but thought that she was a beauty to rival the Madonna painted by Pietro Lorenzetti. She was not and her conversation would have made Donnina pull out her hair. I smiled and laughed at her attempts at wit.

I did learn things from my host, however. He had ousted a rival from the council and Ugolino da Panico was a thorn in his side. I stored the name in my head. If I chose to make mischief in Bologna then such a man would be useful. Before we left, he agreed to my fee, a thousand florins, and he asked if I would take the young noble with me. I learned that his name was Ambrogio Bentivoglio and he was the nephew of the head of the family, the podestà, Giovanni Bentivoglio. I agreed even though I knew that he would be a spy in our camp. The podestà did not trust me. It mattered not. A spy was only useful if his identity was hidden.

Before I left for the inn I said, "Tomorrow, my young friend, wear armour and choose weapons you are comfortable with."

"You think we will have to fight?"

"We are visiting the camp of the company that is holding your land to ransom, what do you think?"

I watched reality dawn on his face. I asked Ned and Edgar to remain in the inn. It meant we did not need to pack everything and I left my finer clothes hanging. They would not need to come with us and the two of them could continue to gather intelligence. My conversation with the podestà had convinced me that I might have to lead my company in this region. I needed to know as much as I could. The two Englishmen were happy to continue to serve. They were old men, quite a few years younger than me, but they had not yet given up on life. In that, they were much like me.

We left almost as soon as the gates to Bologna were opened and rode in a tighter formation although I did not anticipate an ambush. Ambrogio was nervous as we rode and chattered on like a magpie, "Will Ubaldini listen to you?"

"I am not his master if that is what you mean." I sighed as I explained the facts of life to this naïve young noble, "A condottiero is a businessman and his business is war. He does not fight for a flag or a country but for payment. The men he leads are probably true warriors; men who have skills with weapons and wish to be paid to use those skills. In most cases, they will fight for anyone, even former employers."

"Some commit atrocities, Sir John, like at Cesena."

I turned and glared. Many men had laid the massacre of the populace of that town to me, "That was the doing of the anti-Pope. I have not fought for him since that day." I saw the fear on his face following my outburst and I forced myself to be calm, "It makes my point, Ambrogio, condottiere see no reason to slaughter those that they do not fight. There is more profit in hostages and payments to keep their swords sheathed. When there are flags or crosses involved then men lose their perspective. Trust me, a condottiere and the condottiero who leads them will always listen first. We are only in danger if there is profit in it for them. It is why I did not bring your uncle's bribe."

I knew how Giovanni would be operating. He would have patrols out every day. Twenty or thirty lances could raid the land for thirty miles. He would be extracting every coin he could. This was not his full company. It had begun to disintegrate. His success had ensured that. Men had full purses and had simply decided to either go home or enjoy the fruits of their labour. The sunlight glinting off the plate was the first warning that we were close to Giovanni. Men rose from behind low walls as ten horsemen appeared from behind the line of trees to face us. They kept their swords sheathed but I knew that there were crossbows aimed at us.

I recognised the condottiere, "Guiseppe, how is life treating you?"

He beamed and bowed as he recognised me. The last time I had seen him, at Castagnaro, I had been wearing my white plate with a caparisoned horse. "Sir John, I did not recognise you. Zuzzo, Gianluca, it is good to see you too. What brings you here?"

"I seek words with Captain Ubaldini." I was economical with my words. I would reveal my two offers in private.

"He is at Castelfranco. We will escort you. Guido." The men with the crossbows rose and ran to their waiting horses. "Follow as rearguard."

Ambrogio looked nervously around as he saw us surrounded. Guiseppe led us away and I smiled and said, "These are professional soldiers Ambrogio. They survive by keeping to their system. They know me but in our world, you mistrust everyone. We are safe."

The men on the walls of the town were all condottiere. When I was recognised, there were waves and shouts. I had brought them all profit at some time or another. The town was functioning as normal. When we had passed the fields, men had still been working there and the market was busy. Giovanni was keeping the people happy. There would be no regimen of terror. We headed for the castle and dismounted in the inner bailey. I left my archers and men at arms with the horses and followed Guiseppe. Ambrogio, Zuzzo and Gianluca followed me. Giovanni was in the Great Hall. He had parchments on the table and I recognised his lieutenants, or most of them, at any rate. They had been with him at Padua.

When he saw me, his face lit up, "Sir John, a most welcome surprise. Zuzzo, Gianluca, it is good to see you too." He pointedly looked at Ambrogio.

"This is Ambrogio Bentivoglio. He is the nephew of the man who rules Bologna."

"No, my lord, my uncle is merely the head of the council."

I turned and stared at the young noble, "You can perpetrate that illusion in your city, but this is my friend and he needs the truth. Captain Ubaldini, can you and I speak in private?"

"But…"

"Young man, I was happy for you to come with us but I will talk alone with Captain Ubaldini." I left him in no doubt that I would brook no arguments.

I saw the smile on Giovanni's face and he said, "I have a pleasant room where we can have privacy. Antonio, wine and refreshments for our guests. Jacopo, take charge of the meeting."

"Yes, my lord."

Giovanni said, by way of explanation, "Jacopo di Montepulciano is my lieutenant. He is a good man and leads forty lances." So, the condottiero had left the service of Pisa.

I nodded to Zuzzo. I would not need his blades. Giovanni did not speak before we entered the small room. It was simply furnished and cool. He poured us each a glass of wine and waved me to a seat. "The last time you sought me out it was to join me."

"And this time it is to put profit your way."

"And that is always welcome. Speak, old friend."

I sipped the wine. Giovanni knew his grapes and it was a good one. "Before I do may I ask a question or two?"

"Of course. I know how much I owe you and you are the one man in the whole world that I trust."

I laughed, "There would be many who would say that Giovanni Acuto cannot be trusted."

"But you and I know differently."

"You know that Visconti is a venal and treacherous man?" He nodded. "Then why do you do his work? You will be like an old cloak and discarded when he has no more use for you. I know that he does not pay well."

"No, he does not. You know I refused to attack Padua?" I nodded. "I could not fight against the town I had defended. You are the same with Pisa. I am getting old, Sir John, not as old as you but I have no Lady Donnina making my coins grow. I need to take contracts when I can. I am ready to leave his service when I can."

"You serve him now?" He looked down at his wine and so I asked him a blunt question, "Is this a chevauchée or is it ordered by Visconti?"

"I cannot hide from you, Sir John. I was paid a retainer to cause trouble in Tuscany. You are right, Visconti pays us in soldos and not ducats. The fee does not pay my men." His voice lowered, "I am losing men on a daily basis."

That explained the raiding. I finished the wine and poured a second, "Then I can offer you two contracts."

"You are offering contracts?"

"I am the intermediary. First, Florence would have you raid Pisa." He nodded and I smiled, "They will pay ten thousand florins but the payment is really to ensure that you do not attack Florence."

He laughed, "And while you live close to the city that would never happen."

"Cialdini thinks I am old and do not inspire the fear I once did. This is insurance."

"Then I am happy to do so. I send men to Pisa and make easy money. The second contract?"

"It is more of a bribe. Bologna will pay you ten thousand florins to leave their lands."

He beamed, "Then better and better. Twenty thousand florins will pay my men and bring me profit. Between you and I, Sir John, the teat is almost empty. There is little left for us to take. How will we receive the payment?"

"If you send men back with me then I will have the money from Bologna readied. The Florentine money will be sent once you begin your raid on Pisa."

"Cialdini is not a trusting man then?"

"He is a coin counter and your association with Visconti has everyone concerned."

He raised his goblet, "Here's to old friends."

"Old friends."

The business part over we were able to chat. "I hear you have another son." I nodded, "Congratulations. I may have sons," he shrugged, "who knows? I have wandered too much and left women with bulging bellies. I should like to have known a son. It is good for a man to leave his mark on this earth once he departs. A son does that."

"That was your choice. I confess that I am grateful to old Bernabò. Donnina changed my life."

"That she did." He sipped his wine and looked at me, thoughtfully, "Does not England appeal? You have money and, in that land, you only have friends, not least of which is the king. Here you are surrounded by a sea of enemies."

"I have thought of that and my lands and estates in England are profitable but Donnina likes this land too much. So, old friend, give me an insight into the mind of Visconti."

He poured us more wine, "In many ways, he is as easy to read as the trail of an army through a forest. He wants an empire in Northern Italy. He almost has it. Verona and Vincenza are his already. Padua is about to fall. We both know that Pisa is like an egg. The shell is cracked and a little pressure will break it. That leaves Venice, Genoa and Florence as his only failures. He is younger than we two and he is patient. Have you noticed how he never risks his armies? He fears an invasion of his lands. His fortress at Pavia is where he dwells like a corpulent spider. In that rocky fortress, he is safe and his best troops guard him. Milan has never been threatened because he keeps an army there and he hires companies to cause mischief." He gave me a shrewd look, "You would challenge him?"

"I am not afraid of the fight if that is what you mean however I am a sword for hire. I do not have the finances to pay the White Company let alone a larger army. If another hires me I will go."

He leaned forward, "And if that contract comes your way then remember your old friend. I would like a nibble of that particular piece of fruit."

"Who is there now that is to be feared?"

"Jacopo dal Verme is young and skilful. He is about to take Padua and he is Visconti's sword. I am not trusted and I am used." He shrugged, "I am too closely associated with you and Visconti fears you." He stood, "And now we had better return. Your Bolognese friend will fear that we are plotting."

I laughed, "His uncle sent him as a spy but he is out of his depth, he thinks that he is a warrior but he has yet to draw a sword in anger. You could have taken Bologna, easily, my friend."

"And that would simply have delivered it to Visconti. He paid me to make mischief and that I have done."

The look of fear on Ambrogio Bentovoglio's face when we returned, laughing, was a picture. I could almost see the treachery he imagined we had concocted. I had a reputation as someone not to be trusted. My company and the other condottieri knew that I could be trusted but the princes and dukes saw hidden motives in all of my actions. I smiled at him. "It is done, Ambrogio. Captain Ubaldini will send men back with me for the payment. Your mission for your uncle has ended in success, well done."

He preened as though it was his words that had done the deed.

Chapter 6

1388 Casa Donnina

I had made friends in Bologna and, when we returned with the good news that they would no longer be plagued by my friend's company of mercenaries, I was feted as though I had somehow defeated an enemy in battle. I did not disillusion them. It had been easy to dissuade Giovanni from attacking Bologna but they weren't to know that. I took their praise and smiled modestly. I had made an ally of Bologna and, perhaps, a future employer.

The next day, with the payment in my bags, we headed for home. The attacks on the way north had made us wary and we rode mailed once more. Ned and Edgar had learned much in their time in the city. Jacopo dal Verme was very much the new man to be feared. Merchants that they had met told tales of his skill. I took that with a healthy dose of salt for merchants knew money and not swords. However, Giovanni's words, not to mention the intelligence gathered by Ned and Edgar, had given me a warning. I would need to find out as much as I could about this man. We were still at peace but I deduced, as we neared Florence, that war would come. If war did come then my foe would be the new condottiero; one I had never fought before.

I waited at the gates of the city of Florence for permission to enter. It was a formality but I knew that the one time I did not ask I would be punished. After sending my lances, archers and servants back to my estates, my bodyguards and I were escorted to the house of Carlos Cialdini. Michael was there.

Zuzzo and Gianluca stood to one side. Michael's father-in-law simply said, "Well?"

"Captain Ubaldini will raid Pisa and I have managed to persuade him to withdraw from Bologna."

That he was delighted was an understatement. His eyes widened, "How did you manage that?" Bologna was not only an ally but a buffer to the north.

I had no intention of telling him about my fee and instead, I said, "I merely pointed out that a contract to raid Pisa would be more rewarding."

Legacy

"And if Bologna is not threatened then Florence is safe. You have done well, Sir John, and served Florence faithfully once more. We thank you." That was all. There was no payment for having achieved that which he thought impossible. I was kept on a retainer and in the podestà's eyes that was payment enough.

Michael walked me out to my horse. I could tell that he wished to tell me something. I waited. "I think that you may well be hired by the council within the next year." I merely raised my eyebrows. Michael knew me well enough to work out that I was asking a question. "There are spies in Milan who report to us. They have to be circumspect and the news is not always prompt. Galeazzo has hired Jacopo dal Verme and the inference is that Tuscany is at risk. I know that you have few men at the moment and my father-in-law is keen for you to hire more."

"And that means that I keep my company at my expense to serve Florence," Michael said nothing. "Since you clearly now work for Carlos Cialdini then you might as well earn his pay. I will raise more men but I need my annual retainer to be increased."

"You are well paid now, Sir John."

"And have I not just ensured that Florence will be safe? The retainer is not to defend Florence but to be ready to fight when she needs it. The last money for the White Company came from the Pope and not Florence. The last thing your father-in-law needs is for me to have a full company on his doorstep and no war."

It was a thinly veiled threat but Michael knew better than any that I knew Florence well enough to take it at any time I chose. He nodded.

"One thing more, Michael. If you have spies in Milan then gather information about this new condottiero. Be discreet and report to me, eh?"

"Yes, Sir John."

I soon reached home but in a far from peaceful frame of mind. The mention of Florentine spies reminded me that I also had spies in my home. It made me frown as I entered my home. My wife removed that frown when she greeted me as warmly as ever. Many people had often remarked on the disparity in our ages. It did not matter. We loved each other and, more than that, we thought along the same lines. We rarely disagreed about anything. While my wife and I embraced Ned and Edgar brought in the gold and my belongings. Donnina took charge of both. She would have my clothes washed and the payment secured in our vault. I went to change. The roads were dusty and I was hot and sweaty. I bathed before descending to join my wife. I no longer stank of horses and the road. I was perfumed and clean.

Donnina smiled her approval, "It is good to have you home again and the florins are a welcome addition to our funds. They are secured already. We will talk when we have dined and we are alone." She squeezed my hand as she spoke, her eyes speaking with mine, and I nodded. I understood the code. The spy was still in my home.

The girls were now of an age where they were inquisitive. My two eldest were almost young women. They would need husbands in the next five years and when I returned these days, I was no longer pestered with requests for playthings but for clothes, jewels and news. They had inherited their mother's sharp mind. Only Anna remained a young child. I happily answered their questions. Donnina dismissed them as soon as the last of the food was finished.

"Guccio, open a bottle of dessert wine and then you and the other servants have finished for the night."

"Thank you, my lady." He turned to me, "It is good to have you safely home again, Sir John. Will you be here for a while?"

I gave a non-committal smile, "We shall see."

We moved to the two chairs by the fireplace. Although this was Italy and a warm country, the nights could be chilly and we both enjoyed a fire in the evening. For one thing, the smoke kept away the mosquitoes and other flying insects and for another, there was something soothing about crackling logs. When the door closed, Donnina waited for a few moments and then went to the door. She opened it and then reclosed it. I knew why. She was ensuring that there were no eavesdroppers.

After she sat and poured us both a goblet of the heavy dessert wine we both enjoyed, she said, "Your news first."

I told her everything. I kept nothing back. Her smile showed that she approved of all my decisions and the money I had accrued. When she refilled our glasses I said, "And now, the spy. I take it you know who it is."

She nodded, "There is no easy way to tell you this, my husband, but it is Guccio."

I frowned, "I find that hard to believe for his father, Carlos, served us for many years. He was a loyal man." He had died while I had been serving Padua and his son had seemed, at the time, a perfect replacement.

"He was but Guccio waited a long time for the promotion and he has an ambitious young wife who likes pretty things. My enquiries have told me that they both live above their means. I know how much we pay them."

"Have you done anything about it?"

She shook her head, "I had him followed by one of your new archers. He saw him visit Florence every three days. He met one of the podestà's servants and gold changed hands." That was not worrying for telling the council of Florence what I was up to would do me little harm. However, there was more. When we eliminated our spy we would let the podestà wonder what we knew. "He also saw him visit the tavern on the road to Lucca on a weekly basis. Robert said he met a man there. I used Robert Green because he speaks Italian well but he did not recognise the man. I thought to use Zuzzo next time. He might be able to identify the spy's confederates."

"I will speak to Zuzzo on the morrow. We do not need spies here." I told her about the attack on the road. "The spies knew the route we would take. But for a friendly merchant, we might have lost men."

My wife's voice took on an edge I had not heard before and she almost hissed out her words. My bodyguards as well as Ned and Edgar were like family to Donnina, "I feel betrayed. It is good that both Carlos and his wife are dead. They were both loyal. His father would be turning in his grave at the disloyalty. This treacherous pair must pay." My wife had her father's ruthless streak and I shuddered. This would not end well for either Guccio or his wife.

"This is more than disloyalty. This is treachery. Casa Donnina is the one place where I felt secure and happy. Until this threat has been eradicated, I shall not enjoy a moment in its walls."

I did not sleep well, despite the heavy sweet wine I had drunk, for Guccio and his wife had access to every part of the house. I felt soiled at the thought of them watching us. I rose early. I found Gianluca and Zuzzo in the gyrus. I waved them over. They could see that something was amiss for I rarely rose this early at home. I told them what we suspected and they both nodded. "I never liked him, my lord. None of us did. He is an arrogant man who thinks he is better than we are. He was, is, tolerated because of his father who was a good man. What do you need us to do? Would you have us slit their throats?" Zuzzo was more than capable of committing murder for me although I knew it would be an execution rather than a murder.

I shook my head, "Find out who he meets and who his contact works for. Until we know that, we act as though nothing is wrong. Let us deceive the deceivers."

It took two more days for my two bodyguards to discover that Guccio met the servant of a spice merchant from Lucca in the inn on the road west. The innkeeper knew Zuzzo. I think he feared him a little and he happily informed on Guccio and his accomplice. It was always on the same day. Alessandro Soldi was the cousin of Matteo Soldi who was one of the leading wine merchants in Florence. The two had fallen out and Alessandro had set up in Lucca. I suspected that Visconti funded the merchant. Galeazzo Visconti was a planner. Alessandro Soldi would make a good puppet to be podestà if he ever managed to secure Florence for his fiefdom. While that did not tell us conclusively who the two servants ultimately served, we could guess it had to be Visconti. Donnina and I were in agreement about that. My steward and his wife were taking pay from two paymasters and they must have made a small fortune from the selling of news.

We chose the moment of confrontation well. We picked the day when Guccio would normally meet the servant. That way we knew that the man from Lucca would be in the inn. Donnina pretended that we wished to reward Guccio and his wife, Caterina. They were summoned to my office in the middle of the afternoon. Zuzzo and Gianluca hid and once the two entered my

Legacy

bodyguards followed and secured the door behind them. At the same time, John Coe and Peter were sent to the inn to apprehend the servant. My other men kept a close watch on the other servants. Donnina thought that Guccio and his wife were the only spies but it was as well to be careful. Until we had interrogated them, we would trust no one.

Caterina was a bold one and feigned innocence, "What means this, Sir John? Why is the door barred and we are prevented from leaving?" She acted the part of a vulnerable woman seeking the protection of her lord. She was an attractive young woman and she thought to appeal to me as a man. Such wiles had never worked on me and in this situation, there could be no justification for their actions.

Donnina had been angry from the moment she had heard of the deception and she strode up to Caterina, who towered over my diminutive wife and, pulling back her hand, gave her such a slap across the face that the spy's wife reeled and fell against one of the chairs. Her face showed the red imprint of my wife's small hand. Donnina turned and jabbed an accusative finger at Guccio who stepped back, fearing a slap himself, "You were treated and paid well yet you have betrayed us. We know you have met Soldi's man in the inn."

"He is a friend, no more, my lady." Guccio tried to use smooth words and a smile as evasion. He was clearly trying to brazen his way out of this. What he could not know was that I had two men bringing him to my home.

I spoke, for the first time, "Then when he is brought here and questioned, he will confirm your words."

He paled when he realised that we would apprehend his accomplice, and his knees almost buckled, "He is a friend and no more."

"You have a friend from Lucca? Are there not others closer who could be your friends? Why meet him so secretly?"

"My lord, I need a place where I can be private. The other servants resent my wife and me. They think we are too young to run this estate."

"And why do you report to the podestà of Florence? Is he another…friend?"

Guccio pushed himself against the wall as though he needed support. His web was being untangled before his eyes. He had thought that his actions were secret and he had managed to fool us and now it was revealed to him that we knew all.

There was a knock at the door and Zuzzo opened it. He disappeared outside for a few moments. When he returned, he came over to me and spoke in my ear, "John and Peter have the servant. He is without and they are interrogating him. I do not doubt he will tell us all that we need to know. His name is Antonio Carlucci."

I knew we had Guccio now. "So, Guccio, Antonio Carlucci is your friend? He is talking, even as we speak, and John and Peter can be very persuasive."

He paled and dropped to his knees, "Lord, I swear, he is just a friend I..."

I nodded towards Zuzzo and Gianluca, "We were ambushed on the road when we left for Bologna. We could have died. You did not just betray me, you put the lives of my men in jeopardy. Do not expect sympathy. All that I will promise is that if you tell the truth, all of it, then your deaths will be swift and painless. I will let you see a priest." He raised his face and saw the look on my face. He could see that I meant what I said and he nodded.

Caterina had been cowed after the slap from my wife but, as she saw the nod she suddenly shouted, "You cannot!" I am not sure if the words were meant for me or her husband.

Guccio stood and snarled at his wife, "Silence! It is your greed that has brought us to this. I for one would rather have a painless death and the chance to confess than be tortured and still die unshriven. I do not wish to endure pain. They have Antonio and it is all over." He dropped to his knees, "Forgive me, my lord."

I felt sorry for him and I might have relented but for two things: one was the look of absolute hatred on my wife's face and the other was that leaving them alive would put my whole family at risk. "Speak!"

"No!" It became clear that Caterina was the ruthless one in the marriage. She suddenly pulled a stiletto from the folds of her dress and slashed it at my throat. Had it connected I would have died. I was an old man but my body still had the reactions of a warrior. I jerked my head back and the blade tore the top of my tunic. I punched with my right hand and connected with her shoulder and, overbalancing, she fell to the ground. Zuzzo and Gianluca were on her in an instant. Zuzzo had the knife in his hands and he gave me a look which suggested he might use the knife to end her life.

I had no idea why she did what she did. With two bodyguards in the room, it was unlikely that she would escape but perhaps my death might have been reward enough for her. I shook my head, "Let us not make it easy for her. I am unharmed. Fasten her hands and gag her. I wish to hear no more of her screeching. Guccio, your wife's attack is an admission of guilt. You are her husband and responsible for her actions. Speak now."

Once he began, he could not stop. He gave us all the details we needed. It was, of course, Galeazzo Visconti who had used Alessandro Soldi as an intermediary. The servant we took confirmed it too. Once they heard that I was travelling on a lonely road with so few men it was the perfect opportunity. Visconti, through Soldi, had paid Guccio well. He also told us that Carlos Cialdini wished regular reports about where I was and what I was doing. He would receive no more reports. His servant would wait in vain for the arrival of his spy. When we searched their room, we found a chest with three hundred florins within it. We had not paid him a tenth of that amount. His confession, the attack by his wife and the gold we found were evidence enough. They were guilty. I had every right to punish them as I saw fit.

I was true to my word and a priest was brought to hear all three confess and then my wife gave them a draught of poison. I thought that Caterina might refuse but the sight of Zuzzo sharpening his sword with a whetstone left her in no doubt that a refusal to comply would result in a messier and more painful end. It was a painless death for all three; they simply succumbed to sleep and it was a merciful death. It could have been much worse. The poison worked quickly and made them drowsy before they slipped into an eternal slumber. My men buried all three secretly in the grounds. We told the other servants that they had been dismissed for theft. Of course, Alessandro Soldi would wonder about his servant. He might even know that he was taken by my men but he would have to reveal his part in the matter if he tried to bring retribution on my head. He would tell his master and Visconti would send another. As for the podestà, he would be concerned and wonder what we knew. We set in place a system. The guards on the gate would only allow people to leave if they had a pass from Donnina, myself or one of my two bodyguards. We now knew that Casa Donnina was threatened. We would interrogate every newcomer who arrived at my home. We decided that we would not employ outsiders as servants. The ones we had, we could trust, especially with the new system in place. Ned and Edgar took on the role of butler and steward between them. They had proved that they were loyal and any shortcomings as butler and steward were overlooked. Our safety was far more important than having people who understood protocol. Outside of my familia, no one knew of the attack. We knew how to keep secrets.

I felt safe enough to begin to recruit men for my company and the contracts I knew would soon be coming my way. I spread the word that I was seeking men. I had Jack of Derby ride to Robin and secure more men. To facilitate that I went with Zuzzo and Gianluca to Pisa. The man who had protected my position for so many years, Pellario Griffo, was long dead but I had saved Pisa on many occasions and my accountant, William Turner, still lived there. He still handled the revenue from my Bordeaux estate and my Pisan ones. The bank we had built was in Pisa and protected by former White Company warriors but we had a second one on my estate that Donnina and I used for our money. He was a useful man, however, as he was well known in mercenary circles and he could get the word out to more men, quicker than I could.

His wife did not like me and as soon as she saw me dismount from my horse pointedly disappeared so that she would not only avoid speaking to me but also having to look at me. William was far more diplomatic. I had dragged him from an almost slave-like existence and given him and his sister a life. His sister had even borne me sons. I owed him nothing and he owed me everything.

"It is good to see you, Sir John. I have not seen you since your famous, some say, legendary victory. Congratulations." He nodded to my bodyguards. They knew how I viewed my accountant and they wore stoic expressions. "How may I be of service?"

"I need lances for my company."

He looked genuinely surprised, "You have not retired? I thought you would have hung up your sword after Castagnaro. It will be hard to better such a victory."

I ignored the flattery, "I need at least three hundred lances."

"A large number but if you can give me three months then I should be able to manage. No archers?"

"Robin deals with those. I want them sent to me as soon as they have signed the contract." I leaned in, "Spies have tried to get close to me, William. I want honest men and if I find any spies…" I let the sentence hang like a sword.

"I will do my best but how can you see into a man's heart?"

"Try. I assume you will take your usual commission."

He nodded, "The company's funds are in a relatively good state. There should be no problem." He had the bulk of the money of the White Company. Donnina ensured that my money was in Casa Donnina.

"And who is the power now in Pisa?"

"Jacopo di d'Appiano. Although he has a condottiero as an advisor, Jacopo di Montepulciano." He was Ubaldini's man. Perhaps that was why Giovanni had not done as Florence had asked and raided the city.

"A good leader?"

"I get on with him." I knew that he would. William Turner was a master at finding the winning side and staying on it.

"Tell me what you know about Jacopo dal Verme."

He went to a pile of parchments and searched through until he found what he wanted. William kept good records. He knew every condottiero in the land. "Jacopo dal Verme, the son of Luchino Dal Verme and Jacopa de' Malvicini. He began serving Alberico da Barbiano when he was sixteen. He served the Visconti family in the war against the Guelph League and by the time he was nineteen had risen to be Galeazzo Visconti's man. He left the service of Alberico." He looked at me.

I nodded, "A rapid rise and for one so young too."

"He led men in Piedmont and Monferrato for Visconti and even served as a diplomat to Avignon and the anti-pope." He frowned, "He helped Galeazzo take Milan from his brother, Bernabò. He now leads the provvisionati of Milan." He put the parchment on the desk. "He is seen as the next Giovanni Acuto."

I smiled, "We shall see."

I left satisfied that I would be sent good men and three months was a long enough time. I was also happier with the knowledge I had gleaned about Jacopo dal Verme. He had learned his trade with Alberico who had learned it from me. I was still the master.

It was as we left, to head back to Florence, that I thought of the changes over my long and eventful life. Pisa was now in the past and Florence was my home. Men like William were just on the periphery of my world while men like Dai, Eoin, Robert Greengrass and many others were just the memories that sometimes tiptoed into my dreams. They had served me and left to enjoy the riches they had earned following my banner and benefitting from my skills. Even Michael was drifting away from me. The only constants were Donnina, Robin and Giovanni. Now that one of my oldest friends fought for Visconti and his man ruled Pisa, would that bring us into conflict?

William was an efficient recruiter of men. Within a month we had new lances: Corrado Lando, also known as Konrad von Landau, brought fifty lances and Albert Coiser also brought fifty. Corrado di Rotestein and David Falcan brought fifty lances and an invaluable thirty-seven archers. Roger Nottingham came with ten lances and five archers, and William Cook and Richard Croft brought ten lances. Von Landau and Coiser both were renowned condottieri and I had employed them before. Castagnaro and Rimini had reminded other soldiers that Giovanni Acuto was not ready to retire. We lived in Italy and most men answered to an Italian name. Corrado di Rotestein was another German knight, Konrad von Rotestein. Albert Coiser was also a German captain. I found them useful soldiers but I wished that they were English.

Chapter 7

1388 Casa Donnina

As the year drew to a close I found my life filled with work. It was work that I loved for it involved me in making a company. Each company I had commanded had my handiwork and style on it but each one was a little different from the last. They all had more archers and fewer crossbowmen than other armies. We used our squires differently and I had few handguns but they were all similar in terms of proportions. I thought that every White Company that I led was better than the one I had led before. I spoke with every lance and archer who sought employment. I only had to reject two lances. I had no proof that they were Visconti spies but when there was doubt I erred on the side of caution. The rest of the men were just what they appeared to be, swords for hire.

We heard little of the world beyond Italy because, to be truthful, it held no interest for me. Not long before Christmas, however, I was dragged into the world of English politics. A party of horsemen approached my home. I did not fear violence even though there were twenty of them and more than half were mailed for I had two hundred and fifty lances training on my estate. The riders came cloaked and their identities were hidden from me. My guards at the gate had allowed them to enter and that meant they had been questioned and found to be of no threat to me.

Donnina was well aware of our duties to guests. Our policy was to be friendly and hospitable to every visitor until they gave us cause to fear them. I did not know the rank of these visitors but at least four of them wore expensive plate armour and so we would house and entertain them. There were spurs amongst them. I saw that as they rode up and dismounted. They had sumpters and servants. We had enough chambers for those with rank.

Donnina said, as she watched them approach the main entrance to the hall, "I will go within. Ned and Edgar are new to their roles. They will need advice from me."

I nodded and turned to Zuzzo. Gianluca was with the lances, "Do you recognise them?"

He shook his head, "No, my lord, but I do not think they are from this land. Their skin is pale although some are reddening. If I were to take a guess, I would suggest that they are your countrymen or from the north, at any rate."

I did not recognise them but he was right and the plate they wore looked English. Most of the lances who came to me these days were Italian, Hungarian or German but I could always tell the English lances as they wore slightly different plate armour.

They halted and I said, in English, "Welcome, gentlemen."

The leader dismounted and threw back his cloak. I did not recognise his livery. It was red and yellow quarters with a mullet in the first quarter. He was a young man, I guessed less than thirty, and he had the look of an arrogant noble. He had that sneering haughty look I had seen when I served the Black Prince. He said, "I am Robert de Vere, Duke of Ireland, Marquess of Dublin and you must be Sir John Hawkwood."

He sounded the titles as though I should be in awe of them. I was not for I counted dukes and princes as employers and not those to whom I should bow and scrape, "I am, Your Grace." His men had all dismounted, "You wish shelter for the night?"

"Of course. You are a friend of King Richard as am I. I have sought you out for I would speak to you in confidence."

I bowed and gestured with my arm, "If you and your party would enter. Your servants and those without rank will be attended to by Zuzzo here. My wife waits within."

I was intrigued by the visit. I knew the name, de Vere. When Geoffrey Chaucer had stayed with me he had told me that Robert de Vere was a confidante and a favourite of the impressionable young king. He had also said that outside of the court de Vere was despised. Intrigue was tip-toeing into my home and I would be wary. I had enough plots and enemies in Italy without adding Englishmen to that number. The duke was followed by six men. They looked to be the sort of men I might hire as lances. They were young and had plate armour over their mail. Their swords were well-made. All wore the same livery as the duke and I saw that four of them had spurs; they were knights but also they were hired swords. That meant they had left their lands in England to follow this young noble to Italy.

Donnina had changed and she positively glowed as she greeted our guests. Her English was, of course, perfect. Her father had raised her that way and living with me had enhanced it. "This is the Duke of Ireland, my dear. He is a friend of King Richard."

"Then you are more than welcome to our humble home. I fear that your unannounced arrival means that we will not be able to entertain you as your rank and title deserve. Forgive us."

He smiled and, taking her hand, kissed the back of it, "My lady, to be close to such a beauty as you, my men and I would sleep in a stable."

Donnina played a part and gave him a disarming smile although she knew the compliment was a hollow one, "The chambers we have for you are comfortable. Ned and Edgar are both Englishmen and they will show you to your rooms. Ask them anything."

"You are gracious beyond words, my lady."

When they had left us, I said, "Here is a puzzle. Why would a confidante of the king come all the way to Florence?"

"Perhaps he is an emissary from the king."

"The king would have sent Chaucer. No, this is something else. We will be cautious."

Donnina gave me a shake of her head, which told me I was stating the obvious, "Of course." She went to the kitchens. We had larders that were well stocked but entertaining a duke required a judicious selection of dishes.

Zuzzo entered and I said, "Well?"

"The duke is an exile, my lord. John Coe and Peter came with me while I showed them their rooms and they spoke with the servants. There was a rising against the king and the duke was defeated at a place called Radcot Bridge. The king is now confined by men called the Lords Appellant. These visitors are on their way to Rome. The warriors with him are his bodyguards. He has only four knights." That told me a great deal. A marquess and a duke should have a great retinue of lords who owed him fealty. Four was a tiny number.

"I see. Ask John to find out more but with subtlety."

"Of course. Their horses show the effects of a long ride, my lord."

When Donnina returned I told her my news. We still had no idea of the purpose of the visit but at least we had some background. We would learn more while we ate.

Knowing that these were Englishmen decided the menu we would enjoy. We chose the kind of food that they would be familiar with. We always had wild boar for it was one of my favourites and the smell was an enticing one when it was brought in. It was polite small talk that accompanied the boar for the men devoured it as though they had not eaten since England. We had desserts and cheese and they were the subject of comments from the duke as they were Italian. The hot puddings favoured in England were not popular with Donnina. She had given the main course as English, but the rest would be to her taste. The cheeses were also different in taste from the ones that they were used to.

When he had finished the duke wiped his mouth with his cloth and leaned back in his chair, "We have travelled far, since leaving England, my lady, but the food this night has been the finest that we have enjoyed."

She smiled for she had chosen well and she was a perfectionist, "Good, I am pleased. While the table is cleared, Ned, bring the dessert wine, it will help his grace and his men to sleep."

"Yes, my lady." Ned was still learning to be a butler and his big rough hands looked enormous around the decanter of sweet wine which he brought in. He poured generous measures as the servants took away the platters and the detritus of the meal.

There was silence and I could see that the young duke was trying to work out how to broach the subject he had come to raise. I helped him out, "Your servants say that you are on your way to Rome, my lord?"

He looked relieved that I had given him a way to begin the conversation, "I am. I know that you are a loyal Englishman despite the fact that you have lived abroad for most of your life. King Richard speaks highly of you and has told me of your silent and secret service to England. I go to Rome because the Lords Appellant in England are trying to take away the rights of a king. I seek Rome's help in the matter."

"I hope you are successful although in my experience the Papacy responds better to financial inducement rather than moral and legal matters."

He drank some of the wine, "A most excellent wine. It reminds me of the fortified Portuguese wine I enjoyed when I lived in England." He raised his glass to my wife who gave a gracious nod, "There is another matter." He leaned forward, "The Scots invaded England and defeated our men at Otterburn. King Richard needs your men, Sir John. I beg that you take the White Company to England and fight for King Richard and for England."

This was dangerous country. Mercenaries were common in Italy but not in England. I sipped the wine as I formulated an answer that would not insult the duke nor make a return to England, sometime in the future, impossible. I needed the support of the king and the income from my English estates was vital.

"As much as I, Sir John Hawkwood, might like to come to England and fight for King Richard you should know how the company, any condottiere company, works. I have but two hundred and fifty or so lances here at the moment. In terms of men that translates to less than five hundred men. I can get more but it takes time. We are also a mercenary company. We fight for pay. I apologise for the crudity of my words but is the king in a position to pay us?"

His head dropped and he shook his head, "I have sent word to the king's uncle, John of Gaunt, and begged him to return to England but until he does so then the king is fettered. He has no money to pay for men. It is like the time of the baron's rebellion under Simon de Montfort."

I could not see how King Richard, in the short term, would have the finances to hire us so I said, to assuage him, "When the king has the means to pay for my company then send word and I will bring my men to England. I am a loyal Englishman and I have no doubt that I could find the words to persuade many of my men to follow me."

He seemed to like my answer, "And I will continue to seek support for the king. I am glad that I came here, Sir John, you have given me hope."

Legacy

After he left, the next day, Donnina and I spoke with Ned, Edgar, John Coe and Zuzzo. My men had been my spies and had gathered information from loose-tongued servants.

"The duke is not a good soldier, my lord. His tactics lost the battle and he barely escaped with his life. His men say that he lost his horse and weapons and had to shed his armour to escape Henry Bolingbroke. He left the river almost naked."

I smiled at the image. It showed, however, that the duke was resourceful, "Thank you, John. Any other comments?"

Edgar nodded, "The men are not hopeful of a return to England any time soon. John of Gaunt, who is the king's only hope, does not like the duke. It is said that the duke has money he made in Ireland and, I think, that is why his men stay with him."

"After Rome?"

"He has an estate in Flanders, my lord. He will return to Louvain until the king is in power. The king, it is said, is much influenced by the duke."

I spoke with Donnina when my men went about their business. "It seems you are right to advise against a return to England. The king clings on to his crown by the barest of touches."

"And will it affect your income?"

I shook my head, "The deeds and the land are secure in our vault, although if it was an enemy of mine who seized power then they might make mischief. I am just grateful that your uncle has his eye fixed on Italy and has no familial connections with England." I smiled, "It has given me more of an incentive to make up my numbers once more."

Sometimes men came alone to join my company. It was a rare occurrence for most warriors who joined me to arrive without a squire, a foot soldier and either an archer or a crossbowman. The exceptions were Englishmen. John Coe and Peter were two such examples. Robert Daring was another. He came a week or so after our English visitors had left us, on a sorry-looking nag. He was a huge man, and his feet almost touched the ground. With him, he had a rare weapon, a double-headed axe. It was a fearsome weapon which had to be wielded two handed. When he dismounted, I saw that he wore a short hauberk with plates on his upper legs and arms. He had no breastplate. He wore no helmet but had a hood over his head to protect him from the sun. The most distinguishing feature, however, was the long fresh scar that ran from above his right eye down to his chin. He still had his eye but he had been lucky to keep it for the scar was deep. Normally I would have dismissed him out of hand, not for his wound but for his weapon. It was hard to see how he would fit into my company. Even John and Peter had adapted so that John and Peter were now both lances and had employed a squire and a foot soldier. They had made enough money from me already to become condottieri.

I was intrigued by the wound and before I dismissed him, I decided that I would speak to him. "Gianluca, fetch food and wine for this weary soldier."

I spoke in Italian but the man showed me that he had understood the words for he said, in English, "I would prefer ale if you have it, Sir John."

"Ale then, Gianluca." My bodyguard nodded and left us. "What is your name, soldier?"

"Robert Daring."

"A family name or did you earn it?"

He smiled and with the scar, it gave him a cockeyed look, "Earned, my lord. When you use this weapon, you find yourself in the heart of many combats, my lord, and I never shirk from a fight."

"Is that how you came by the wound? I cannot help but notice that it is fresh."

He placed the axe on the ground as servants, led by Gianluca, brought food and ale. He drank half of the ale before he spoke. He grinned, "Good ale, my lord, and the first I have enjoyed since I fled England. Do you mind if I eat before I speak? The road has been a hard one."

I nodded, "Gianluca, stable Robert's horse. Come my intriguing friend, and shelter beneath the portico for it is hot." I bent and picked up the axe, "I will carry this weapon for you." Carrying his platter of food and his precious mug of ale he followed me to the portico where we would be sheltered from the sun. The axe was heavy but I found it well-balanced and I was able to carry it one handed. In my days as an archer, I might have been able to wield it one handed in battle but those days were long gone. We sat on the bench there and I allowed him to finish his food. As I studied him, I saw what he meant about the road being a hard one. For a man with his frame, he was thin, almost gaunt.

He put his platter down and emptied the mug. I waved over the servant who took it away to refill.

"Now my tale. I fought for the king at Radcot Bridge or rather I served in the army led by his incompetent lieutenants. Henry Bolingbroke is no fool but even a simpleton could have beaten Robert de Vere." Luigi returned with more ale and Robert drank once more. "He fled and the other leaders did too. We were left to fend for ourselves. Sir John Constable did this to me. The brow of my helmet saved my life." He chuckled, "And cost Sir John his leg and, I daresay, his life. I managed to escape the battle. I was the last of the men who had begun the battle and the rest lay dead. Losing my life would have been pointless. I found the nag I now ride wandering the field and took it. She may look fit for the knacker's yard but she has brought me here."

"You came all the way from England to find me?"

"I would not serve those who oppose the king, he may not be the best king but he is the son of the Black Prince. I know that while you are a mercenary, Sir John, you are still an Englishman. Crécy and Poitiers are a testament to that loyalty. If I cannot fight in England, at least I can fight for a noble Englishman. Your name is well respected in England by real warriors."

His story made me change my mind about his employment. I nodded, "Your weapon and the fact that you are alone would normally cause me a problem but I can see that you are a warrior. Can you use a lance?"

He smiled, "If I have to, aye, but if you are asking can I use one while mounted then my answer would be nay. I like the ground beneath my feet, my lord. Plant me next to you and I promise that none would get close to you."

Even as he spoke, I was working out the best way to use him. My days of leading charges were long gone. Zuzzo and Gianluca had made it quite clear that my place was behind the front lines and directing the battle. I had fought from the back of a wagon before and that would be how I would fight in future. Robert

Daring and his weapon would be perfect for the defence of a wagon.

I waved over Zuzzo, "I have a new man, Zuzzo."

I saw my trumpeter and bodyguard scrutinising the Englishman. Zuzzo was a good judge of men and while I was happy to employ Robert Daring I would use Zuzzo's opinion in my decision of how I would use him.

"His name is Robert Daring and he has ridden all the way from England."

Zuzzo looked at the horse which was eating the few weeds that grew next to the entrance to my hall, "On that? I am impressed, my friend." Zuzzo could speak English.

"Have him sign the contract or make his mark and give him a surcoat and a bed."

"A surcoat?"

Most of the company did not wear the surcoat with my livery upon it. They were reserved for my bodyguards and those like my four Englishmen, my familia. "Yes, we will see if he can work with you and Gianluca. He will need to learn Italian. That is your appointed task." Zuzzo nodded. "And when you are cleaned up and dressed return to my hall. I would introduce you to my wife and learn more about the state of England."

"Yes, my lord and, Sir John…"

"Yes, Robert?"

"Thank you. You will not regret this." Somehow I knew that I would not.

Donnina liked the gruff soldier from the first. He was like a piece of clay in her hands. He towered over her, he was even taller than I was and yet around Donnina, he was a gentle giant. I think he was a little in love with her. Certainly, he became tongue-tied and hesitant when he was in her presence but I saw in his eyes something that could not be hidden. Loyalty. Donnina was my wife and he was my man. Warriors like Robert have a code which is unshakeable. Zuzzo and Gianluca were the same. I suspected it when I first met him but I learned, as time went on of the veracity of that first impression.

He told me of England and I feared for my homeland. I had heard about the king and about England from those who served him, men like Chaucer and de Vere. It was a jaundiced view.

Legacy

Robert was an ordinary man who saw England for what it really was. A land in chaos ruled by a troubled king. Italy seemed, somehow, a safer place.

Legacy

Siena and its neighbours 1390

Chapter 8

1389 June Siena

My new bodyguard, Robert Daring, now that he was eating regularly, began to put on weight and fill out his frame very quickly. He would be a giant once more and Zuzzo remarked that he would be like two bodyguards. He got on well with Zuzzo and Gianluca although, at first, there was a problem with the language. He overcame that and they became closely bonded.

Our training was coming on well but it was expensive to maintain the men I had and it was with some relief when Michael came to speak to me. "The Florentine council wish to hire you, Sir John. It is for six months and it pays five hundred florins a month"

"And where do we go this time? Bologna?"

He shook his head, "No. Montepulciano, as you know, is an ancient ally of Florence. The Sienese have hired Paolo Savelli to take the city."

I frowned for I knew the name. Paolo Savelli had been one of Alberico da Barbiano's lieutenants many years earlier. "And who is Savelli's paymaster?"

"Your old friend Galeazzo Visconti."

The tentacles of the Milanese were spreading and I now understood why Florence was happy to pay me on top of my retainer. I knew that we could double the pay by raiding around the borders of Siena.

"Does Siena know that Visconti will swallow them, Michael?"

The Florentine council had many spies who were constantly working to keep Florence safe. "They do not. Savelli has a thousand men but Jacopo dal Verme is gathering more men. The council thinks that they will be used to reinforce Savelli."

I knew what would happen then. It had been Verona's fate. Visconti had helped them in their war with Padua and then simply swallowed them up in the aftermath of their defeat. "Am I to be bait? I only have one thousand men."

I looked into his eyes as he answered to see if there was deception. He shook his head, "No, Sir John, you are only to keep Savelli from Montepulciano. Of course, if you were to raid Sienese land then that would please Florence."

Siena, like Pisa, was an ancient enemy of Florence.

"And the contract ends?"

"Six months from now, Sir John."

That was generous. It would take at least a week, perhaps two, to reach Montepulciano. "And the payments?"

He handed over a purse, "Here are the first five hundred florins. The rest will be delivered by me to Lady Donnina each month."

That was acceptable as I trusted Michael. "Then all is well." He turned to go but I said, "Did you find out about Jacopo dal Verme?"

He nodded, "I did. I am sorry I did not bring it to you earlier. We have been busy in Florence." The report he gave me confirmed what William had told me. I was happy to have two accounts which tallied with each other.

Donnina was delighted with the contract. She gave a rueful shake of her head as she said, "A good contract but the payment arriving each month ensures that you have to fulfil the whole contract." If we had been paid the whole amount then my clever wife could have invested it and made it grow.

"I have yet to let anyone down."

"They will not see the good in you, my husband. You are a mercenary and tarred with the same brush as those who are less than honest." She smiled, "This means you can use Montecchio Vesponi as a base."

I shook my head, "I do not wish to risk damaging that estate. Besides, we will live off Sienese land."

Her half-brother, Carlo and his men had also joined me. He was a young condottiero but a good warrior and he hated his uncle more than anyone. I would use him and Konrad von Landau to command my Italian lances. I used John Balzan and John Edingham to command the English elements. Jack of Derby was my captain of archers.

We left my home to head for Robin and my estate in the east. I would not stay there but I wanted to be in a position to raid the Sienese lands on that side of the city. That way I would have easy access to arrows and archers too. Three weeks after leaving my home and having visited Robin to pick up four more archers and arrows, we arrived at Montepulciano. Our route had not been the shortest. That would have taken us through Sienese land. We had skirted the Valdichiana. It was a large area of lakes, rivers and bogs that protected the eastern side of the city-state. When we arrived, I sent my company to the west of the city to set up camp and Konrad von Landau and Donnina's brother, Carlo, to take their companies to scout out places we could raid. I visited with the rulers of the city, the Del Pecora family. They were relieved both by our arrival and the fact that I had kept my company from the city. I noticed that they did not offer any soldiers to defend their own land. It was telling.

The condottiero, Savelli, was not close so we spent a week raiding Sienese land. It gave us food and plunder but the sooner we could bring Savelli to battle the sooner we could end the threat. It was also an opportunity for me to see my new men in action. I rode with each party of raiders over that first week so that I could see how they blended. We used Italian and English soldiers together. We had a few Germans and Hungarians in my company and that seemed to work. We kept ourselves well supplied with food and supplemented our pay. Our raids worked and forced Savelli to bring his company to meet us. My scouts found him at Sinalunga. He had chosen a good place to confront me as one of his flanks was protected by water while the mountains guarded the other. I did not mind his choice of battleground as he could not use his entire force to attack me. The narrow field negated his superior numbers. I regretted not having a wagon. I would have to address that in the future. I learned that only half of his army was made up of mounted men. I stored that information although, in the coming battle, it would have no effect.

My three bodyguards all had a unique function. Zuzzo had my trumpet, Gianluca my standard and Robert Daring, my new Englishman, had his axe and his job was to keep the three of us safe. Robert was not mounted. He could not wield his axe from the back of a horse. As I had no intention of fighting myself that suited me. I chose a piece of ground that was higher than the land before me and I surveyed the battlefield. I had my lances dismounted and they presented a wall of weapons facing the enemy. Behind them I had my archers and before the lances the fifty or so crossbowmen brought by Carlo. The spearmen guarded my flanks. They were not as well armoured as the lances but they could move easier than mailed men. The slightly rougher ground suited them better than mailed men. The squires guarded the horses and were a mobile reserve. If I had to use them I could. The enemy had a similar formation but they were without archers. They did, however, outnumber us. Unlike me, Savelli intended to fight alongside his men.

As soon as the battle began, the enemy advanced. I could see that Savelli had learned from me and that this would not be an easy battle. He would do nothing rash and wear me down with his weight of numbers. He would try to grind us down. Neither of us could use the flanks and this suited me as we had smaller numbers. This would be a brutal encounter with men who had the same weapons, the same armour and the same experience. The crossbowmen fled back through the lances after loosing their bolts. The enemy's rapid advance to close with my front line negated my archers and when the two sets of lances came together it sounded like a thousand blacksmiths all hammering at the same time. All we could see, from my elevated position, was the movement of men as lances collided. As the lances were shattered and swords were drawn, we saw the rising and falling of weapons above the heads of helmeted men. My leaders knew their business and the front rank was rotated. It was part of the training and it paid off. The newer men pushed the enemy back and it began again. In this fashion, we gradually pushed back Savelli and his men for they did not rotate. I admired the way that he joined his men at the fore to rally them. It was clear to me that my men were causing more casualties than the enemy but the enemy could afford the losses. They outnumbered us two to one.

Robert turned to me as the men in the front rank were rotated once more, "My lord, if I was there with my axe then there would be a hole big enough to drive a wagon through."

"And I might lose a bodyguard. Your place is here, Robert. We are doing well enough."

Zuzzo said, "But we cannot win, my lord."

"I know." I turned to the squires behind us and pointed to one, "Edward, mount your horse." The eager squire did as I commanded. He was just nineteen and was keen to impress me. "No heroics, boy, just deliver my message."

"Aye, Sir John."

"Tell my captain of archers to withdraw his archers without fuss, and have them secrete themselves behind us along the road back to Montepulciano. Then go to Captain von Landau, Captain Balzan, Captain Edingham and Captain Visconti and tell them that when I sound the horn they are to fall back in good order. Tell them to make the enemy think that they are winning." He nodded. "You understand the orders?"

"Yes, my lord."

"Good. Then be off with you."

Although he soon passed his message to Jack of Derby, it took some time for him to make contact with my four captains. He had to dismount and make his way through the ranks of lances. By the time he returned, the archers had withdrawn and were in position and I was almost ready. All the time that this was going on men were blunting weapons and wounding opponents but we were not being pushed back. Our rotation helped us.

"Now, Edward, ride to the men on the flanks, the ones by the water first. When the horns sound I want them to pull back too."

By the time Edward was on his way back an hour had passed since I had first sent him. Both sides were tiring. As Edward passed me, I said, "Have the squires mount and tell them to take the archers' horses to them. Lead the horses of the lances, do not ride them, down this road and wait for me." If the enemy saw men mounted they might know what we were about.

"Yes, my lord."

"Zuzzo, sound the horn."

We took Savelli by surprise. I think he expected us to rotate and push him back once more when the horn was sounded. There was a gap of twenty paces before he realised what we were doing and when he sounded his horn, his men were too eager. Lances and spears now faced the enemy who ran at us with swords. They fell to longer weapons wielded by my men. I waited until the first of the lances reached me before I said, "Robert, mount, it is time we pulled back." He mounted. As we passed my archers I said, "Jack, keep yourselves hidden. Let the enemy pass you and then send five flights into their flanks. When that is done follow us. Do not be dainty about your retreat. Ride as fast as you can."

"Yes, Sir John." There were squires holding the archers' horses; one squire to four horses. My archers could mount and ride in a heartbeat. The enemy soldiers were on foot and would never catch mounted men.

I led my bodyguards down the road and, after we had joined the squires, we waited at the side as my lances moved back. The first to pass us were the wounded. I counted at least twenty. They would need time to recover. Then came the men who had been last in the front rank. They carried swords.

"Halt here and face your front."

The last to arrive were the men with lances and spears jousting with their opposite numbers. There was little damage to either side. When John of Derby chose his moment perfectly and sent his arrows into the enemy there was a huge amount of damage. It was close range and their bodkins punched holes in plate armour. It was almost carnage as my ambush was sprung. At that range, they were capable of penetrating plate but my archers were so skilled that they also could aim at the parts of the enemy protected only by mail. They lost many men before Savelli realised he had walked into my trap. I heard the enemy horn and knew that he was summoning crossbowmen.

"Zuzzo, sound the retreat. We are done here."

Robert said as the strident notes echoed from the hills and mountains, "We are defeated then."

I shook my head, "The enemy thinks we are defeated but we are not for I planned this withdrawal. We did not win and the enemy holds the ground but he is welcome to it. When he camps here tonight, he will be plagued by flies and mosquitoes. With luck, dysentery and disease will race through his camp. We have not won but neither have we lost. Welcome to Italy, Master Robert."

As I had expected Savelli did not spend long by the water. After a few days of enduring swamp-like conditions, he headed away from the area. Our wounded recovered. The rider from

Florence reached us just a fortnight after the battle. There was a letter addressed to me from the Council. They had heard of the victory, those were their words and not mine, and I had more instructions. I called a meeting with my captains. Konrad and Carlo had impressed in the battle and I felt more confident about using them. "Savelli has shown us his intentions. He will try to bring us to battle." I held up the letter, "The Council has paid us an additional one thousand florins to make mischief in Siena. They wish us to hurt Siena and make them sue for peace. Let us use our advantage for we are well mounted and make him chase us all over the land of Siena. We will race across the land and take from the Sienese. We have many horses and they do not. If we strike quickly we can move on before they can find us. We will be the fox that is in the hen house and gone before the farmer awakes. At the end of the month, I will send to the leaders in Siena and ask for…what shall we say? Forty thousand florins?" Carlo and my German captain, not to mention my English ones, could not help but bang the table in pleasure. "If we do this right then they will pay and we shall all end the contract as richer men."

They agreed and we pored over the map I had brought. "Let us be bold. Poggiolo is a mere thirty miles from here. We make a night ride and raid it."

Carlo frowned, "Sir John, the city is not far from Siena."

I smiled, "And can you not conceive of the effect our raid will have? They will think we intend to attack Siena. We do not. When we have ravaged Poggiolo, we shall head down the valley of the Arbia River towards Montalcino, which is a twenty-five-mile ride. Let us keep Savelli and the Sienese guessing where we will strike next."

We left our camp two days later not long after dusk. We planned a route which avoided castles and fortified towns. We passed, like ghosts, through villages where every door was barred. They would speak of our passing but by the time any others knew of it, we would be gone.

We reached the small town just before dawn. With my archers watching the roads, we gave the townsfolk a rude awakening. It was a small town but it had not only food but the people who lived there had coins. We took the coins and their food before setting fire to the buildings. No one died and we left not long after the sun was at its zenith. We passed the walls of Siena; they were three miles to the east of us. I knew that they would have seen the smoke from Poggiolo and their walls would be manned. We were taunting them. They did nothing to bar our progress for they had no army to meet us. They had hired Savelli to do their fighting for them. We neared the town of Val d'Arbia and I was about to order my men to attack when emissaries came from the town. My banner was recognised.

"Sir John, we beg you not to attack us. We will pay you a thousand florins and feed you if you do not take from us."

It was easy money and my men had ridden hard. I frowned and made the town councillors think I was debating the matter. When I nodded my agreement, their relief was almost laughable. We camped outside the town and after the florins were brought to us, we ate.

Robert Daring had never been on a raid before and he could not believe how easy it was. "Sir John, if this is the way of war in Italy why have you not returned to England with all the money you have earned?"

Zuzzo shook his head, "Because my English friend, we are not always successful. Sir John is the best of leaders but sometimes we are not paid or we find ourselves fighting against another company which is the equal of the White Company. What is it you English say, 'make hay while the sun shines'? Although from what I have heard from your countrymen, the sun rarely makes an appearance in your land."

Robert had finished cleaning the flesh from the fowl he had eaten and he tossed the bones towards two dogs who were attracted to the smell of the food, "So we ride to, where did you say, Sir John, Montalcino?" I nodded. "And will they open their gates to us?"

"They might but it matters not if they do not." I wiped my hands on the cloth hanging on my left shoulder and pointed to the walls. "The men who guard these towns are without mail and plate. They are like the constables back in England. They are there to keep the peace and apprehend wrongdoers. We are too great an army for them to stop. Savelli has the only force that can hurt us and he does not know where we are. He has too many infantrymen to follow us closely."

"Do you fear the enemy company, Sir John? Do you not think that they might call out the militia to aid them?"

"Here, Robert, they call them feditore and I fear no man but this is harvest time. The Sienese have hired Savelli so that their farmers can harvest the grapes and the crops. It was a mistake for them to threaten an ally of Florence. I am guessing that they now regret that decision."

We spent two months ravaging Siena. Sometimes we were paid off and sometimes we had to take the towns and villages. We lost not a man and we were becoming richer. Savelli and his company were always too late after we had struck and moved on. They were left chasing shadows. Even better was the fact that they were going hungry as we had taken all that there was to offer. By the end of September, we were at San Galgano. We had ridden hard and I decided to use the town to rest for a week. The contract would be up in a couple of months and we had done all that Florence had asked and more. I sent Carlo to Siena to ask for forty thousand florins. He returned two weeks later with the news that they would only pay us ten thousand.

"Then let us head to Colle di Val d'Elsa and raid there. It is close enough to Siena to encourage them to increase their offer."

Carlo was a little disappointed, "The contract runs until November, Sir John. "

"And Florence pays us five hundred florins a month. If we end the contract a couple of months early we lose a thousand florins. The money from Siena will more than make up the shortfall."

Carlo was young but he was learning how to be a condottiero by watching me. By October we had taken more plunder but had our first serious mishap. The town of Monteguidi had manned its walls and in our assault, Konrad von Landau was wounded. We still took the town but the German's wound and the eight men we lost took some of the shine from the victory. Konrad had to leave us and his deputy took over while he recovered from his wound.

I sent Carlo back to Siena and the price for us to depart was raised to fifteen thousand. We took it and as we headed back to

Legacy

Florence we received another contract. Lucca would pay us a thousand florins to protect them from Galeazzo Visconti. It was an easy contract for word of our Sienese adventure had reached Visconti's men and they backed away. We ended the year back at Casa Donnina, richer men.

I was a rich man once more and my reputation was intact. I returned to my wife and I disbanded the company. That is to say, I allowed them to either enjoy the fruits of our labour or to seek other work. I retained my Englishmen, both archers and lances, for the Luccan contract. As there was no threat from Milan and Lucca was close, there was no need to ride west. Many men chose to spend winter with me. I would feed them and there were inns and whorehouses close by where they could enjoy the fruits of their victories.

At the end of November, I was visited by Ghino di Roberto, Giovanni Orlandi, and Piero Baldovinetti. They were all Neapolitans and in the service of Queen Margherita of Hungary. Her son Ladislaus was the new king of Naples. The Pope had recognised him but all that Ladislaus controlled was the fortress of Gaeta. The three men tried all that they could to persuade me to join them but I was becoming weary. The three stayed with us and it was as we were eating in my hall that they let slip that Galeazzo Visconti was supporting the anti-pope and Louis of Anjou, who claimed the throne of Naples.

Carlo was staying with us and I saw his knuckles whiten as he gripped his knife. "He has even more ambition than I thought. We should take this contract, Sir John."

I shook my head, "Gaeta is a long way from here. I have spent too long in the saddle. You could go."

Donnina laughed, "My brother might well become a great condottiero, husband, but do you think that he would have more success than you? You are the man that they need." She turned to the Neapolitans, "How long is the contract?"

Ghino smiled and spread his hands, "For as long as Sir John can spare."

I chewed the wild boar thoughtfully.

Carlo said, "It would spite Visconti. After running Savelli ragged in Siena it would enhance your reputation."

"And you think my reputation needs to be enhanced." I cocked an eye.

"I am sorry, Sir John, I meant no offence."

I spoke to the three men, "And I can return when I tire of the saddle?"

"Of course, Sir John."

"You realise that I must leave most of my company here in case Lucca needs them."

"It is you and your sword we need, my lord."

"And I can bring my Italians too, Sir John." Carlo was keen to get revenge on his uncle.

"Then I shall come."

I took just my bodyguards and we returned once more to the warmer south. That was the only advantage that I could see in this but Donnina had persuaded me. As we rode through Rome, we visited the Pope who gave us his blessing. As far as he was concerned we were doing God's work and fighting the anti-pope.

In all, we spent just two months in Gaeta. We never fought a battle but, in the couple of skirmishes we endured, we got to see Robert Daring with his axe and he was an impressive warrior. I had to draw my sword once too when an eager mercenary tried to claim my head. He failed. The measure of our success was that all of Ladislaus' enemies within forty miles of Gaeta were defeated. He still had to reclaim Naples but my influence and advice enabled him to gather allies and soldiers. With his mother's money, he was able to hire other companies too.

Two things made me leave: firstly, I became ill. It was a recurrence of the headaches and shortness of breath I had endured before and secondly, word came to me that the Florentines needed my service. With my bodyguards and Carlo Visconti, we returned to my home at the end of January.

Chapter 9

April 1390 Bologna

Carlos Cialdini, the podestà of Florence, came to my home at the start of March. He had heard that I had returned. I suppose now that he had no spy in my home he was forced to rely on the gossip in the city. He had with him his son-in-law Michael. Many of my company had returned to ask to recontinue their employment having either spent their money or decided that they wished to earn more but I still felt that I did not have enough men to go to war. My men were busy training. The larger number of men staying on my estate meant that we were spending more money than we were earning. We needed another source of income. Donnina and I had money but not so the White Company. The days when I would spend my own money were in the past. I would have to try to get money from Florence and then delay when we began to earn it.

"Sir John, it is good to see you." The podestà was polite.

"And you too, my lord."

"How is your new son, Sir John?" Michael was genuinely interested in me and my family. His question was sincerely meant.

"Growing day by day, Michael, and becoming noisier. His sisters no longer find him to be as cute as they once had. I pray you sit. Ned, Edgar, fetch wine and refreshments."

"No Guccio, Sir John?" Carlos Cialdini had been surprised when it was my men who had opened the door. He must have wondered why his spy had not been delivering information. Now he was trying to seek an answer. Was this the purpose of his visit?

I smiled and waved a hand suggesting that the matter was unimportant, "No, Podestà, there were problems and he and his wife left. Ned and Edgar may not have the skills Guccio had but I am comfortable with them and Lady Donnina is learning to live with their idiosyncrasies." My former squire seemed happy with the explanation but the podestà frowned as he tried to see beyond the mask I had adopted.

Donnina sat with us and I smiled at the frown that creased the face of Carlos Cialdini. Not only was he worried about his spy, but I knew that he did not approve of women in such meetings. Unlike me his view was that women had no place in business, "So, my lord, how can I be of service?"

"I will come directly to the point, Sir John. Jacopo dal Verme has left Milan at the head of his company and some Milanese troops. Their route suggests that first, they will raid Bologna, but we believe that their ultimate aim is to take Florence. We wish you to lead the Florentine army and your company. Your contract will be to stop their advance." So, the information from both William and Michael was correct. Jacopo would be my opponent. The Florentine spies in Milan had to have told the podestà that they were heading for Florence.

I looked at Michael, "And will you be with the army?"

"I will." He quickly added, "But we will obey all your commands and orders, Sir John."

"And the pay?"

Carlos' head jerked around as my wife spoke. He looked at me and I just stared back at him. If he thought I would chastise my wife for her interruption then he did not know me or my wife. We were partners in all things. He answered but looked at me, "Thirty thousand florins."

That was a cheap price to pay to keep not only an ally safe but also to prevent any threat to Florentine land. Peace was profitable.

"Is that for my husband or for him and his men?"

The merchant gave a silky smile, "Your husband and the White Company."

She shook her head, "That is not enough. My husband alone is worth thirty thousand and the company needs to be paid. The last contract on behalf of Florence was insufficient for the service the White Company provided and my husband was forced to raid to pay his men. This time he cannot do so for he will be in friendly territory and he might suffer desertions if the pay is inadequate. It is not right that the pay for our men comes from our purse. We have raised a company as you asked and kept it at our expense. Now we need to have recompense for that."

Legacy

"Sir John, who rules here, your wife or you?"

I smiled, "We are a democracy, and we jointly rule." I looked at Michael, "I would have thought that you might have let your father-in-law know that, Michael."

He flushed and I saw Donnina smile.

"How much for the company then, Sir John?" He pointedly asked the question of me.

"Let us say ten thousand for the White Company. After all, they are the most successful company of condottiere in Italy."

I saw his face as he wrestled with the decision. He had lost his spy and did not know the state of my finances. I knew that Florence could easily afford the payment. As for not raiding...I had no intention of staying close to Bologna. Even in the short time we had been talking I had been planning my campaign. My mind held a map of the land and I knew that the lands around Modena could be raided. The nod from the podestà confirmed that I had judged it correctly.

"Very well you shall have the payment. When can you leave?"

"As soon as the forty thousand florins are in my vaults then we will march to Bologna. My men are eager and hungry for war." I saw the frown as he baulked at the delay. "Many of my archers are in Montecchio Vesponi. It will take three days for them to reach us. You have time to send the money, I think."

"Very well, it shall be delivered." He suddenly snapped, "And your friend Ubaldini has not fulfilled his contract. He has not yet raided Pisa."

I shrugged, "And as the contract was for him to be paid once he began his raids, you have not had to pay out the money anyway." He was silent. "My lord, you just wanted to keep my friend away from Florence and Bologna. That has been achieved, it seems, at no cost to yourself. The small payment you made to me was worth it, was it not? Ubaldini did not cost you an extra florin and he has not raided. Do you care where he raids?" I confess I did not know why Giovanni had not raided. It did not upset me but I was worried. It was out of character.

He shook his head, "I suppose."

"And I will need to speak with Michael. As he is here now this seems an appropriate time, does it not?"

105

Legacy

It was as though I had dismissed the podestà. He had a grand view of himself and thought, like many doges and podestàs, that he was the equal of a king or a duke. I knew that Carlos Cialdini lived in a palace but he was still just a merchant who had bought his way to power. "Very well. Farewell, my lady." It was a cold goodbye.

Donnina held out her hand for the Florentine merchant to kiss. He did so and she smiled, "Always a pleasure to speak to a gentleman."

When he had gone, she rose, "I will go to attend to John. Will you dine with us, Michael? I am sure that you and Sir John will have much to discuss."

"An honour, Lady Donnina."

She pecked my cheek as she left.

"Ned, Send for John Coe."

While we finished the wine and the refreshments on the table we chatted about our families. I wanted Michael to feel comfortable with me.

When John arrived, I said, "Take two men and ride to Montecchio Vesponi. Tell Robin I need my archers now. We go to war."

"Yes, my lord."

"Warn John Balzan and the others. They need to prepare the men. As soon as the archers arrive, we shall leave for Bologna."

My relationship with Michael was not as close as it once had been but I still viewed him as a trustworthy soldier and a friend whom I could trust. "So, first, the opposition. Are these regular soldiers from Milan or has Visconti hired swords?" The distinction was important. The nobles of Milan were rich men and if it was they who were heading for Bologna then it would be a hard fight. Each one would have their own retinue and they would be well-armed, mounted and armoured. Mercenaries would be more pragmatic and, as I had either fought with or defeated most condottieri, fighting mercenaries was always preferable.

Michael shook his head, "Provvisionati but led by a condottiero. Visconti will use his nobles judiciously. If Milan is threatened then he will send them into battle. He has gold looted from Padua, Verona and Vicenza. He is paying and the soldiers all come from Milan. Some are the remnants of Ambrogio Visconti's Company of St George and the other companies whose leaders have retired. Some may even be men who fought in the White Company."

I snorted, "I doubt it although if they were in the White Company they were not the best. The best have either retired or still serve me. Those I might fear fighting now enjoy a life in England. And Jacopo dal Verme? All I know is what you told me. What is his company like?"

"He brings with him a mixture of Italian, Hungarian and German lances. The crossbowmen he has are not Genoese and there are no archers." Michael knew how to give a report without me having to ask many questions.

That was important. Although we did not fear crossbowmen, the Genoese were the best that there were. They were brave and well-led not to mention highly skilled. They also employed their own pavisiers who worked well with the crossbowmen. They were a good team. If they fought then there would be a problem. I would be able to overcome it but this way it was one less difficulty.

"Will the Bolognese provide men?"

"They will send feditore and some nobles."

"Then the cavalrymen would come from the White Company and Florence." He nodded, "In that case, you shall command the cavalry although it may well be that this battle will be fought on foot."

He looked surprised, "How can you say that? You do not know where the battle and the war will take place."

"Have you learned nothing from me, Michael? I will choose where I fight the battle. Castagnaro showed me that horsemen can win a battle but men fighting on foot can prevent a defeat."

"You do not think that you can win?"

I sighed, "I did not say that. However, Michael, my long career has taught me one thing, to win a war does not mean winning every battle. The secret is to survive the defeats with as many men as you can. I have never fought dal Verme. I need to know his strengths and weaknesses. We have to get into his mind so that we can predict what he will do. The contract is an open one, is it not? We have to stop Jacopo dal Verme from fulfilling his master's aim of taking Bologna and Florence?" He nodded, "Then it will take time."

We then went through the Florentine troops at my disposal. Michael would command a large number but their strength lay in their numbers and not their skill. They would be largely foot soldiers and have the most basic of armour and weapons. If we were successful then they could be equipped from the looted battlefields. The battles and the war would be decided by my lances and my archers. We would number less than a thousand men but they would be worth the whole of the Florentine and Bolognese elements combined. It was late in the afternoon when we had finished. Donnina had arranged an early meal and she asked about Michael's family. The two got on and despite the slight estrangement since his marriage, she was keen to rekindle his affection for my family. Donnina was protecting me. I knew that Michael would be as loyal as any, but my wife often believed the worst in people. She had learned that from her father.

As he was mounting his horse he delivered some disturbing news. "Our old comrade in arms, Giovanni Ubaldini, has been fermenting trouble."

"Where?"

"He is in Siena. He joined Savelli as soon as we left. I think he chose not to fight you, but he sent a confederate, as a spy, to Florence. The spy was caught and revealed his plot."

"Who was it?"

"Jacopo di Montepulciano."

He was the man who had been, briefly, it seemed, the adviser to the podestà of Pisa. My old brother-in-arms was now engaging in dangerous work. Was he trying to be like Visconti? Had his association with that most treacherous of men changed my old friend? He had told me he was planning for his future and it looked like his future was that of a plotter. Michael took my frown to mean that I did not know the man.

"He was an exile from Montepulciano. Before he was executed, he revealed that our old comrade now works for Visconti. It seems that the Lord of Milan is using our old friend's knowledge to thwart us. He may not be leading Visconti's army but he is Visconti's man now. I thought you should know."

"Thank you." I was disappointed more than angry. I tried to think back to the moment we had ceased to be close and I came back to the Battle of Castagnaro. He had asked me to lead the army and we had won. Had there been some resentment I had not seen?

After he left and the children were in bed, Donnina and I spoke of the campaign. She was not a soldier but she understood the needs of a campaign. "You are no longer a young man, John, you need to take things easier."

I laughed, "And that will be all but impossible." She cocked a questioning eye. "I intend to take a wagon which I shall use not only as a bed but a command post. The last campaign in Siena not to mention the long ride to Gaeta showed me that I am getting too old to spend all day in the saddle. I do not intend to ride into battle although if I can avoid a battle I will do so."

I could see that she was curious, "Avoid a battle?"

"I am fighting with new men and against a new opponent. I knew the Veronese, the Sienese and the Neapolitans. Dal Verme and the Milanese are something new. I will not commit to a battle until I know that I can win. I expect to be away for at least six months but it may well be longer. Galeazzo Visconti will want his money to be well spent and even if I do defeat them then it would take a huge victory to make the Milanese leave. He has the north of Italy and Bologna and Florence are the last major opponents for him to take. Pisa is a spent force. Siena is almost his. His ambition knows no bounds. He will throw gold at this attempt to win a kingdom. He lived in the shadow of your father, Donnina. He had him murdered but Bernabò Visconti casts a long shadow."

"Promise me that even on the back of a wagon you will wear your armour."

"Of course."

"And keep your bodyguards close."

"That goes without saying."

Robin brought the archers quickly. When he rode up, my spirits rose for I wondered if he would come with me to command the archers. He quickly dispelled the thought, "No, my old friend. I came to see your son and your wife and to ensure that all the archers I trained had arrived. Unlike you, I have no desire to put my body in harm's way. I enjoy my life and I am making up for lost time. By my reckoning, I have sired six sons since I stopped drawing a bow and many more daughters. My work is now to make the world a better place thanks to the blood of an archer."

I could not help but smile although Robin did not look as well as the last time I had seen him. Perhaps that was no surprise. He was almost as old as me. That night I enjoyed a good meal with my family and the man I still considered to be my best friend.

The wagon with the florins arrived the next day. Michael escorted it personally. "And now you are ready to leave?"

"Tomorrow, I will lead my men to Bologna. We rendezvous at the city."

"Do you want help to unpack the florins?"

"No, we shall do that and you may take the carters away with you. I will loan them horses to ride."

"But the wagon?"

"Is a sturdy one and will suit me nicely. Tell your father-in-law I thank him for the bonus."

Michael saw the grins on the faces of Robin, my bodyguards and my lieutenants. He shook his head and left. He would not argue.

When they had gone and the gold was removed, I said, "Zuzzo, this will be my command post and bed on the battlefield. Prepare it so that it can be used as a moveable home and a command post. Pack chairs and tables that can be folded. We need a cover to keep out the rain. Have come canvas oiled. I am content to sleep beneath that."

"We will pack blankets too and have a pailliase for you to sleep upon." He turned to Gianluca and Robert, "We three can sleep beneath the wagon. It will be drier."

The more I thought about the wagon the better the idea became. Robert Daring had told me that he was no rider and he would make the perfect driver. Ajax and Blackie could be tethered to the back and my armour safe from the rain beneath the canvas.

We left at dawn. There was little point in delaying our departure. The road through the mountains would take us longer than when we had last visited. The one disadvantage of the

Legacy

wagon was the lack of speed. I did not ride on the wagon for the first twenty miles. I rode at the head of my company. I wanted the world to see Sir John Hawkwood and the White Company go to war. The people would talk of it and Carlos Cialdini would think his money was well spent. I rode the grey horse I had captured at the Battle of Brentelle, Ajax. Wearing my polished armour and white surcoat I knew that I made an imposing sight. Gianluca carried a huge war banner. It was too large for battle but as we rode close to Florence it was a sign for the people. Sir John Hawkwood was leading the White Company to war and cheers rang out when we passed people working or travelling on the road. Once we reached Bologna then the banner would be stored and we would use the smaller one that was easier to hold in battle. I knew how to strike a pose but I also knew when to be practical. If I had to ride into battle I would use Ajax. When I wished to be anonymous, I would ride Blackie and cover the white livery with a black cloak.

The Florentines clearly knew my purpose for I was cheered as I passed the outskirts of Florence. Voices called out to me, "Giovanni Acuto!"

"Kill the snake that comes to strangle us!"

"The hero of Castagnaro!"

One of these days I would be able to ride through the city and receive the accolades of all people. That would only happen when the council learned to trust me completely.

By the time we reached Pian di Voglio, I had ridden enough. We stopped in the village where we could water our animals and buy food. Michael and the Florentines had not passed and that was good for us. I halted outside the Leaping Hare and waved my men forward so that the tiny village thoroughfare was not too congested. Guiseppe came out and waved me and my bodyguards into his inn. He beamed, "We cannot feed all your men within but we shall do our best."

"Thank you and if I were you, I would cook even more food for once my company has passed then the Army of Florence will follow and you can profit from those with fat purses."

His face beamed from ear to ear. He could make more in one day than in six months of normal trade.

Robert had grown used to Italian food in the time he had been with us but he still yearned for English ale. He had a skin filled with ale from my estate but he would have to husband that. He sighed, "I will make do with wine I suppose."

Zuzzo shook his head, "You English and your beer. Robin was the same. What is it about beer you enjoy so much?"

Robert, my giant, shrugged, "We are brought up on it. What food will they serve here?"

Zuzzo said, "The last time we were served rabbit. Is that something else you English do not like?"

Robert shook his head and beamed, "It is something I love. The trouble is that one rabbit rarely fills me."

Gianluca laughed, "It is hard to know what will fill you, my friend. At least when we go to war if the enemy tries to get at us, we will have a walking barrier before us."

He nodded, seriously, "With Bettina," we had learned he had named his axe, "then no one shall pass. You will be safe, little man!"

The banter of the three of them was a good sign. They were comfortable in each other's company. I knew from the gyrus that they admired the skills the others possessed. Even my master swordsman, Zuzzo, recognised the skill of a master axeman.

We camped, for the night, at Lodole. When we had passed through there, before the ambush, I had seen the potential of the small village. The ground was flat and the river was close by. The horses could graze. There was no inn but the village would be able to sell us rabbits and milk as well as seasonal vegetables. I had already set aside a sum of money for food. Once we reached Bologna then the Bolognese would provide the food. One day and a night of buying food was no hardship and it endeared us to the villagers of both Lodole and Pian di Voglio. Mercenaries could not afford to make enemies. Aversa had taught me that.

We had fires lit and food bubbling away when the leading elements, the nobles, of the Florentine army arrived. There was still enough space for them to camp for neither element would use tents, but my men had the flatter ground and easier access to the river. I had planned for this. The life of the White Company would be as pampered as I could manage to make it.

Legacy

We reached Bologna before the Florentines. We were welcomed at the gates but that was as far as the White Company was allowed to go. They had to camp outside the walls. The Florentines would also have to use tents or hovels. Hospitality in Northern Italy was not a universal gift. There was little trust between any of the city-states. Florence might be coming to the aid of Bologna but that did not mean that Giovanni Bentivoglio would risk allowing us to stay in his city. The exceptions were me and my three bodyguards. My previous service on behalf of the podestà was not forgotten. Even Michael had to camp with the army. We were even given, for the duration of our stay, a house. Antonio del Mogli had been found guilty of collaborating and conspiring with Milan. His trial had been swift and his punishment was death. It was not a large house but it was comfortable.

Robert grinned when we walked in. He had to duck his head in the small doorway but once inside he said, "I could get used to this life, Sir John."

Zuzzo said, "Make the most of it, my friend. Once we discover where the enemy soldiers are to be found it will be the rocks beneath the cart that is your bed."

I was invited, alone, to dine with Bentivoglio and his nephew, Ambrogio. The young noble would lead the Bolognese contingent. Before we ate, I was taken to the library in the palace. Giovanni Bentivoglio pointed to Ferrara and Modena on the map that was hung on the wall, "The last reports we had were that Jacopo dal Verme and his army are north of Modena. These two towns are ruled by the Este family and, as we all know, they have strong connections to the Holy Roman Empire. Neither Jacopo dal Verme nor his master are willing to take on the Empire, not yet at any rate, and so he will either negotiate a passage through their land or pay a bribe. I suspect the former." He looked me in the eyes, "Dal Verme thinks you are an old man and that you lead a rabble."

"Uncle, that is not fair!"

He sighed, "Ambrogio, Sir John is old but I know he can defeat Captain General Jacopo dal Verme. As for leading a rabble…the men you lead have yet to fight in a battle. You have never led men in war. We do not have a martial reputation. As for the Florentines…they are little better. This whole campaign hinges on two things: Giovanni Acuto and the White Company. I think that the Milanese and Captain General Jacopo dal Verme are in for a surprise. I am a realist, Ambrogio. If Sir John loses, and I do not believe he will, then I will negotiate peace with Jacopo dal Verme. He is a mercenary and gold is often the best weapon to use." He shrugged, "I hope you are not offended."

I shook my head, "Everything you say is true and I concur with your conclusions. What I intend to do is to move, in the next days, when the army has rested, north and west towards Modena. Like our enemy, I will not risk the wrath of the emperor even though I think he is a toothless hound. I will seek a place to fight the Milanese that is as far away from Bologna as possible."

Ambrogio said, "That is your plan? A little vague is it not?"

"Despite what scholars might think the science of war is not precise. Timing and luck are the two most important weapons in a general's armoury." He nodded but I could see he was dissatisfied with my answer. This was not school and I was not his teacher. If he was to learn how to be a leader, it would be by watching me as Michael had done. "Now the order of march: have you men who can scout?" His frown told me he did not, and I said, "In that case, we will use my company to lead and I will use archers. Ambrogio, you will have your Bolognese behind mine and Michael will be the rearguard and protect the baggage." Michael would be happy enough in that role. I was pinning the unknown that was the Bolognese contingent between two smaller bodies that were more disciplined.

Giovanni Bentivoglio leaned forward, "I cannot impress enough on you, Sir John, the need to keep war away from the land of the Bolognese. We are not as rich as Florence and we rely heavily upon the income generated from our farms." He hesitated and then spoke, "Mercenary companies live off the land and I would rather that land belonged to another."

"And we need to be fed too, my lord. Your men are unused to fighting on campaign. Empty bellies and the proximity of their homes may encourage men to return before we have won. The food you send will be for your men too."

Even condottiere companies suffered when troops were hungry. It was always easier to raid than to defend. Dal Verme's

Legacy

men could take whatever they wanted from whoever they chose. Even the lands of Ferrara and Modena would not be safe. He would not risk sacking cities but the farms and estates along his route, unless protected by a castle, would be fair game. That was an unknown. The Este family had never employed me. Their two cities, Modena and Ferrara, were both rich. I wondered why, if there were condottiere close to them, they had not sought an alliance with Bologna. My arrival had clearly not been a secret. What were the Este family up to?

"Tell me more about this Jacopo dal Verme. I have some information but you cannot have too much."

Unlike his nephew the podestà had knowledge and he shared it. "He has worked for Visconti in the Piedmont and France. He knows how to use mountains and passes to cause trouble. He is well respected amongst his employers for, like you, Sir John, he has always kept his word and fulfilled his contract." I knew that was not always true. He went through what he had heard about the condottiero and when he had finished I had a better picture of the man. The information about the passes and the mountains was valuable.

It was late by the time we retired for I had given Giovanni Bentivoglio a great deal to think about and a list of tasks that needed to be completed.

The next morning, I rode to our camp. I was greeted by my men with ironic cheers, "Did you enjoy the soft bed, Sir John?"

"Any scraps from the high table?"

"What, no jug of wine for us?"

It was banter and I took my hat off and swept it in a greeting, "And good morning my White Company. I brought you nothing for I would have you lean and hungry and not fat and replete like me." That brought a laugh. "The lands to the west of us are like an unpicked plum tree, they are ripe, juicy and ready for plucking clean. We will be the first condottiere to take from them. There you can 'fill your boots'." The English expression made them all laugh. I was keeping them in good humour. I knew that there would be harder days ahead.

My lieutenants had heard me and as I dismounted John Balzan said, "Sir John, the lands to the west of us owe allegiance to the Emperor. Is it wise to tweak his nose?"

Legacy

I handed my reins to Gianluca and took the wine from Zuzzo, "The Emperor is far away and, if I am to be honest, I am unconcerned with his reaction. Imperial troops sound grand and fearful but the reality, John, is that they look better than they fight. I hope for a short campaign but if not then it will still take time for the Emperor of the Holy Roman Empire to hire a company such as ours and send them down to this land. Dal Verme is clearly the best of the condottieri. Who else is there?"

John Balzan smiled, "You mean apart from you, Sir John?"

"There is not enough gold in Italy to make me work for Galeazzo Visconti."

Michael had wandered over and he said, quietly, "Giovanni d'Azzo degli Ubaldini. He did not go to Pisa as asked. He went to ferment trouble in Siena and who knows where he and his company are to be found now?"

He was the unknown and I wanted to know where he was to be found. "He is not here, yet, and if he comes then we will deal with him. I am only interested in who I face and not those I might have to fight." I had wondered, as had Michael's father-in-law, why Giovanni had not taken the Pisan contract. I suspected that he had approached Jacopo d'Appiano and been bribed to stay away. Perhaps his man had been part of the deal. The last time I had spoken to him his company had been haemorrhaging warriors. Giovanni had tried to be a plotter but it was clear he was not very good at it.

I waved over my vintenars, "I want our best scouts to ride to the north and west. I want to know exactly where the enemy warriors are to be found. We need the scouts to remain invisible. I need to know the numbers. The metal snake that insinuates its way through Reggio Emilia will be easy to see. Remember Parma is now Milanese. That is the bolt hole that dal Verme can use when he is defeated." My confidence made my lieutenants and vintenars smile, "If his army is still there then we have little to fear for a while."

Zuzzo said, quietly, "Except for the flight of the Bolognese."

I sighed, "Zuzzo, dal Verme needs to strike and strike quickly. I will protect the Bolognese until we have a victory secured and as their confidence grows so shall our successes."

Legacy

Sir John Hawkwood at the gates of Milan

Chapter 10

1390 Summer The Modenese Region
The wagon was proving invaluable. While there were often houses for me to use the wagon was an easier way to travel and I found I could study maps while Robert drove it. The folding chairs and table meant I was able to write and plan. I could use my time on the move usefully and it enabled me to hold conferences with Carlo, who commanded my Italians and John Balzan who now commanded my English contingent, as we rode. Captain Jack also found it easier to report to me when his archer scouts returned.

My plans had been made before we left Bologna. I had decided to push towards Padua. Dal Verme had taken the city and I knew that the Carrara family would be grateful if I was able to defeat the Milanese. Il Novello was clinging on to the Paduan land to the east of that city between the Polesine and Castelbaldo. By heading to Padua I was helping Il Novello who might be able to draw off some of the men led by Jacopo dal Verme. It would also fulfil the brief given to me in Bologna. It would keep dal Verme far from either Bologna or Florence. My men were also able to raid and to do so with impunity. The lands were either ruled by the Milanese or the Holy Roman Emperor.

Konrad von Landau, my German condottiero, had not returned to me after his wound. He was in Perugia and the Marche where he and his company were raiding and plundering. The Germans who had recently joined me were under the command of Heinrich von Altinberg. Konrad had fallen out with Heinrich and was another reason why Konrad von Landau had not rejoined me. I could not work out why. I found him to be, for a German, quite pleasant. Some of my unhappier encounters in my past had been with either German or Hungarian condottiere. Heinrich was always willing to take on the less well-rewarded duties. He would take his men and scout out prospective targets for us. Such patrols could be long ones and rarely resulted in rich rewards. Often they just exhausted men and horses. I sent him to Modena to negotiate a passage through the lands of the Este family. I had been assured in Bologna that while the Este family were not allies, they were not enemies. My aim was to raid Parma before turning to approach Padua.

It was while we were on the road that I received news about my friend, Giovanni Ubaldini. Robin sent a messenger with the news. He had been in the service of Siena and had attacked Florentine land; I knew he would have taken advantage of my absence. It was bad news for he had died. Robin said, in the letter, that the official reason was that his heart gave out. I knew that was a nonsense. Giovanni had always been a fit and healthy man. Robin suspected that he had been poisoned by the Florentines with a bowl of cherries. That sounded like the way Carlos Cialdini would do it. I was sad, as we headed along the road to war. Giovanni and I had drifted apart over the years and towards the end of his life he had let me down, but he was still a brother-in-arms. My victory at Castagnaro was as much down to him as to me. I put the letter away and kept a blank expression on my face. I would mourn him but in private. How was it that brothers-in-arms could drift apart? At least I still had Robin as an old comrade in arms and a friend. I had far fewer of them now.

We spent July raiding and found ourselves close to Modena. One afternoon, while we awaited the return of the German, I spoke with Carlo, Donnina's half-brother, and John Balzan. "If Ferrara allows it, I will head for Padua from the west. I believe that Francesco Carrara is to the north of us in the Polesine area. The eyes of the Milanese in Padua will be looking south and east and not west."

"Will he fight alongside us, Sir John? Did he not try to have you arrested after Castagnaro?"

"He did, Carlo, but that was in the past. It is in his interest to help us. At the very least his presence will protect us from a flank attack."

When Heinrich returned, the next day our hopes were dashed, "My lord, the Marquis of Ferrara is no longer an ally. He has joined the Milanese. The passage to Parma is barred."

It was a bitter fruit to swallow. I had suspected something along those lines. Visconti had not sent Jacopo dal Verme to raid either Ferrara or Modena. He had used gold to bribe the Marquis of Ferrara instead. I studied my maps. If we went directly north then Ferrara, another city ruled by the Este family, would also

Legacy

bar our passage. The land between was also ruled by them but the only two castles were at Modena and Ferrara. "Tomorrow, we head north and east. We will try Cavezzo and then Carpi."

When the others had left us, I said, "Carlo, I would have you lead your familia and scout out the road."

Detecting the unease in my voice he asked, "What is wrong my lord?"

"I do not like to be forced to take a direction I did not choose. This may be a trap. Be cautious and question everyone that you meet. We will not race into a trap. At best we will test the water first."

Even before Carlo had returned, we had discovered that it was a trap. Some Bolognese merchants had found their way barred ahead by a small army. It was not Jacopo dal Verme who was ahead of us, that much we knew. It was Ugolino da Panico and that concerned me for he was a confederate of my old friend Giovanni Ubaldini. He had been exiled from Bologna. Giovanni would never have faced me in battle, he knew he would lose but he knew my tactics. He had mentored Ugolino and I saw the hands of my old friend all over this trap. I hoped that Galeazzo Visconti was paying Ugolino well for I would destroy him.

I gathered my captains and lieutenants. "We have a battle to fight. I will have more information when Captain Visconti returns but the information I have is that Ugolino da Panico is ahead of us with an army the same size as ours."

John Balzan said, "I am sorry, my lord, but an army that is the same size as ours poses little danger."

"Perhaps but what if there is another army, perhaps led by Jacopo dal Verme, that is coming to attack us when we are engaged?"

Heinrich said, "My lord, I am new to this company but it seems to me that if you had my men at the rear and were watching for this other enemy we could give you a warning. I would like to offer the services of my company for this task."

"A good idea. Then tomorrow, when we march, you will be at the rear, half a mile behind the baggage."

"And I guarantee that you will be safe." He was a confident young condottiero.

Legacy

Once the order of march was decided we retired. Robert Daring, my new bodyguard, had something on his mind. I had learned to recognise his mood changes. Sometimes it was hunger that made him irritable but we had just eaten and we had been well fed. He had also drunk sparingly. "Come, Robert, sit and tell me what is it that has you prowling like a cat on the hunt for a mouse."

"It is that German, my lord. I do not like Germans. I do not hate them as much as the French but it is close." We all smiled. No Englishman ever liked a Frenchman. "There is something about him that makes my hair prickle. I can explain it no better than that."

Many men would have dismissed the opinion of a man who admitted his prejudice but I had learned to trust such instincts. "Zuzzo, find Heinrich and ask him to come to my wagon."

"Yes, my lord." He left.

"Satisfied?"

He grinned, "Yes, my lord. I am content and I can now sharpen Bettina. If we are to fight on the morrow then I need to be prepared."

Before Zuzzo returned Carlo arrived and I knew that something was up for he galloped in hard and was alone. "Is there a problem, Carlo?"

He leapt from his horse, "Aye, my lord. There is treachery in the camp. I found an enemy scout, we found four actually, but three fought and were killed. The fourth told all before he was executed. Dal Verme is marching from the direction of Modena. He intends to attack our rear once we are engaged by the enemy. I left my men watching their camp."

I smiled, "We suspected that, and we have a plan. Heinrich von Altinberg will be the rearguard and warn us of an attack."

He shook his head and his words brought a chill to my heart. "He is the traitor. The man we captured told us that he and his company had met with Ugolino da Panico. He is to attack our rear once we are engaged with Ugolino and his men. We have a wolf protecting our sheep."

Just then Zuzzo returned. He and Heinrich were sharing a joke but I also noticed that the German had ten of his men with him. I was not wearing my mail but my sword was to hand. I nodded to Gianluca and Robert.

Zuzzo spread his arm and then stepped to one side. Heinrich said, "A change of orders, my lord?"

"In a way, yes. I do not need you to guard my rear for we will not be fighting tomorrow. Captain Visconti has brought information that changes my plan. Instead, we will head to Modena. If the Marquis of Ferrara is not an ally then he should be punished. You and your men will be the advance guard."

"Is that wise, my lord? Who knows who is behind us?" His shifty eyes confirmed what Carlo had told me. The man was a traitor.

I smiled, "Oh, I think that you know exactly who is behind us, Heinrich. The information that Captain Visconti brought was that you visited the enemy camp and it was your job to attack us in the rear."

It was only at that moment I realised that I had underestimated my enemies. The five of us were outnumbered two to one. Heinrich saw how few we were and shouted, "Kill them all!"

We would have all died but for two things: Robert's Bettina and Zuzzo's fast hands. As Robert swept his axe at the three men who ran, with drawn swords, to end my life, Zuzzo pulled his sword and long dagger and parried the blow from one German before sliding his dagger into the man's belly. Robert's axe sliced one of the Germans in two. I had my sword drawn and Heinrich came for me. Carlo might have come to my aid had not two men charged him just as two men raced at Gianluca. They saw my bodyguards as a threat and believed, perhaps, that their young leader could take me.

Heinrich was wearing mail and he also had a slightly longer sword than I did. As I blocked the two-handed swing intended to take my head, I used my left hand to pull my dagger from my belt. He was mailed but he wore no helmet. Had he done so in camp it would have looked suspicious. I lunged at his eye with the dagger. He jerked his head back but not before I had given him a scar almost as long as Robert's. My English axeman had taken out three of the Germans and the odds were rapidly coming in our favour. All that would mean nothing if the German captain succeeded in his attempt to kill me.

As he reeled back and the blood spurted, I swung my sword at his thigh. He had mail there but no plate. The years I had spent as an archer made my right arm like an oak sapling and I shattered links and hurt his leg. The blade had damaged the muscle and, perhaps, cracked the bone. I saw him wince. I slashed again with my dagger and he had to take another step back. He might have been a better swordsman than I was but what I lacked in skill I made up for in experience. I knew how to fight. His mail now became a hindrance for the broken links hung down. He was bleeding from his cheek and his leg was injured. I was working out how to best defeat him when Robert Daring took matters into his own hands. He swung his axe at the middle of the German's back. The links shattered as though they were parchment. The blade bit into flesh and then severed the German's backbone. I saw the light leave his eyes as he crumpled at my feet. I looked and saw that his companions were all dead.

Men had come racing at the sound of battle. "John Balzan, take men and apprehend the rest of the Germans. They are traitors."

"Yes, my lord."

Robert said, apologetically, "I know you could have beaten him, Sir John, but I was angry. I am sorry."

I sheathed my sword and patted his back, "Do not apologise, Robert. You did what a bodyguard should do. You protected my body. I thank you." I turned to Carlo, "And I am in your debt too. Now we need to extricate ourselves from this trap."

By the time John reached the German camp, the rest of his men, having heard the swordplay, had realised that the game was up and they fled. The eleven horses and weapons that were left in the tents were the only things that they did not take. They would ride to Jacopo dal Verme and tell him that the plan had failed. That would hasten the arrival of the Milanese condottiero. I needed to act and react quicker than he did.

"Break camp! I want to be on the road in an hour."

Carlo said, "Where to, Sir John?"

"Back to Bologna. I need to work out what we do next."

Legacy

I had the easiest time for I just sat on the wagon. As we moved through the night, with scouts all around us, I was able to plan my next move. Carlo had also discovered that the Paduans had been victorious in Polesine and Jacopo dal Verme would have to use men to bolster the defeated Milanese in that area. Of course, had the plan succeeded and we had been destroyed then the Paduans would have been attacked by both condottiere companies. We reached Bolognese territory by dawn and we camped. No one objected to having to do extra duty. The treachery of the Germans had been a close call. On the positive side, the pay that was owed to the Germans would now be shared by the whole army.

We spent just one day inside the Bolognese borders. Men we had left hidden in the area where we were supposed to be attacked reported that dal Verme and his army had reached the scene of the treacherous attack. Realising we had fled, the Milanese Captain General led his army north to meet up with da Panico. That meant we could move. It was the perfect time for us to race toward Reggio Emilia for the Milanese were to the north and had left the road west unguarded. The Modenese cowered behind their walls as we passed and were impotent to prevent us from taking the animals they had failed to take within their walls.

Carlo Visconti nodded admiringly as my men drove the cattle and pigs that they had found from the farms they had looted. "Clever, Sir John. The Modenese thought we were either defeated by dal Verme or falling back to Bologna."

I nodded, "Speed of action and a firm decision are always the way to win. Of course, it helps if you are in sole command. That is why we were less than successful in Naples. There were two others who were trying to make decisions."

We continued to raid the lands around Modena. By the time August had ended, we were close to Parma. We had taken more animals than we could eat and some had been sent back to Bologna along with chests of treasure. They would be safer in the city and we could continue to raid. Reinforcements arrived as we progressed along the road to Parma. It meant we now had parity of numbers with Jacopo dal Verme and his brother who had joined him, Taddeo. With the treacherous Heinrich von Altinberg dead, Konrad von Landau also returned and having

Legacy

another lieutenant I could trust made life much easier for me. We made the road between Bologna and Parma our own. The Marquis of Ferrara was a realist and once our raids began to hurt he defected from the Milanese alliance. He did so because we had raided him so much. I still could not trust him but at least the land close to Bologna was safe and it was only when we neared Parma that we had to be wary.

It was October when we almost came unstuck. I do not think that we were over-confident and we had developed systems to keep us safe. The German treachery had affected the whole army. When we camped, we kept a good watch and had defences around our baggage and booty. It was the night after we had received news from Padua that the Carrara family had allied with Bologna and Florence when I held a council of war at my wagon. The new alliance had changed my plans. We had spent the evening after we had eaten planning a march not to the northwest but to the northeast. My wagon was a luxury. We had padded the base with blankets so that it was as comfortable as a bed. My men sleeping underneath seemed to make my bed warmer and with a canvas cover, I was safe from the elements.

That was the night we were attacked. I am still unsure if the men who raided our camp were trying to take animals or to take me. We never discovered the reason but the thundering of horses as horsemen galloped towards us woke the camp. I left my wagon as fast as I could and found myself surrounded by my three bodyguards. We wore no mail and just had cloaks but we were armed quickly. The advantage night raiders held was a simple one; they came from the dark and those in the camp who had just been rudely woken were disorientated and did not know where the enemy soldiers were. The two hundred lances had overcome the night guards and were galloping through the camp. What they had not taken into account was that my archers could string a bow quickly and, in the dark, could find cover from which to release their arrows. It was they who thinned the ranks of the horsemen. Carlo and Konrad von Landau quickly organised half-naked men to make a wall of spears and lances that prevented the horses from causing damage. By the time dawn came, the attack was defeated. The odd prisoner we had each told a different tale. Some said they came to kill me while

Legacy

others said that they wanted the gold chests they believed we were carrying. We captured horses and took plate but our march northeast to Padua was delayed by a day. We learned that Jacopo dal Verme was still in command but he was leaking men. Il Novello's success in the Polisene area had cost him men and our raids had also hurt him.

One casualty of the night raid was Michael. He was wounded in the attack. Whilst not serious he relinquished his command of the Florentine army to return to his home. When he recovered, he would rejoin the army. It was a blow for Michael was solid and reliable. More importantly, he led the men of Florence. I put another in command but he would not have their total trust. The brunt of the fighting would have to be borne by condottiere. The feditore led by Ambrogio Bentivoglio were just numbers. If we fought then they would have to be a reserve. I could not rely on them in an attack and until Michael returned the Florentines were the same.

We crossed the Po and headed to Padua. I wondered if Jacopo dal Verme would fight me before we reached Padua. I knew that the Paduan army was making its way from the east. Would it be a battle or would dal Verme hide behind his walls? As we neared the city of Padua, it was with some relief that we saw the flag of the Carrara family flying from the city walls and towers. The Milanese had fled and Padua was recovered.

As we neared the walls Zuzzo, who had his horse next to my wagon, said, "It will be interesting, Sir John, to see if you are welcomed or shunned."

Robert, driving the wagon was confused, "Zuzzo, I thought we were allies of the Paduans. I know I am new to Italy but if we are not welcomed then I do not understand this land at all."

I explained the situation to the Englishman I now trusted to watch my back, "It is complicated, Robert. Zuzzo is right, Francesco da Carrara leads the Paduan army and he is now an ally of Florence and Bologna but he does not like me. He tried to have me arrested after the Battle of Castagnaro. I may not have a warm welcome but the army will. I have a thick skin and I will bear any insults that come my way."

His greeting was, thankfully, a warm one. In the years since Castagnaro, he had won his own victories and did not seem to resent me as much. We spent Christmas at Padua. It was the heart of winter and my men were weary. We had been fighting since June and both animals and men needed rest. I ensured they were all paid what was due. Some spent it on whores, drinks and clothes. Others squirrelled it away. My money had been sent to Casa Donnina with Michael. This was not like campaigning in Apulia or Naples. We were close enough to home to be there within a couple of days.

Il Novello and I were not idle. We pored over maps and worked out our best strategy.

"Galeazzo Visconti does not, it appears, like to spend his money. The enemy has not been reinforced and is losing men. Dal Verme does not seem to have the funds that he needs."

Francesco nodded and jabbed a finger at the map. "If we take Vicenza first then our right flank is protected and we can then move on Verona."

"We need to force dal Verme to fight a battle and then we can win this war in one stroke. We have as many men with us now as we did at Castagnaro and the Milanese fewer. When Galeazzo Visconti wakes up to the fact he needs to hire more men, it will be much more difficult."

"Then we are decided. We take Vicenza and then Verona. For once, Sir John, it seems that things are going in our favour." He waved over a servant, "Send for Alessio Nicolai." When the man had left he said, "He may be able to offer us some advice."

"I have not heard of this soldier. What is his background?"

Francesco laughed, "He is not a soldier but an astrologer. He studies the science of the stars. It was he who predicted that I would prevail and regain Padua."

I kept a straight face. I was sceptical of such things but I did not want to jeopardise this new accord. I would smile and listen for the alliance. The man was learned. Like all scholars, he had the ink-stained fingers that came from making marks on parchment.

"Alessio, this is Giovanni Acuto, the renowned condottiero."

He bowed, "It is an honour. How can I be of service, my lord?"

Francesco said, "We need to know the most propitious time to move into the land of Verona."

Legacy

The astrologer had with him a wax tablet and he made a few marks and notations upon it. "My lord, when were you born?"

I shrugged, "Seventy years ago and in the autumn."

"You do not know which star was in the sky when you were born?"

"No."

He frowned, "That makes it difficult but not impossible as I know when Lord Francesco was born. You were born in England?"

"I was."

"That helps. It will take me a day or so, my lords, but I will return as soon as I have a perfect date and time."

Left alone Il Novello said, "I have used this man since Castagnaro and he has never let me down."

I smiled and, in my head, began to make plans. We had more men than when I had first arrived to face dal Verme. The arrival of the Lord of Faenza, Manfredi Astorre, had helped for his Company of the Star were fresh and keen to impress. Since retaking Faenza for Manfredi, they had rested on their laurels. I would use them in the fore. My men and Il Novello's had endured six months of war. We needed the fresher men he brought. I pictured the land north of the Adige River. Verona was a mighty nut with walls and towers but the land around could be plundered. I had learned that was the best way to draw out an enemy. In the case of the Este family, it had encouraged them to make an alliance with Bologna and Florence. I also wanted to strike sooner rather than later. We had confidence and the enemy had suffered reverses. I wanted to capitalise on both factors.

When the astrologer returned, he brought an assistant. He had with him both papers and charts. I sighed. He was going to bombard us with science. All I wanted was for him to cut to the chase and give us a date. Francesco was paying the man and he seemed quite happy to endure a lecture. It took an hour and Francesco, who had clearly listened while I had daydreamed, seemed inordinately happy. Like a conjurer at the end of the trick the astrologer said, "The fifteenth of January at dawn is the time to attack, my lords."

Francesco beamed and said, "There, did I not tell you?"

Legacy

I feigned astonishment although I had already decided that the middle of the month would be a good time and I always like to move at dawn. "That is most miraculous, Master Alessio. We shall be in your debt when we rout our enemies."

He preened, "This is the future of war, my lord. You are the soldiers, but we scientists will determine the time and place of battles and wars."

The two of them were deluding themselves. War would never change. Battles would still be won by the best leaders with the finest troops and I knew that my White Company were without peers.

Chapter 11

1391 Padua
We headed for Castelbaldo and crossed the Adige. This was familiar territory for it was close to Castagnaro. Our target was Verona. The Milanese troops in Verona knew that we were coming. I had defeated Della Scala at Castagnaro and I hoped that our presence might make the people rise in revolt against Milan and recall Della Scala. He had been deceived and swallowed by Milan. I hoped he would now be more amenable as a leader. I was seeking help from the Veronese. If we took the city, it would be to free it from Milan's tentacles.

For the first time in a long time, I had enough archers. There were five hundred of them and my captain of archers had quickly established his authority over them. With three thousand lances and four thousand infantrymen, we were a formidable force. Of course, the drawback was that with so many infantrymen I could not move at the speed I would do normally. The Bolognese and Florentine armies were largely foot soldiers. However, Verona was a place that had to be defended and I hoped that our raids would draw the condottiere to us. We closed with Verona. Dal Verme must have been confident for he fetched his army from the walls to face us. So far, he had avoided battle with us. Was this the day when I would finally meet him sword to sword? The river protected the north, west and east of the city and the only approach was from the south. To that end a canal had been dug and it was a barrier behind which the Milanese occupiers of Verona waited. The canal and the river meant that we would not be using horsemen.

I gathered my leaders for a council of war and explained my strategy. "We cannot win here today. If we are successful dal Verme will merely withdraw behind his walls. What I intend is to make him bleed and lose more men than we do. I hope that the people of Verona will rise against their Milanese occupiers. Captain Jack, you and your archers will begin the battle. They have crossbowmen, destroy them. When that is done, I want a shower of arrows to thin their numbers. Captain Manfredi, you will lead your company and assault the enemy over the canal.

Carlo, you will lead the Florentines as well as your company, Francesco the Paduan and John Balzan the White Company. Captain von Landau, your company will be the fourth. Ambrogio, your Bolognese will be our reserve. You will be the steel wall to protect our backs." The young noble believed my lies. I was just keeping the feditore from Bologna safe. They were unreliable. "All of you, listen for the calls from my horn."

We drew my wagon up so that it was just behind the lances and the infantry. There were bridges across the canal but we had manufactured more so that we could cross at various points. The archers were spread out to my left and right. I might no longer be an archer but I felt closer to my archers than anyone and it was comforting to have them flanking me. We had pavise in front of the waiting foot soldiers and the archers were hidden behind both the pavise and the serried ranks of my men on foot. The crossbowmen we had were spread out behind the pavise. The men who would send bolts and arrows at the enemy would be hidden from the Milanese mercenaries.

"Are you ready, Captain Jack?"

"Aye, my lord."

"Zuzzo, the horn!"

Five hundred arrows soared into the air and even before they had descended a second flight was on its way and then a third. We heard the sound of men crying out as they were hit by the falling arrows. The Milanese pavesiers could protect the crossbowmen from horizontal flights but arrows falling from the skies was another matter. The archers sent arrow after arrow. Crossbow bolts also slammed into pavise and any pavesier foolish enough to raise his head. My archers were a beautiful sight to behold for although seemingly effortless I knew the hours of training that resulted in such discipline. From my vantage point atop the wagon, I saw the survivors, the crossbowmen, race for the walls. A couple of flights of arrows had ended their threat.

I shouted from the vantage point of my wagon, "Captain, the crossbows have been cleared."

Captain Jack shouted, "Switch targets." It was not just the targets that would be changed but the arrows. My archers would now use bodkins. They could penetrate armour plates although

Legacy

we could not guarantee a mortal hurt. Some of the enemy still had shields and it would take luck to find a weak part of the armour or a gap. Men would, however, be hurt. I waited until ten flights had been sent and then said, "Zuzzo, sound the advance."

The archers, hearing the horn would compensate and send their arrows further back in the Milanese lines. The armoured lances were in the front ranks and my men would switch to war arrows which were cheaper. If we held the field at the end of the battle then they would recover the arrowheads but Bologna had sent us many hundreds. It would not matter if we failed to find any.

With a watery barrier before us, my men could not simply run and use their weight. The four companies strode over the canal. They were shoulder to shoulder with lances and pole weapons before them. There were nine columns and without crossbow bolts to slow them they reached the enemy lines with no losses. As usual, the two evenly matched lines jousted and sparred with their lances and spears as they clashed on the Veronese side of the water. Men would be hurt and my men knew how to fall back to allow fresh men to join the fray and for the wounded to be taken to safety. The nine bridgeheads spread out and more men filled the gap behind until the two sides were engaged in a deadly duel. It was the archers and their arrows that did the damage to the enemy. Their arrows fell amongst the rear ranks. The reinforcements for the front lines were hurt before they got close. I saw that the Milanese were weakening and being forced back as we were able to feed more men into the battle. It became clear that unless something dramatic happened they would be pushed back to Verona's walls. Jacopo dal Verme could also see that they had lost the initiative and he had his own horns sounded. The Milanese hurried back to their walls. The crossbowmen who had fled from the arrow attack had joined others on the wall and before too many of my men were hit, I had Zuzzo sound the retreat. We had done all that was necessary. We had hurt them and forced them to fall back and take shelter in Verona's walls. My men came back in good order with a bonus of one hundred and fifty captured men. I had my priests ride to the walls with demands for ransom.

Legacy

We cleared the surrounding area of all food over the next week and then moved west to the village of Santa Lucia. At first, Francesco wondered at my decision, "We could besiege them in Verona, Sir John."

"And suffer disease in our camps? I think not. Besides, if we chose to come back, we could repeat what we did here the first time. I do not think our enemies have an antidote to our archers. We will wait here and see if the people of Verona rise up. If they do not, then we will raid the land between here and Mantua."

While we waited to see if Verona rose, they did not; and we raided. Mantua was a fair target as they vacillated their allegiance between Milan and Venice. Both were enemies of Padua, Bologna and Florence. At the moment, they sided with the Visconti and that made them fair game. We took Valpolicella and Valpantena easily. The towns were looted and our coffers filled. We took their food and then made our way to Mantua. The leader in Mantua was Francesco I Gonzaga, Podestà of Mantua. His wife was a half-sister to Donnina but that meant nothing to the Visconti family. Old Bernabò had spread his seed far and wide. We plundered the land of Mantua to within four miles of the walls and then we halted. It was February and after a battle and a couple of weeks of raiding we needed a rest. So far, the Veronese had not risen as we had hoped and I spent the evenings planning our next moves.

It was as we rested that Michael returned to the army. He was recovered and he had news. His face was like that of the young warrior I had taken under my wing all those years ago. He was clearly pleased with what he had to tell me and his words poured forth like a torrent, "My lord, you are made Captain General of the whole alliance. The councils of both Florence and Bologna are delighted with the way you have waged war. You have kept both lands safe. In addition, your wife has been negotiating with the Florentine council. Your annual pension is raised by two thousand florins and your three daughters are each to be granted a dowry of two thousand florins, payable when they marry."

The title meant nothing. I was Captain General no matter what my employers said. I had earned that right. However, the dowries and the increased pension were generous offers. My annual pension was more than doubled and, if I chose, I would never need to lead a company again. For my family, it was even more generous. Ginnetta and Caterina were growing up. Within the next couple of years, both would be of an age to be married. Even Anna, at ten, would not be far behind. Men would say that we were rich enough to pay our own dowry, but my wife knew how to extract every last florin from our employers.

    I might have been able to enjoy the accolades had it not been for even more treachery that manifested itself. I had planned on striking again at Verona for the populace had not risen. Even as I sent for my leaders to tell them my plan, I discovered that Manfredi Astorre and his Germans had changed sides. We were betrayed by Germans once more. When the ransoms arrived and after we had shared the plunder he defected to the Milanese in Verona. It was like Heinrich again. Visconti knew how to bribe and corrupt. He would never attempt such a thing with men like Michael or Konrad von Lando but clearly, Manfredi Astorre was susceptible to financial inducement and the promise of power. I cursed him but I was impotent to stop him. We had such a large camp that I could not keep my eye on everyone and by the time his defection was discovered it was too late. I was forced to leave Mantua and head back to Padua. I now did not have enough men. The Company of the Star was as big as the White Company. We had been within touching distance of taking Mantua and making Padua much safer but with a large part of our army now serving Visconti and my plans revealed, we would need the safety of Padua's walls. It felt like a defeat and yet it was far from one. We had completely vanquished our enemies and raided wherever we chose. We had not suffered a single defeat and yet we were retreating. We returned to Padua while we built up our supplies and I planned my next move. It took two months for us to be reinforced sufficiently to allow us to return to the area around Verona and Vicenza.

    One of the leaders who brought fresh troops from Bologna was a German warrior, Konrad Passberg. As with every condottiero, he had made his name Italian and was called Corrado Prospero. He had served under me once before and I had liked him for he was a skilled warrior. Back then he had been a condottiere but he had since achieved the command of his own company and was a condottiero. Bologna was paying him

Legacy

eighteen florins a lance and that was good pay. It showed what Bentivoglio thought of him. Part of that pay was due to his skill at tournaments. He was one of the few warriors I met who could best Zuzzo. He did not do so all the time but, as we trained and practised outside Padua, I saw that he was a man that other warriors liked. I was no fool and such men are to be nurtured. However, my experience with Germans was somewhat tainted. I invited him to dine with me in the house I had been loaned by the Paduans.

"So, my young friend, I lost touch with you after Lucca. Tell me your tale and entertain an old man."

"I was hired by Bologna to follow the banner of Captain Ugolino Ghisleri and fight against the Malatesta family in Romagna." I saw him hesitate.

"Konrad, I will be honest with you. Some of your countrymen have let me down. I have been betrayed by Germans. We are here and not sitting in Verona thanks to the treachery of Manfredi Astorre. I need to know as much about you as I can. I am the Captain General and the other leaders I have are all known to me. As a condottiero, you are new. Speak honestly."

He sighed, "Captain Ghisleri is a fine soldier but he is one better suited to defending walls than conducting a campaign. He did not handle the attack against Malatesta well and we were defeated at Rimini."

He was not telling me anything new. Ugolino was Bolognese and the Podestà of Bologna, Giovanni Bentivoglio favoured him. He might be the best that Bologna had to offer but as Bologna hired more condottiere than most it was not a great endorsement.

"Niccolò Malatesta captured all the survivors. We lost our horses and weapons and then we were freed. The march to Bologna was humiliating. We had to endure insults and attacks from all the towns and villages we passed until we reached Bologna. I seriously thought to return to my family's estates at Allgau in Swabia. My father might welcome me, who knows?" I knew that the condottiero were, in the main, hated and unless we could defend ourselves, we would be attacked.

I liked him because he was personable. He reminded me of Michael. I leaned forward and poured wine into his goblet, "Listen, Konrad, serve me and when we have done with Bologna you shall have a place in the White Company." He smiled. "But do not let me down. Heinrich von Altinberg did so and paid with his life and when I catch up with him then Manfredi Astorre will suffer the same fate."

"I will not let you down, Sir John. I have admired you since I was a boy. Every condottiere I have met says you are the greatest warrior in the whole of Europe. It is said that your king admires you above all others. When I served under you at Lucca I hoped to learn from you. This time I will stay as close to you as I can."

After he had left, I spoke with my bodyguards. They acted as my servants and their eyes and ears were invaluable. They sat around my table and drank. Robert had managed to find some beer and while it was not English it was better, in his eyes, than the wine we drank.

"What do you think of him?"

"He is good with a sword, my lord. I know that is not a skill needed by a condottiero but men like a leader who can fight."

I smiled, "And coming from you, Zuzzo, that is praise indeed."

"His men are loyal to him. They do not blame him for the defeat at Rimini. When they were harried back to Bologna it was his company that stayed together. Ghisleri's disintegrated." Gianluca took a piece of bread to eat, "It is telling, my lord, that the Podestà of Bologna sent Corrado Prospero here with fresh troops and Ghisleri now commands the garrison at Bologna. The Bolognese leader knows his worth."

"Then watch him. I do not want another German to betray me."

Zuzzo frowned, "My lord, although Corrado Lando is German a more loyal man I have yet to meet."

"Zuzzo, I have seen more than seventy summers by being cautious. You may be right. Certainly, my instincts tell me that I can trust him. I feel the same way about him as I did about Michael but I must be wary. I will not be betrayed by a German a third time." My tone made them all nod. "We will leave here in by the middle of April. Be subtle but watch him."

They nodded and then Gianluca said, with a smile, "Then that task is appointed to Zuzzo and me, Sir John. If our English giant watches him then his men might fear for his life."

Legacy

Robert did not take offence. He smiled and his face took on the twisted shape of a half-carved pig's head. The scar was no longer red but it gave him a terrifying aspect. "And unlike you pretty Italian boys, this Englishman does not care if he terrifies others. In battle, that gives me the edge but you may be right, Gianluca, subtlety is not a strength of mine."

Before we resumed our campaign, we had to wait for the deliberations of Alessio Nicolai. Our victory at Verona and the success around Mantua had made Francesco even more dependent on the astrologer. Alessio loved the attention he was receiving and he took even longer, not only with his deliberations but also his delivery. This time it did not matter to me what he said. We would leave whenever he decided because I now had the measure of Jacopo dal Verme. He feared battle with me and that meant he would wait for our arrival and react to whatever I did. That is always a bad characteristic for a general. A good general took charge and did not simply wait for his enemies to decide on a course of action. I would determine my own campaign. I was the Captain General.

At the end of his rambling report, he said, triumphantly, "If you leave on April the 23rd, Sir John, then you will enjoy the victory."

I was genuinely pleased with the date he gave me for that was the Saints Day of St George. As an Englishman that was always a propitious date. My smile was not a faked one, "Excellent, we shall leave then and end the threat of the Visconti."

Once the men knew the date we would be leaving they were able to prepare better. New weapons were acquired. Spare horses were found and all the food that could be bought in the land in and around Padua was purchased. Our men knew that we would win and that meant profit. The weapons, food and horses were an investment that would be repaid with interest.

The extra two weeks while we waited resulted in more orders from the council of Florence. The rider brought a sealed parchment and would not even let Zuzzo touch the leather-bound document. It was for the Captain General. I showed the orders only to Michael. He was the head of the Florentine army and I did not want to upset the council. It was good news, of a sort.

Legacy

John, the Count of Armagnac, had been hired by Charles Visconti, the cousin and enemy of Galeazzo Visconti. He was to attack Milan from the west with his French mercenaries. Florence had added their florins to the payment. It meant that we now had a slightly different purpose from that of the Paduans and the Bolognese. Once we had defeated Jacopo dal Verme, we were to take on the Milanese, in Milan. That changed everything. My whole life seemed to have led to this one point. I would finally have vengeance on the man who had fought me for the last twenty years or so. The nagging worry I had was that I would be reliant on another. Even the huge army I had was not enough to take Milan. I needed the Frenchmen of the Count of Armagnac. I could plan my part of the campaign but too much was outside of my control for my liking.

Legacy

Chapter 12

Verona 1391
We returned to raid Veronese land. I wanted to take as much from the region before we moved west. The winter crops were being harvested and by raiding we not only fed ourselves but denied our enemies their food. Jacopo dal Verme declined battle once more. I was learning about this Italian condottiero. He would only fight if he had walls behind which he could hide and superior numbers. I could also see that he liked to use treachery. Heinrich and Manfredi had taught me to be vigilant when it came to captains I did not know. The enemy general squatted like a toad behind Verona's walls and we took from every town that had no wall. By the end of April, there was nothing left to be taken.

We returned to Padua. I sent my gold back to Casa Donnina and we received more welcome reinforcements. Our success was breeding success. Florence, Padua and Bologna had more offers from other mercenary companies who were eager to follow the White Company. For the first time in a long time, the Lord of Milan was not having things go his way. He had lost Padua and had his nose bloodied in the lands around Verona. While we refitted and resupplied, I had messages from Count John. His company was still heading from France. I knew the region through which he would have to pass. It was through the Alps and Piedmont. When I had first come to Italy, that had been where I had enjoyed my first success but I knew that the passes from France could be blocked and guarded. The French condottiero would not have an uncontested journey. We would have to be patient if we were to defeat Galeazzo Visconti.

I knew that we had spies in Padua and I made no secret of our plans. I let it be known that we were heading for Milan. It was a calculated risk. Jacopo dal Verme served Galeazzo Visconti. Their fortunes were irrevocably entwined just as mine were with Florence. Neither man could afford to simply let me march my army across the San Martino Valley. Captain General dal Verme would have to stop me. I was gambling not only that I would have my battle with my opponent but that I would win.

Legacy

My plan worked. Instead of simply placing his army before Verona's walls, my enemy planted his army across the road west. He was using his cavalry to defeat us. He had more cavalry than we did but it was a gamble. He thought to charge us and sweep us from the field. The advantage they had was they could flee to Verona's walls if they were defeated. That told me he was not as confident as I was. That he had an escape route showed his fear.

Our reinforcements had included a thousand crossbowmen and I placed them on the right flank of our army where they were protected by the canal. I dismounted my army and had my archers placed behind the lances. Whilst only half the number of the crossbows, they could send five times the number of missiles. On my left flank, I placed the infantry, the Bolognese. Their nobles apart they had poor mail and armour. Thus far, I had protected them but this time I could not. I had stakes embedded before them as an illusion of safety and I placed Captain Coiser's Germans behind them. I had Carlo and his company next to them. They were solid and dependable men. The only place that Jacopo dal Verme and his brother Taddeo could attack us with horsemen was in the centre. To encourage him to do so I placed my wagon behind the third row of lances. I had the horses unhitched to show that I would not run. Gianluca took my largest banner and he held it aloft. There, helped by the wind from the west and the north, it fluttered above the wagon, like a shining light to draw the enemy to me. I wore my polished armour and that too reflected the sunlight. It was a beacon intended to draw the Milanese moths to me. I know that many men said it was arrogance but I was using my name to make me the target and not the weaker elements of my army. I also knew that my men, the White Company, would fight hard to save their leader.

I saw that he was leading one wing of horsemen and, from his banner, Taddeo, his brother, the other. My dispositions were different from the last time we had fought. For one thing, I now had Konrad von Landau, Michael and Corrado Prospero. They were an unknown factor for the Milanese. I had their three companies before me and placed my White Company on the left flank closer to the more vulnerable infantry, the Bolognese led

Legacy

by Ambrogio Bentivoglio. The Paduans I placed on the right flank close to the crossbows. The squires waited some fifty paces behind my archers and the baggage with the horses. If Jacopo wished to stop me then he would have to charge and, with a cacophony of horns, he duly obliged and initiated the attack. I was in a perfect position to watch my new Captain, Corrado Prospero. The last time he and his men had fought they had been soundly defeated and disgraced by the loss of weapons and horses. This was their first real test since. Raiding and plundering told a general nothing about his men.

The thundering of the hooves of charging horses could inspire terrifying fear in those waiting to be struck. Men would find themselves needing to empty their bowels or make water. Those in the front rank would wonder if those behind would stand and protect their backs. All of them would hope that their pole weapons did not shatter in the first encounter. They would look at the shaffrons worn by some of the horses and seek an easier target for their spears and lances. They would scrutinise the horsemen to see if the horses' trappers concealed mail. The feditore would be scared beyond words while the provvisionati knew what they had to do. Each soldier would choose his own target but they were shoulder to shoulder. Professional soldiers knew how to fight as one unit. The feditore just watched out for themselves. Any weakness and lack of resolve would result in disaster.

I rarely used my voice in battle but that day seemed an appropriate time. As we waited I shouted, my voice carrying across the serried ranks, "Today you fight under the banner of Sir John Hawkwood. Remember Castagnaro. We have yet to be beaten by this enemy who has hidden behind his walls for he cannot face you. These horsemen fear you and their charge will be shattered on your weapons. I stand here with you on my fortress of wood and I will be as a rock. I shall not move. God is with us and we have the right!"

The words worked and everyone cheered. To the charging horsemen, who had not heard my words, it might cause doubt to creep into their heads as they saw men raise their weapons in acclamation. In a charge confidence was everything and any doubt a potential disaster.

Legacy

Robert was eagerly looking forward to the fight. He had shunned a helmet and was simply hooded but as he wore white too, he looked almost ghostly. With the scar on his face, he would draw the eyes of the enemy. Zuzzo and Gianluca had chosen poleaxes with which to defend my wooden fortress. With a hammer, a spike and an axe head, they were a weapon that could kill three different ways. They both wore, as did Robert, breastplates and mail beneath their white surcoats. I did not draw my sword but held my baton aloft.

I watched the enemy line as it approached. It was not straight. A cavalry charge rarely was. Horses were different and the men riding them too. Some were eager to show their courage or to get to grips with an enemy. It was more serpentine in nature. It was not a straight iron bar. They would not all hit us at exactly the same moment. From my vantage point, I was able to work out where they would strike us first. It was Corrado Prospero's company, my new German condottiero, Konrad's men who would be hit initially. This would be a good test for him. It was only then that I noticed that some of the men in Corrado's front line had shields. That showed me that my new condottiero had planned for a cavalry attack.

I turned to Zuzzo, "Sound arrows."

He gave the call for my archers to loose.

Captain Jack said, "Draw! Loose!" The two commands were close together. An archer did not hold at full draw for more than a heartbeat.

I heard the arrows like a flock of birds rise from behind me. The bodkin-tipped arrows plunged down as another flock rose. Not all the horses wore shaffrons and I saw at least six horses struck, their riders hurled over the dying horses' heads. Their riders would die, trampled by the rest of the horses. The plate would merely slow their death and make it even more agonising. Four arrows also hit riders who fell. A falling man or horse caused the line to lose even more cohesion as men swerved to avoid the fallen. The line was even less straight than it had been. The result was that when the second flight struck there were even more casualties as horses tried to avoid the carnage before them and were hit in the side. Horsemen were not looking for the arrows but for the obstacles in their way. Five more flights hit the horsemen before the now irregular line of horses struck my men. The gaps ensured that some horses and riders were hit by three lances. More men died. Corrado Prospero and his company weathered the attack well. Their shields protected them and Konrad had shields pushed into the backs of those in the front rank so that they did not buckle. They reeled a little but no more than the other companies did.

Once the horsemen closed with my dismounted lances then the effect of the archers was somewhat negated. They had fewer targets. The horsemen now also had the slight advantage of height. This was where men armed like Robert would have been useful. A double-handed axe or poleaxe could take the legs from a horse. It was Michael's Florentines that weakened first. They were not provvisionati. They were Florentine nobles and feditore paid for by Florence. They began to fall back towards the wagon and our line bowed. As Michael and his men were the closest to my wagon, another factor was that the Milanese were trying to cut the head from the snake and I was that head. My reputation might prove to be my Achilles heel. If they killed me then my men would lose heart for Giovanni Acuto did not lose.

Zuzzo recognised the danger and shouted, "Florence you must hold the enemy. You must fight and hold for today we earn our florins."

I put my baton in my belt and drew my sword. Sometimes fate intervenes or perhaps luck follows some men more than others. As I drew it, a shaft of light struck the polished blade and it flared like lightning. My archers saw it and cheered. That cheer unsettled the Milanese. They still came on but I saw in the faces of those with open sallets and bascinets, apprehension. Was the flashing sword a sign from God? Soldiers are never atheists and they are also superstitious. Such signs were important.

Four lances, their faces hidden by helmets, forced a gap through the Florentines and their lances jabbed towards the four of us in the wagon. We could have simply retreated to the rear of the wagon but that was not our way. Robert roared a challenge and swung his axe in an arc as Gianluca and Zuzzo chopped down at the lances. The weapons of the enemy broken, they jabbed at us with the stumps. Zuzzo placed one leg on the side of the wagon and swung the hammer part down to smash into the head of a Milanese warrior at the same time as Gianluca took a sideways swing at the head of one of the horses. The horse had a swift death. The rider fell to the ground. The Florentines close by who had been forced back by the four men hacked his prone body. When Robert emulated Zuzzo and stood on the wagon he was able to swing his axe and his blade smashed through the plate and into the neck of the horseman.

Michael shouted, "Florence! We must defend the Captain General. Close ranks."

It had the desired effect and when the Milanese horns sounded the horsemen pulled back. "Zuzzo, sound arrows."

Our horns sounded and Captain Jack was able to send his arrows at the backs of the fleeing horsemen. The whole line cheered. It had been the four companies in the centre that had borne the brunt of the fighting but we had survived an attack by mercenary cavalry and that was a cause for celebration.

I alone did not celebrate. We had defeated the enemy but he had not quit the field. He had not used his infantry and his crossbows. They were still whole and outnumbered us.

That night as I spoke with my leaders, I shared with them some of my thoughts. "Visconti must be worried about us that he commits so many men. Perhaps he knows of the advance of Count John of Armagnac and hopes to defeat us before they arrive."

"Let us rid ourselves of the nuisance of dal Verme and push on to Milan."

I smiled. Il Novello was still as aggressive as ever. It had almost cost us the battle of Castagnaro. I kept my voice even as I explained my plan, "We are outnumbered here and these troops fighting for Milan are not Milanese. The Lord of Milan will have many times this number waiting for us at his capital. No enemy has threatened it, well, certainly not in my lifetime and its defences will be formidable."

"But the river there is not like the Adige or the Po, we can cross it easily."

"And scale the walls, Francesco?"

Michael nodded, "He is right, my lord. I would baulk at risking the men of Florence in such an attack."

Legacy

He nodded but he still wanted us to take a more positive approach to the campaign, "Then what is your plan, Sir John?"

"When we finally defeat Jacopo dal Verme he will have to retreat. He will need to cross the Mincio River and the Oglio River. The best bridging points are to the north. Let us make him move by cutting off his retreat. We will let it be known that we intend to head for Bergamo. The land there has yet to be plundered and there are allies along the way, Guelphs who hate Visconti as much as we do. The Veronese might not have risen in revolt but the ones in the San Martino Valley will. First, we defeat dal Verme when he comes forth again to battle with us."

"And how do we do that?" Corrado Prospero was keen to learn. His question was one of curiosity.

"He will feint the next time he attacks with his cavalry but he will make his main attack with infantry. His cavalry were badly hurt today. He lost good men and many horses. He will take away that he got close to my wagon today. He will send men at my wagon."

"But that will not be the focus of his attack?"

"No. He will see the Bolognese as a weakness." I gave an apologetic shrug in the direction of Ambrogio Bentivoglio, "I think they will see them as canaglia, neither nobles nor provvisionati. We will lay our own trap for him. Michael, I would have your Florentines in the place that the Bolognese occupied yesterday. Corrado Prospero, you will be before me and to the right of the Bolognese and then we will have your men, Ambrogio. Captain Balzan, my White Company will be behind the Florentines. With Captain von Landau on your right and the Paduans protecting the far right then dal Verme will push towards the Bolognese. Captain Albert Coiser, your Germans will be the reserve and they will be mounted. I will have Zuzzo sound the retreat. I will judge the moment. That call is for the Bolognese only. Ambrogio, you will move your men through my White Company and Captain Balzan will charge the men who think they have broken through. You must explain to your captains that this retreat is a feigned one. There must be order. When they are through the White Company, they turn to support my men."

I saw nods for it was a good plan.

Legacy

Captain Jack said, "And my archers, will they be the same as today?"

"No, Jack, the majority will be behind the White Company. Use our best archers there for they will have to launch their arrows a great distance. When their arrows fall and Captain Balzan's men charge, I will sound the advance for the whole army. Captain Michael and Captain Corrado, you will try to envelop the ones who follow the Bolognese. Il Novello and Konrad von Landau, your men will have to hold the rest of their line, can you do that?"

Both men could see that I had placed the onus of victory on my White Company, the Bolognese, Michael and Corrado Prospero. They nodded, "and when we have won," I saw the smiles appear on their faces as I said the word, "then we push on. Captain Coiser, your Germans will take Verona and hold it. With the Milanese gone, they should surrender easily enough."

"Yes, my lord." Corrado and Konrad apart, I did not trust Germans and whilst Coiser had not shown any signs of disloyalty, the two who had betrayed me had not done so either.

The attack did not come for a few days. Dal Verme was planning and preparing but we did suffer raids. Fortunately, I had men who were vigilant and when the men tried to enter our camp and drive off our horses, men were ready for them. The raiders died and my men did not.

I spoke to Michael and Il Novello about the attack, "That confirms what I thought. They are trying to slow us down. They want us on foot and as slow and ponderous as they are. I fear that Visconti has heard of the approach of Armagnac and seeks to defeat him first. If they drive off our horses then we lose the ability to strike quickly. From now I want the squires to guard the horses at all times. They will not be used to fight. We must remain mobile." I also thought that there must be a spy in our camp who was reporting to the enemy. Our move to Bergamo would not succeed unless we were highly mobile.

Dal Verme sent more men the next night but the squires were ready and not a raider returned to the Milanese lines alive. We formed our lines up, just after dawn, as we had each morning for the last few days. The Milanese had done the same but they had just faced us. Perhaps they thought I would be foolish enough to attack them but being outnumbered I had no intention of doing so. The two dal Verme brothers were with their leaders and I saw them pointing at the Bolognese. My men had placed themselves according to my battle plan each morning and the enemy now knew where we were weakest. The men under the command of Ambrogio were brave enough but they had little discipline. While the rest of my army waited in straight lines the Bolognese milled about. They gestured and gesticulated at the enemy all of which encouraged the two generals to believe they were the weak area. My White Company wore cloaks over their distinctive livery and their helmets lay on the ground. Their cloaks gave the illusion that they were part of the Bolognese.

This time the army that advanced towards us had two elements, the mounted element that was heading for our right flank and a dismounted force. The cavalry would test the Paduans but von Landau was a good and steady leader, they would be supported. The main attack came from Taddeo dal Verme. He had dismounted lances protected by mounted men at arms on their flanks and crossbowmen to the fore. They marched steadily.

"Captain Jack, stop the crossbowmen from hurting the Bolognese. Let us not make it too obvious what we plan to do."

"Aye, my lord. War arrows."

I waited until the crossbowmen, behind their pavise, stopped, and then I shouted, "In range, Captain."

"Draw! Loose!" The two commands were almost simultaneous for my archers knew their business and their actions made them seem like a single entity rather than individuals. The timing proved perfect for the crossbowmen raised their weapons to release their bolts just as the arrows descended. A few bolts were sent at the Bolognese but most of the crossbowmen missed. In some cases, it was because they had ducked too quickly behind their protection while others were distracted by the descending arrows. My archers also managed to kill more than twenty. The cheers of derision from the Bolognese drifted over to the enemy. By the third flight of arrows, the crossbowmen had endured enough and they fled. Ambrogio had to stand before his men to hold the line. They saw the retreat and believed that they had won.

Legacy

The infantry that came on moved at a faster pace than the crossbowmen had and my archers did little damage to the plated lances. When the infantry struck the Bolognese, unlike Corrado Prospero's men in the previous battle, they reeled. I heard Ambrogio exhorting his men to hold but Taddeo's men came on and the Bolognese were forced back. On their flanks, Corrado Prospero's men and Michael's Florentines did not budge an inch so that as the Bolognese fell back Taddeo and his men were being enveloped. My wagon proved decisive. I was able to see, quite clearly the perfect moment to sound the horn. John Balzan had my company already with open channels through which the Bolognese could pass and when I said, "Zuzzo, sound the retreat," the Bolognese fled. The Milanese flooded forward and as they did so Corrado and Michael closed the gap behind them. My archers drew back their bows and sent arrows at the Milanese who were racing to support what they viewed as a breakthrough. As soon as the White Company struck their lines then the battle was over. They were surrounded and facing the best of warriors. Taddeo sounded the retreat and he fought his way from the trap. By the time the battlefield was cleared, we had captured sixty men at arms and two hundred infantrymen. More importantly, we held the field.

    On our right flank, Konrad von Landau and Francesco da Carrara had easily held the enemy and the German reserve had not been needed. Even while we celebrated the Milanese were pulling back. Under the cover of darkness, they abandoned Verona. The next day I was able to enter and receive the thanks of the Veronese. I did not know if Della Scala would return but with Coiser and his Germans in control, the city would be ours.

Chapter 13

Brescia June 1391
I was proved right, once more, for men flocked to our banner as we headed towards Brescia. These were men who had suffered under the rule of the Visconti family. These were the Guelphs who had been defeated by Visconti in the Guelph War. They wanted vengeance. Having learned my lesson with the two Germans I personally interviewed all the leaders and nobles who sought to follow me. I found none to be suspect and I formed them into a company. As they came from many families and clans, I appointed one of my men as their Captain. Roger of Nottingham, who was used to command having led his own ten lances and five archers, was a reliable warrior; as a condottiero in his own right he could lead the disparate men who were coalesced under the single banner of Guelph. That he could speak Italian also helped. When I named them the Guelph company they were pleased.

The fleeing army evaded us and we made steady progress west towards Bergamo. Even if Jacopo dal Verme turned to face us now, we would have parity of numbers and we had the advantage of being more confident than his army. He had suffered defeat after defeat at my hands. The new company helped us almost immediately. Not all had mail but there were young warriors who were keen to impress me. They rode ahead as scouts and it was they who told me of the enemy who were waiting for us on the other side of the Mincio River. That they would offer battle on the opposite bank of the river was telling. They feared to lose. If they lost on this side of the river then many would drown or be captured at the single bridge that spanned the water. They also made the mistake of not preventing us from crossing the river. I was allowed to cross with most of my army before they prepared their men for an attack by horsemen. As they had nine thousand cavalrymen, when they finally did launch their attack, it would be a stern test for us.

I quickly organised my men. I would use my lances this time. Unlike the Milanese, I had not lost many fine horses and good riders already. Jacopo dal Verme and his brother had been profligate with their men. We were all well-mounted and still had our best lances. I allowed each company its own frontage and they rode beneath their own banners. They made a stirring sight. My White Company was in the centre and I followed with my wagon and Gianluca held the smaller of my two banners. We had just half of his number of horsemen. I sounded the charge and ensured that our archers were mounted. They would follow and if they had the opportunity then they would support the cavalry. The infantry, largely the Bolognese and Florentine elements, followed behind. The Milanese infantry, in contrast, waited with their baggage. Our baggage was guarded by our squires.

    I held a hurried council of war with my leaders. My wagon was proving invaluable as I was able to be seen by all of them as they gathered around it. "The Bolognese and the Florentine infantry will form a triple line. Captain Falcan, you will command the infantry. When we charge you will follow but at a steady pace. I do not want a mad charge."

    "Yes, my lord." David Falcan was a reliable English leader. He commanded seventy-nine of his own lances as well as thirty-seven archers. "And my lances?"

    "Will ride with the White Company."

    I saw the pride on his face as he said, "An honour, Sir John."

    "The archers will be on the right flank and the crossbows on the left. The lances of the White Company will be in the centre. Captain Michael, your lances will be to the right of the White Company and Captain Konrad von Landau to the left. Captain Ambrogio, your lances will join Corrado Prospero and the two of you will be to the right of the Florentines. Il Novello, your lances will be on the left flank, next to Captain von Landau. Between you will be Captain Visconti and his company. Captain Roger, the company you command will be the reserve and advance with me. If there is a gap then you will exploit it. I want our new men to feel part of this army but I will not risk them in the first encounter. The enemy lances outnumber us, but we have the advantage of being better mounted and confident. We have beaten them at every turn. They seek to stop us, but we will sweep through them. We do not halt but race for the Oglio River before they can organise."

I saw, from the faces of my leaders that there was no dissension. Even Il Novello no longer questioned my every decision.

"Zuzzo will sound the charge. When he sounds the recall then stop. We have some way to go before we reach Milan. That is our aim! I want no glory hunters chasing the enemy across this land. We do not hunt a fox but the snake that is Milan."

When I reached my wagon, Zuzzo was ready with my helmet. Robert helped me up and Zuzzo placed it on my head. "Today, Robert, Bettina will not be needed. I want you as a carter. Keep us as close to the rear of the horsemen as you can."

"Aye, my lord. I suppose it is a Christian thing to do. This way there will be fewer widows amongst the enemy." Zuzzo and Gianluca smiled at the Englishman's arrogance.

It took time for the six companies to form up. Each one had a similar formation. They rode three ranks deep. The front rank would have levelled lances. They had all trained well together and could ride closer than the Milanese. There would be no gaps. Jacopo dal Verme had gambled that his superior numbers would hold us. He had not made the ground before them into a killing ground. The wind came from the west and that was a good sign for us. While it made our flags fly behind us as we charged, it made the enemy flags snap, crack and fly in all directions as they charged. Theirs would look like washing on a line. It was a little thing but my infantry, moving behind would be stirred by the sight while the enemy would be disheartened.

"Zuzzo, the charge!"

The horns sounded and the horsemen before us moved off at a walk. The gap between each of the companies was just two men wide and when they neared the enemy that gap would be closed. The walking pace for the rest, twenty or thirty paces behind, enabled us to keep close to the men led by Roger Nottingham. Captain Jack and his mounted archers loped easily behind the lances. They would dismount to fight. As the walk became a canter, the infantry struggled a little to keep up and when the lances began to gallop there was a clear gap. I glanced behind and saw that Captain Falcan was not panicking. He and his men were marching in straight lines. There was a gap but by

Legacy

the time the two sets of horsemen had closed then they would have the chance to catch up.

I heard the cheer as the two sets of horsemen came closer to each other. I knew that it was my men who cheered. Even from the vantage point of my wagon, I could not see the effect of the collision. I held on to the wooden post that Robert had fitted. I heard the crash and the crack of metal-headed lances shattering on plate armour. I even saw some of the splintered wood as shards flew into the air but the wall of men and horses before me hid the carnage that I knew would follow such a collision.

Suddenly there was a gap for the White Company and Michael's Florentines had broken through. On the flank, I saw that Corrado Prospero had routed the men he faced. Captain Roger took his new company to ride obliquely to help Captain Prospero. I realised that our infantry would never reach the battle in time to be of help. The enemy had broken after the first charge. There would be no slogging match. The enemy lances had crumpled like parchment. When my wagon reached the site of the coming together of thousands of horses, I saw that the majority of the dead animals and lances were Milanese.

"Robert, we can stop here." I watched the line of horsemen, no longer in neat blocks as they chased the enemy from the field. I waited until they were a mile or so away and then said, "Zuzzo, sound the recall."

Captain Jack was close enough to simply bring his mounted archers back quickly. They had not been needed. Even as the last notes sounded, the infantry, crossbows, baggage and squires had reached us.

"Captain Falcan, we will camp here. Have the dead buried and butcher the horses. We will enjoy meat this night."

I heard from the north and west, the sound of the horns of my companies as they echoed my call. It would take time to bring them back. Some would charge a little further after the horns sounded and plead temporary deafness. Others would carry on to take more prisoners and gather more horses. I would excuse those. There would be prisoners to take and the dead to strip. My bodyguards unhitched the horses as I took off my armour. I had not needed it but if I had not worn it then I would.

Legacy

By the time the weary horses returned, the dead had been stripped and buried, the dead horses butchered and hovels erected. It was summer and we needed no tents.

My leaders reined in, "Well, Captain Michael, did we lose any?"

He shook his head, "Less than ten lances fell and we have prisoners."

Francesco da Carrara was particularly ebullient, "Sir John never mind Bergamo, the road to Milan is open."

I shook my head, "Until I have word from Count John that his Frenchmen are in place we will keep our swords in the Milanese back. We will encourage the Guelphs in this land to revolt and we will take his cities." I turned to Corrado Prospero, "How many men did we slay this day? You were at the fore and saw all."

"More than five hundred, my lord. I think the true number of losses for the enemy will be twice that for many were wounded and I saw men fleeing in all directions."

I turned back to address the Lord of Padua, "So, my lord, we lose ten and they lose fifty times that number. It is a war of attrition and we are winning."

That night, after we had feasted on horsemeat once more, I held my usual conference with my leaders. I wanted them to know my intentions and I also wanted them to have the chance to speak to me. So far none of my professional soldiers had brought up the fact that the men they led had yet to be paid. The men from Bologna, Padua, Florence and now the Guelphs were not expecting any pay. We had taken enough from the enemy to ensure that the provvisionati were well fed and their purses had increased but when the contract was up they would need to be paid. I did not want a resentful army that would not fight. I would send back to our paymasters for some payment.

"This is a land of rivers, valleys and bridges. To that end, I want not only the squires to guard the baggage but also the archers. Captain Jack, you and the archers will be the last to cross any bridge."

"Yes, my lord."

I turned to Konrad von Landau, "You know Bergamo the best, can we take it easily?"

Legacy

"No, Sir John, it is like Verona with strong walls and natural defences." I liked my honest German. He was blunt and that was what I needed.

"Then as with Verona, when we reach the city, we will have the Bolognese besiege it. Captain Ambrogio, I entrust that task to you. I have no intention of making men bleed to take its walls. While the rest of the army makes merry in the land around Bergamo you will keep dal Verme trapped inside the town. Hopefully, they will have to resort to eating their horses."

"Surely we will not be there long enough for that, Sir John?"

"Ambrogio, I like not this delay as much as you, but we are dependent on the Count of Armagnac. Who knows, even now he may be enjoying as much success as we."

Captain Prospero smiled, "But you think not, eh, Sir John?"

I liked the personable young man. He was honest and open, "No, I think not. The French have never impressed me."

Captain Falcan chuckled, "As one of the last men to have fought at Crécy and Poitiers, that is understandable."

We moved towards Bergamo.

The Oglio River was not like the Po or the Adige. In places, it was less than thirty paces wide. We did not head for the bridges in case they were contested. Bridges could have gatehouses or castles. This was land held by Milan and its allies. We captured many wagons and made them into our own pontoon bridge. While the horsemen could swim, we simply marched the infantry over. My foresight in keeping the archers and squires with the baggage was vindicated as we crossed the river. The horses and infantry had passed over and there was just my wagon, the squires and the archers left to do so when seven hundred horsemen appeared from the east. They had used one of their own bridges and sought to ambush us by attacking our baggage. If they took the wagons then they would deny us food and rob us of our booty.

It was Zuzzo who saw them, "Sir John, Milanese horsemen."

"Captain Jack, archers! Squires, protect the wagons."

The squires were all warriors but young and largely untested. Most lances like to wean their squires into war. The young men, lightly armoured, wearing metal studded leather and helmets took their shields and spears. They bravely stood around and on the wagons. My bodyguards armed themselves and I donned my helmet and drew my sword. If I had not placed archers with the wagons then I am convinced we would have lost squires, wagons, arrows, spare weapons, coins and, perhaps, me.

"Archers, string your bows." That was always the lengthiest part of the procedure. Once strung an English archer could send ten arrows in a minute. In the time it took for them to string their bows, select an arrow and nock it the enemy had closed to within three hundred paces.

"Draw!" A heartbeat later, "Release!"

Once they had sent their first arrow then the other flights followed so swiftly that it appeared as though a black cloud was moving east. Horses and horsemen fell but, seeing the archers, they had spread out in a looser line and the arrows did not have as much effect as they might have done against a solid block of horsemen. I knew that some would reach my wagons, my squires and me. I had ridden my wagon in every encounter. They knew my wagon and they knew me. I was as much a target as the supplies.

I drew my sword. Robert held his axe aloft. He loved war and his shout was a sign of that joy, "Come on, you bastards! Bettina lusts after your flesh!" He shouted in English and few of the enemy would have understood his words, but it had an effect on the squires who were forming up around the baggage. They cheered. As many of my captains were English even the Italian squires could speak some English.

As I had expected, not all of the arrows struck either horse or flesh and some of the horsemen made it to the wagons. I was impressed with the courage of the squires. When the Bolognese had been charged, some had fled, not many, it is true, but some did run. The squires, in contrast, stood their ground. They held spears and as they had wagons around them then the horses could only close to the length of a lance. The squires also had shields. Even so, some fell. I hoped they were just wounded as I did not want to lose such courageous youths.

"My lord, they come for us."

Gianluca had seen a group of lances detach themselves from the mêlée around the wagons and were heading for me. It was not just to seek glory. If they killed or captured me then the heart would go from my army. This was not simply arrogance on my part. My leaders and bodyguards had all told me so. We had shields in the wagon and I picked one up. The six men who charged at our wagon had no squires to deal with, they were doing as I had ordered and guarding the wagons. One of the men coming at us was struck in the shoulder by an arrow. It had to be a bodkin for it penetrated but the warrior was tough and he kept coming. Gianluca and Zuzzo had their poleaxes and I was confident that my three bodyguards had the skills, the weapons and the armour to stay safe. Once the lances struck us, I had no more chance to observe the attack. A warrior who was less than vigilant died.

 A warrior wearing a red surcoat with golden stars upon it came at me. I blocked the lance that came at me with my shield and I used it angled so that the lance's head slid upwards. I was helped by the fact that the rider was below me. I swung my sword at his lance. I did not hack it in two, but I weakened it. He pulled his arm back to thrust at my middle and this time, when I blocked it with my shield, the wooden shaft shattered. He was beyond my reach but if he drew his sword, he would have to close with me and then I would have him. I saw blood on Robert's left cheek and wondered if it was his or his enemies. There were now just four lances trying to get at us. The numbers were more even. The lance with the red surcoat and golden stars drew his sword. He was more than proving his courage for while he would only strike at my greave-covered legs, his head and his upper body were within my range. I had my shield held by the guige strap rather than the brase and I dropped the shield to hang before my legs. It guaranteed that he would not do much damage to my lower limbs. The sword struck the shield and it absorbed most of the force. He swung again and had the same effect. As he pulled his arm back for a third attempt, I brought my sword down to hit his head, encased in a bascinet with a face mask. He had no shield and was concentrating so hard on hurting me that he did not defend the blow. I hit the helmet. While it was well-made, my arm was strong and the sword was an expensive one. Its edge was sharp and it was heavy. When I struck the helmet it was as though I had hit him with an iron bar. I saw the helmet as it dented and then cracked. His sword arm dropped and I

Legacy

switched my strike to hit him hard on the side of the helmet. He fell from the back of his horse. I do not know which blow killed him but his body, lying by the wagon, told me that he was dead.

I took off my helmet when I saw that my bodyguards had killed the others. It was easier to see the scene that way, "Is that your blood, Robert?"

My English bodyguard put his hand to his face, and it came away bloody, "Aye, my lord, but I do not think it will be as bad as the other."

"And we have six fine warhorses, my lord. They are worth more than a few ducats." Gianluca said.

"And they are yours to share. The armour and weapons I will keep."

Zuzzo said, "See, the attack is over. They are defeated."

Captain Jack mounted his horse and rode over, "Are you hurt, my lord?"

"No, Jack, and it felt good to be a warrior once more and not just the general ordering men to their deaths. Have the wagons taken over and tell the squires that I was impressed by their duty this day. The plate from these dead knights and their swords can go to the six squires who showed the greatest courage."

Jack nodded, "And I know who they are. We kept a closer eye on them than you, my lord for we knew you had the finest of armour and the best of bodyguards."

As we crossed the pontoon bridge the cheers rang out from both the squires and the lances of the White Company who had returned to see if they were needed. I raised my sword and the cheers increased.

Legacy

The Milanese campaign

Chapter 14

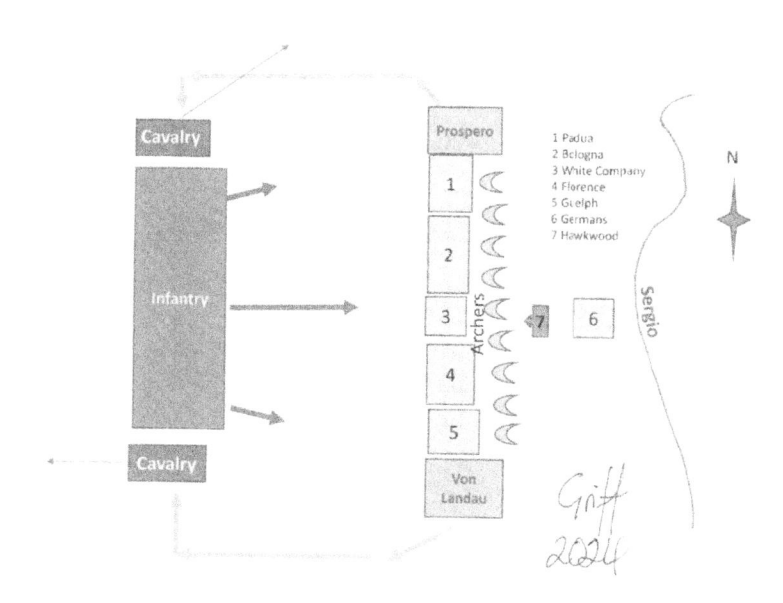

The Battle of Bergamo

Bergamo Summer 1391

We reached Bergamo at the start of June. Jacopo dal Verme had nowhere left to run. The question was, would he offer battle or squat inside the walls of the city? To encourage him to fight us, once we had made a fortified camp on the eastern side of the Serio River, I sent some of the mercenary captains and their companies to raid and ravage the land surrounding Bergamo. It proved to be rich pickings. The land was so close to Milan that they enjoyed the close protection of the Lord of Milan and had never been raided, at least not in the recent past. We had so many men that the protection from Milan was an illusion. Our lances took advantage of the freedom I afforded them and took animals and gold. They were earning more than the contract provided and they were all more than happy to do so for as long as I asked. Their pay from Florence and Bologna might not be needed for a while.

Legacy

After a week of such raiding and with more Guelph reinforcements arriving on a daily basis, Jacopo dal Verme had no choice but to bring out his army and fight us. I had chosen our campsite because we had the river behind us and that was useful for both grazing and watering but also because we had no obstacle before us if we chose to march to Milan. Jacopo dal Verme could not possibly know that I was not going to do that until the Count of Armagnac sent me word and so he had to shift us.

He brought his army before the city and we prepared to do battle once more. He had learned his lesson and had more lances that would fight dismounted. It may have been that we had destroyed his elite horsemen, I do not know, but he had just two blocks of horsemen on his flanks. That decided my own battle plan. I used Konrad von Landau to lead one company of lances and I placed them on my left. Corrado Prospero and Donnina's brother, Carlo, were on the right with more horsemen. Konrad would command as he had more horsemen than Carlo. The two got on well and there would be no rensentment. I made sure that each group of horsemen would outnumber their enemies. For the rest, I used dismounted lances intermixed with blocks of infantry. I had the White Company in the centre with the Bolognese on their right and the Paduans to their right. The Florentines were next to the White Company and the Guelph contingent of soldiers, led by Roger Nottingham, were close to the Paduans. Captain Coiser had joined us having been relieved in Verona by fresh men. After his march from Verona, his men were tired and they would be my reserve. The line of archers, which always looked too thin to me, were behind the infantry. If nothing else the campaign had shown me that when it was over I needed to visit with Robin and secure at least two hundred more. My archers had been worth their weight in gold.

There had to have been communication between Milan and dal Verme for, once more, the Milanese began the battle. I had Galeazzo Visconti worried and he wanted the threat that was Giovanni Acuto to be removed. He feared that I would win and move to attack Milan. That was the last thing he wanted. He had always been secure in his northern stronghold. When other cities and leaders had been threatened, he had enjoyed a comfortable

Legacy

life at his palace at Pavia. He was now paying the price for murdering Donnina's father. Such sins always come back to haunt the perpetrator of such a foul deed. I had a personal reason for victory and it was not simply gold.

The enemy horsemen were static. That told me they were there to protect the flanks. The line of infantry, bolstered by the feditore of Bergamo, moved forward with drums beating and horns sounding. The distant walls of Bergamo were filled with flags and defenders. I knew that this would be a long and hard day.

"Zuzzo, order the cavalry to charge."

We had devised signals using a mixture of new cavalry calls and the waving of flags. The two condottieri who led the horsemen for me were intelligent leaders and knew my mind. They would know what to do. The signals given, the two groups moved, not directly towards the enemy horsemen but across the face of the enemy so that when the charge was made it would be from the flanks. They halted and turned and then I heard the sound of the horns, just a heartbeat apart. The enemy horsemen had been forced to shift their positions to face the new threat from their flanks. Both German condottieri had complete control over their men and had timed their charge to perfection. The two groups of Milanese horsemen were still in the process of dressing their ranks and preparing to receive the charge when my cavalry struck them. I was half a mile away with a perfect view of the battle from my lofty perch. I heard the crack of my lances as they first hit and then unhorsed and killed many of the enemy horsemen. The survivors facing Captain von Landau now turned and fled back to the city. Konrad was too good a leader to miss such an opportunity and he hurtled after them. The men who were fighting Captain Prospero were also hurt in the initial charge but the leader must have survived for he ordered a retreat, not back to the city but north and east towards the bridge over the river. Corrado Prospero ordered the pursuit. The effect of the charges and the flight of enemy horsemen was to make the two flanks of the enemy line slow for infantry were always wary when there were horsemen on their flanks. They were now without protection and there were two companies of horsemen who could return at any time.

Legacy

The Milanese in the centre knew nothing of the defeat and desertion of their cavalry and they marched on with good plate armour, fine helmets and lances held before them. They knew that they outnumbered us and the proximity of their walls gave them an illusion of safety. It made their line more like an arrow.

Zuzzo would give the order for the archers to release on my command. My lofty perch was perfect and I knew, better than any, the range of my archers. They had bodkins ready in their hands and the arrows would descend and bring death to the enemy infantry, especially the feditore who wore little armour. That descent would add to their speed as they plummeted from the sky. I waited until the enemy soldiers were about one hundred and fifty paces from us. I could have given the order earlier but this way they came on thinking, perhaps, that we had used all of our arrows up.

"Zuzzo, the archers."

The horn sounded and I heard Jack's command, "Nock." He had time to make this a perfect strike. The archers had chosen their best arrows. "Draw!" The creaking of the bows sent shivers up my spine for I knew the power that was in every archer's arms. "Loose!"

Such was the speed of commands and the release that the enemy line had moved just six paces closer. The sound of metal bodkins striking plate armour and helmets was like a hundred blacksmiths hammering away. The second and third flights followed so quickly that the noise rolled on like thunder. The effects were clear. The arrows had made holes in the advancing line. The bending of the Milanese line and the arrows' effect had made the advance into a sort of wedge and the point of that wedge would strike just between the White Company and the Bolognese led by Ambrogio Bentivoglio.

Robert said, "My lord, Captain Prospero and Captain Carlo are driving the enemy cavalry into the river."

"And Captain von Landau is reforming his men and they are returning."

"Thank you, Gianluca." I peered at the right flank of the enemy infantrymen. Those at the rear had seen the return of horsemen. They stopped their advance and turned to present a wall of spears that would, they hoped, deter the horsemen whose horses would be blown. The effect, of course, was to slew the enemy line around even more as those to the left of the men who had turned, slowed.

"Zuzzo, order Captain Nottingham to advance."

I knew that Michael, leading the Florentines, had enough skill to edge a little closer to the Guelph warriors who would move forward. If Captain von Landau could keep the right flank of the enemy occupied then we had a chance to break the right side of the Milanese army.

There was a mighty crash from before me and I turned to see that the Milanese had clashed with the White Company and the Bolognese. The sprinkling of nobles in the Bolognese contingent gave some stiffening to their ranks but behind the mailed men of the front rank were warriors who had no armour. While the White Company held, as did the Paduans, the Bolognese buckled and Jacopo dal Verme, sensing a breakthrough, threw his reserves into the rear of the men pushing the Bolognese back. When they broke it was so rapidly that I barely had time to give my orders.

"Zuzzo, signal Captain von Landau and Captain Prospero to support the Bolognese."

The horn sounded and the flag was waved. The word support was the wrong one for the Bolognese soldiers who broke and fled towards the river had no order. We had a huge gap in our lines. All that I could hope was that our cavalry could remedy the situation. My position, along with my archers was also perilous.

I shouted, "Captain Jack, fall back behind the Florentines."

"Aye, my lord. You heard the order, now shift yourselves."

The advantage my archers had was that they wore little armour and could run. Even so, it was a close-run thing. Captain Falcan had managed to echelon his men around to attack the flanks of the Milanese who were pouring through the gap left by the Bolognese.

I saw that Captain von Landau was attacking the Milanese right as were the men from Guelph and Michael's Florentines were also adding their weight. Il Novello had turned his Paduans and the men who were trying to exploit the breakthrough found that they were attacked from both sides. When the two groups of

Legacy

horsemen closed with the leading men from two sides and my archers poured war arrows into them then the gap was plugged. It now became a close-fought battle with lines that were serpentine in nature. I had not drawn my sword for it was the White Company that was before my wagon and they would not let me be in danger. Captain Balzan had lost his lance but he was wielding a poleaxe to great effect. He was a true leader. He had many of the qualities of my old friend, Giovanni Ubaldini but he had the added qualities of an Englishman, a stubbornness and unwillingness to flee the field. They held.

Robert, with no heads to cleave, was giving me a commentary of what was going on behind us, "The river is claiming both Milanese and Bolognese, my lord. Those with armour have no chance and the others…"

Gianluca finished the sentence, "Will also die. Men cannot swim. Those who jumped in are foolish. If they surrendered, they would live."

The Milanese had feared our horsemen while the Bolognese showed that they did not have a martial spirit. Ambrogio, if he lived, would be mightily disappointed.

Inexorably the two wings of my army closed around the Milanese. It was when the noose was about to be completed that Jacopo dal Verme ordered the retreat. The walls of the city were manned by his crossbows and archers. When I saw the puff of smoke from his handguns, I knew that it would be foolish to lose men close to his walls.

"Zuzzo, sound the fall back. We have the field this day!"

Our men obeyed my signal for they were weary and weary men do not charge the walls of a fortress.

There were many dead. Zuzzo did a count for me. So many men had fallen into the river that a true number would never be known. He estimated that more than four thousand men had died that day. The difference was in the quality. We lost a handful of lances and the majority of our deaths were in the feditore of Bologna. The Milanese had lost all of the cavalry from one flank and half of the rest. We found the bodies of eighty Milanese men at arms. We took their plate and then allowed the Milanese to claim their bodies. We had a truce for a day. Some men returned to us by the end of the day but no Milanese came back to their stronghold. It was a victory.

I held a feast and we dined on horsemeat once more. We ate in the open and within sight of the walls of Bergamo. I wanted the Bergamese and the Milanese to see us celebrating. We had the city surrounded and it was in a state of siege.

I praised all my men at the feast, singling out Captain Prospero and Captain von Landau as well as Carlo Visconti in particular. I made sure that Captain Balzan and Michael received due praise for what they did and, of course, Il Novello and Roger Nottingham. I did not mention the men of Bologna nor Ambrogio Bentivoglio. For one thing, they had almost cost us the battle but, more importantly because Ambrogio almost hid himself away at the end of the table. Had I mentioned his name or the men he had led he would have been shamed.

"And now we take Milan?"

I shook my head, "No, Lord Carrara. Dal Verme still has a large army within the walls of Bergamo, and we do not know where Count John is to be found."

Captain Coiser asked, "Do we assault the walls, then, my lord?"

I laughed, "I think that our enemies would love that. We would bleed on them. We raid the land to the north of Bergamo and see if dal Verme will fight us again. Only when he is no longer before us will I risk a march on Milan."

That night, after most of my leaders were in bed I confided my fears to Michael, Carlo and Corrado Prospero. The three had become close and Prospero reminded me so much of the young Michael I had mentored and nurtured that it was like travelling back in time. "My fear is that we are too reliant on the arrival of Count John and his Frenchmen. We face the greatest threat from Milan and yet we have won at every turn. Is the Frenchman to be trusted?"

"The alliance has paid him well, Sir John."

"Michael, when has that ever made a difference? I will raid for a week and then we shall see if Jacopo will respond to a formal challenge of war. I will send him a bloody glove."

Konrad asked, "A bloody glove?"

Legacy

Michael nodded, "It is a challenge to combat. Usually, it is between two knights but Sir John will do so as Captain General. If Jacopo dal Verme refuses then he will lose face and his men will have even less confidence than they have now."

When it was clear, after a day or so, that he was not coming forth we left Bergamo and raided the land around. We took from Trescore Balneario and Cenate, breaking into the Val Cavallina. It was there that we were opposed. It was not dal Verme but Lombard warriors who contested a bridge. I sent in my archers and the bridge was cleared in five flights of our arrows. We crossed Ponte San Pietro, and then Presezzo, and Bonate Sopra, where we constantly plundered the surrounding territory. We passed through Brignano Gera d'Adda, Pandino, and Villanova, before reaching Ghiaradadda to the southwest of Bergamo. We had not crossed the Adda River for I wanted to be close enough to Bergamo to battle with the Milanese if they came out.

We stopped at Cassano d'Adda. I planned on spending some days there. The day after our arrival was St John the Baptist's Day, June the twenty-fourth. I gave a prize of twenty florins and held a horse race by the river. I knew it would please the whole army and with the Bolognese keen to make up for their showing at Bergamo, they acted as sentries while the rest of us watched horses racing and, inevitably, gambled. The priests amongst us disapproved of course but I needed some way to help my men enjoy some free time.

That done I took the decision, encouraged by Il Novello and the Guelph contingent, to march towards Milan. I do not know if it was the word of our race reaching Jacopo dal Verme, our alarming movement towards Milan or if he had orders from the Lord of Milan but whatever the reason he brought his army from Bergamo. We were now within fifteen miles of Milan and having crossed the bridge at Cassano d'Adda, we must have been a worry for the Lord of Milan. One advantage the Milanese army had was that they had the support of the people in this region. It had been we who had raided and plundered. It meant that they could cross the rivers anywhere they chose and without a dispute. They also began to attack our supply lines. That was the real reason I chose to head to Milan. Better to live off Milanese land than starve. The campaign had cost us men. The battle at Bergamo had cost us the largest number but now we endured more desertions. The condottiere did not desert, they were fighting for pay but some of the Bolognese, Guelph and Florentine warriors did. Our army was becoming smaller and there was still no sign of the Count of Armagnac.

When Jacopo and his army appeared before us, I sent him, with a herald, a bloody glove. He declined to fight us. Although my men cheered and roared with laughter the fact remained that if he did not fight us, we would soon starve to death.

The day after the glove was returned, we woke to find the Milanese army had disappeared. We spent the next two days seeking them but to no avail, they were not to be found. Scouts rode almost to the walls of Milan but they had vanished. We began to raid and plunder the land to the east of Milan. We were close enough to the city so that the smoke from the burnt-out buildings we left could be seen from that city.

The lance and his squire who reached us at the start of August were French. We could identify the nationalities of most lances by their armour and this was a Frenchman. The man at arms had no lance and the two of them had nothing else to identify them on their horses. As they neared me and my wagon Gianluca said, "They have been in a battle, Sir John."

I nodded. Zuzzo said what was in my head, "And they have come straight from that battle."

When they neared us, I could see that their surcoats were bloody. The squire had no helmet and there appeared to be a cut about his head. Their horses were lathered and exhausted. They had been ridden hard. They dismounted and the lance bowed, "Sir John Hawkwood?"

"I am he."

"I am Gaston de Foix and we have come from the battle that took place some days ago at Alessandria. My master Count John of Armagnac is dead, and his army is scattered. We were sent to bring news to you."

My heart sank. In that moment I knew that this campaign was over but I kept a brave and stoic face. My leaders had wandered over. My face was expressionless as I said, "Robert, see to the squire and the horses. Gaston, come into my tent. Zuzzo, refreshments." We crowded into my tent. There were just two

Legacy

camp chairs and I sat on one and gestured for him to sit on the other. There might have been many nobler men present but at that moment the most important man in the whole camp, me included, was the Frenchman. I waited until he had a goblet of wine. The way he downed it told me that they had not eaten or drunk very much since the battle. "Tell me all and spare me nothing. That this is a disaster is clear but I need to know the scale of it."

"We fought our way through Piedmont. You know the land, Sir John, it is perfect for ambushes. Count John defeated all before us until we neared Milan. Six thousand knights were sent to Castellazzo Bormida and it was then the Lord of Milan himself brought an army. Count John sent for those besieging Castellazzo Bormida. With those we would have been evenly matched with the Milanese."

"How many men?"

"Ten thousand." He held up his goblet and Zuzzo refilled it. "We might have beaten them too but men slipped into the rear of our camp and captured our horses and then another army joined them."

I sighed, "Jacopo dal Verme."

"Yes, my lord. With the extra men and the horses and squires captured it was a foregone conclusion that we would lose. Count John gave me orders to find you and tell you that he had failed. Even as we mounted our horses to find you, he was slain and by the time we had quit the field the army had surrendered. The six thousand knights in the army would fetch a good ransom for the Visconti."

"By my reckoning, you have ridden more than sixty miles. You have done well."

He shook his head, "I was the count's man and now I have nothing save my sword."

"Are you weary of war?"

His face hardened, "No, my lord. So long as Gian Galeazzo Visconti is the Lord of Milan, I will fight him."

"Then join the White Company. We always have need of stout knights and you are one."

"Gladly."

Legacy

"Zuzzo, take this warrior and see to his needs. Have him sign the contract."

"Yes, my lord."

The seat vacated, Il Novello sat down. He shook his head, "If they have combined their men then we are lost. Our numbers have shrunk."

Michael said, "We were outwitted. It is no wonder that dal Verme refused battle. He must have been in constant communication with Milan and they trapped Count John."

It was typical of Jacopo dal Verme. He had tried the same with me when Heinrich had defected. I smiled, sadly, "And had we pushed on then it would have been we who were trapped by two armies. The difference is that the French were also close to the mountains and the mountain men of Lombardy were able to take their camp. This is the end of our attempt to take Milan." I looked around at the faces, Il Novello, Bentivoglio, Michael, Lando, Prospero and Balzan. "You concur?" They nodded. "Alessandria is to the southwest of us. They can cut us off and here we are surrounded by enemies. We head for the Adige and Castelbaldo."

Francesco smiled, "At least that bodes well for us, Sir John. That is close to Castagnaro."

"Francesco that battle is in the past. Do not dwell on it but look for the next victory. If we are to save as many of this army as we can then we will need a victory that is even greater than Castagnaro. We break camp now and head for the Oglio River and Calcinato and Montichiari. If we can cross the river then we have a chance." I sounded confident but I knew that an army in flight soon disintegrated. "Captain von Landau, you will be the vanguard and Captain Carlo, the rearguard. The squires will guard the baggage."

I had to hold them together. Sir John Hawkwood would have to show the world that he was not yet ready to retire.

Chapter 15

August 1391 The Oglio River
From the moment we packed our tents and turned east we began to haemorrhage men. They were neither lances nor were they archers. Some Bolognese nobles fled and most of the Guelph nobles took to their heels and headed, not for the Oglio river, but their homes. They had bloodied the nose of Visconti's men but now it was a moment for discretion. We would be hunted and the Guelph nobles hoped to escape the gaze of Galeazzo Visconti. Many feditore ran. By the time we camped, at the end of the day, we had lost more than a thousand men. I was less concerned than the Lord of Padua, Il Novello, who had his men stand guard to stop others from fleeing.

The next day as we headed east once more, I rode next to him, "Francesco, we can do nothing about the men who wish to flee. Do you think that by making them stay they will fight?" He looked at me as though I was speaking a foreign language. "All that we will do will be to make our lines weaker when we fight. The mercenary companies have not deserted. The condottiere are ready to fight and while we may be outnumbered, we still have our minds."

He took in my words and glancing around him, saw that the provvisionati were still marching confidently. We had not been beaten and that was all that mattered to those professional soldiers. It had been another, a Frenchman who had been defeated. He smiled, "And you, Giovanni Acuto, still have the mind of a fox." He nodded, "We might not have achieved all that the alliance hoped but we have done more than any other army. We have taken the war to the very doorstep of Visconti's Milan. I can return to Padua and make it stronger. I have learned much from you." He smiled, "I am not the young arrogant noble from Castagnaro, the one who thought he was a better general than Giovanni Acuto."

Dal Verme caught up with us at Pontoglio in Cremona. We were some miles from the river. Between us and the river was a forest and the road passed through it. We had stopped where we could graze our horses. If they weakened then all would be lost.

Legacy

Corrado Prospero had grown during the campaign and he was now a confident and clever leader. He rode in with the news that the Milanese were coming down the road in great numbers. They were trying to trap us against the river. I called a hurried council of war.

"It will take some time to cross what remains of our army across the Oglio River. He thinks that he has us but we still have some tricks we have not played. Corrado, how far away are the Milanese?"

"Five miles but they have scouts a mile ahead of the main army."

"Excellent. Captain von Landau, I want you to take your lances and secrete them along the road that runs through the forest. Carlo, take your men with him. Captain Jack, your archers will go with them. We will take them when they least expect it. I want everyone to be prepared to break camp but we will only do so when we see their scouts. We make them think that we are fleeing and we rush headlong down the road. When their advance guard pursues us then you, Captain von Landau and you, Jack, will ambush them. Hurt them and make them fear to follow too closely. I want them damaged and fearful of another ambush. We will ford the river and your men will follow."

Their smiles told me that they approved.

As we loaded the wagon Zuzzo said, "Soon we will need to abandon your home, Sir John. It is slow and cumbersome. We have enough spare horses to carry the arrows and food. The other wagons should be abandoned sooner rather than later."

"Thank you, Zuzzo, and will you next teach me how to suck an egg? I know that we will have to take to our horses soon enough but now is not the time. We can ford the Oglio with the wagons and if my ruse works then we will do so in comfort."

"Sorry, my lord."

To the scouts who appeared just half a mile from our camp, we looked to have been caught unawares. Fires still burned and it looked as though we were cooking food. It was an illusion. The pots had already been emptied and their contents devoured. The horses were hitched to the wagons and all was ready for flight, or feigned flight. As soon as the scouts turned and raced back to tell the main army that we had been caught unawares, pursued

Legacy

somewhat half-heartedly by Corrado Prospero, the hitched horses began to move the wagons, the men were mounted and with the feditore leading we headed along the forest road. The feditore from Bologna ran. They were not acting flight. They were fleeing. We had less than half of the Bolognese still with us but they played their part to perfection. The ones on foot were running for the river as fast as the horsemen. The feditore from Florence had more composure as did the Paduan contingent. Leaving Robert on the wagon I mounted Ajax and waited in the forest with von Landau and his men. Zuzzo and Gianluca flanked me. The last of the squires and the baggage had just passed when we heard the thundering of the hooves as the advance guard of the Milanese army arrived. They had seen the slower-moving wagons. They had to have come to know that the baggage was just guarded by squires and they saw their chance.

The shout, "Loose!" was the start of the ambush. Using a flat trajectory Jack's archers sent arrow after arrow into the Milanese men at arms who led the pursuit. As more Milanese appeared, von Landau gave the order to charge and I heard, in the forest, Jack's distinctive voice give the command for the archers to leave. Von Landau's well-trained warriors demolished the advance guard as well as the ones who came to support them.

When the survivors fled down the road, I gave the command to fall back. Zuzzo's horn brought Landau's men back from their attack. Some had taken swords, horses and even plate such had been the swiftness of our attack. We reached the river and I saw that there were just the squires, the baggage and Landau's men to cross. The four men we had left in the forest to watch the enemy reached us after the last of the wagons had crossed the river and reported that the Milanese were coming through the forest but had scouts in the woods, looking for another ambush. We had bought time to get ahead of our pursuers. However, I was not a fool. The next time they caught up with us Jacopo dal Verme would be warier.

We rode hard for Calcinato. More men deserted. Horses were stolen and we needed a double guard on the herd. It added to the tiredness of the army. I, too, was feeling my age. I was no longer a young man and the rigours of such a long campaign were taking their toll.

Legacy

When we crossed the Mincio I was told that we had lost another five hundred men. The weariness of our men also showed when forty were drowned in the crossing of the river. I chose that moment to knight twenty men, amongst them Corrado. He became Sir Konrad Passberg. I also gave spurs to John Balzan. He had been as a rock. The joy on the faces of the twenty new knights was also reflected in others. They saw that I had rewarded the bravest and the best. It would encourage others to acts of valour and it cost me just twenty of the many spurs we had taken from the battlefields.

My inner core of leaders and I dined together. The others were genuinely pleased that I had knighted not only Corrado but Jack too. Like Robin, he was now a knighted archer.

Il Novello drank deeply for one thing we had in great store was wine. We had taken many barrels at Calcinato. "If we can make the Adige, Sir John then we have succeeded."

"That is many miles hence and I think that is where we will have to rid ourselves of the wagons. It may be too deep for the wagons to ford. We shall see."

I saw him look ruefully at the wine in his hand.

The Adige River was a mighty one. It was not as powerful as the Po but it was the most important river in this part of Italy. The banks had been built up to stop it from flooding the surrounding land. When we reached the river, I risked taking the wagons across. I ordered that the empty wine barrels be tied to the wagons as well as the half-empty ones to make the eight wagons we had left float. With riders using ropes, we forded the river. It was at that crossing that we lost many men. Most were the feditore or infantry. Some lost their grip on the wagons while others were just too weary to fight the river. When we reached the other side, we were wet and exhausted and we made camp. Men were sent downstream to try to rescue as many from the river as they could. A mere fifty were fished from the water. We would now be vulnerable if Jacopo dal Verme could bring us to battle.

I ordered food to be cooked. We were almost within touching distance of Castelbaldo and that was both symbolic and represented safety. It was close to there that I had turned defeat into victory and destroyed my enemies at Castagnaro. Once more, I had done what many thought was impossible. I had extricated my army from a trap. We had lost men but we had stayed together and the ones who remained at my side had not become a rabble. I held another council of war.

"We have not rid ourselves of the Milanese. They hang on to our cloak still. From here until we reach home, we abandon the wagons."

"Yours too, Sir John?"

"Yes, Ambrogio. I want us to move as fast as a fox that is hunted by hounds. We pack everything onto the draught horses: food, arrows, spare weapons and water. Each man will carry his own weapons, bedding and purses. Zuzzo, have the gold we have taken divided amongst the men according to their rank."

He nodded. The feditore might get a florin or two, the squires twenty or so, the archers a hundred and the leaders and captains would need small chests to carry theirs home. Our losses and desertions meant that there was more for all the survivors.

Jacopo dal Verme was a worthy opponent. While we emptied the wagons and distributed our supplies he was upstream of us and he had another trick to play. I was one of the fortunate ones for I slept in the wagon. The rest of the camp had a rude awakening. The Milanese had breached the embankments of the river and we were rudely woken to find ourselves in a new lake. Many men drowned as the water inundated our camp. Food was ruined and the half-full barrels of wine, which we had intended to empty before we left, were dashed and smashed by the floodwaters.

Even as we rescued what we could a herald came from the Milanese. He had with him a gift. There was a box covered by a cloth and carried by the herald's servant. "Captain Hawkwood, my master says that you have done all that you can but this is the end. It is time for your surrender." I nodded and said nothing, "This is a gift from my master. He hopes you will take its meaning."

When the cloth was removed, I saw that it was a fox in a wooden cage. Il Novello snorted, "This is an insult, my lord." His hand went to his sword.

I held up my hand, "This is a herald and he merely delivers a message. Give me the beast." I saw it was a young scrawny

Legacy

male. Dal Verme had taken an easy victim. I said, "I see the animal is not sad, it means it will find its way." I broke one of the wooden bars and when I placed the cage on the ground, the fox fled and my men cheered. The herald coloured. I smiled, "Tell your master that this fox is not yet in the cage. We are wet and we are dirty but we can still fight. If he wishes to take us then here we shall be when he comes and we will make a fitting end for this glorious campaign."

When they had gone, Il Novello said, "Surely we are not going to try to fight him."

I laughed, "Of course, not. We emulate the fox. Zuzzo, do not use the horn for that will alert the herald but go around with Gianluca and tell the ones who are not in hearing distance of my words to mount. We leave as soon as we are all horsed." I felt no remorse for my actions. Dal Verme had called me a fox and like a fox, I would do all that I could to survive. I had lived this long by choosing when to fight and when to run. I mounted Ajax and Robert mounted Blackie. His old nag would carry our blankets and treasure. I waved my baton and led the race to Castelbaldo. When the Milanese reached the camp, they would have to negotiate the detritus of the flood: the wrecked equipment and abandoned wagons. The wreckage would slow them. That there would be nothing left for them to ransack would not be immediately obvious. We had a head start and I intended to use it. We rode hard. Once we had passed Castelbaldo we turned north to head for Padua and by the time we reached Montagnana, we were weary but we were safe.

This was Paduan land and Il Novello ordered a local lord to send men back to Castelbaldo to watch for the Milanese. They returned late the next day with the news that Jacopo dal Verme had given up the pursuit. He was heading back to Milan. How the Lord of Milan would view the news was open to debate. We had hurt him and raided freely for many months. We had not been defeated in open battle and had trounced his armies in most of the battles. The defeat of the French was his only true victory. I did not know how either Florence or Bologna would take the news but we could have done no more than we had.

Legacy

We spent a week in Padua and I was richly feted by the Paduans. With a much-depleted army, we headed south for, first Bologna, and then Florence.

I rode with Michael and Corrado Prospero. The three of us got on well. "What are your plans, Sir Konrad?" Although we referred to him by his Italian name when I gave orders, he had let it be known that, just as I preferred to be called Sir John, he liked to be called Konrad.

"I confess, Sir John, that I had not thought beyond reaching Florence. Will you be paying off your men?"

I nodded, "I normally do but I am lucky. I know that when I have a new contract they will flock to my banner. Success breeds success. Why not spend some time in my home? I know that my wife would like to meet you."

As soon as his face lit up I knew that he had been seeking just such an invitation. "I would like that and I would be able to see Sir Michael and his family too. He has invited me to spend some time with him and his wife."

As we neared Bologna, I spent more time with Ambrogio knowing that I would see the other two in Florence. Konrad von Landau had shown me that he was the best of the captains who had served with me. He had commanded the vanguard for the most dangerous part of our retreat and he would also return with me to Florence.

"Well, Ambrogio, you came to learn. I hope that you have seen that there is more than one way to fight a battle."

He nodded, "I will never be a condottiero like you but I believe that I can lead the men of Bologna and we will not be embarrassed as we were at Bergamo."

"The men you led were not provvisionati, they were feditore and far from home. Many of those who fled will be waiting in Bologna. Do not treat them harshly. They have paid the price for they have not enjoyed the rewards we divided at the Adige."

"Will you stay in Bologna?"

"I will need to speak to your uncle for he was part of the alliance who sent me forth. I need to know if he requires any more of me."

"And what next for you, Sir John? Will you rest your baton? Is this the last campaign of Giovanni Acuto?"

Legacy

I laughed, "Retire? I think not. If nothing else this campaign has shown me that there are few who are as good as I am. When it is time to retire then I will know."

It was when we reached Bologna that we learned our service was not yet over. The Este family had changed sides again. The podestà of Bologna did not know if this was coercion, bribery or simply treachery. They might have heard of our flight and taken it to mean I had been defeated. What was known was that the Lord of Ferrara had hired Ugolotto Biancardo, Antonio Porro, and Antonio Balestrazzo to raid Bolognese lands. We were tasked with ridding the land of them before our service was over.

Michael's Florentines were ready to go home and I did not want disgruntled men so I left them in our camp outside the city. It ensured that our baggage and horses were safe. I also left the infantry of Bologna at the city. Bologna now had better warriors for the ones who had returned from the campaign were far more reliable than the ones who had gone to war with young Ambrogio Bentivoglio. It meant that while I had a smaller force it was far more mobile. I had the White Company as well as the Bolognese nobles. The three companies I had, Captain von Landau's, Captain Coiser's and Sir Konrad's were almost as good as the White Company.

We headed for Modena. I knew the land there well and I was confident that I could not only ravage and plunder but also draw the enemy into a battle on ground of my choosing. Our mobility ensured that I had five companies to spread themselves around the Modenese land. The enemy had no idea where we would strike and for four days we raided with impunity. The scouts Ambrogio used knew the land well and they reported that the enemy warriors were moving towards the camp we had established to the east of Modena. I had taken over the village of San Cesario Sul Panaro. It was more of a hamlet than a village but I had chosen it because it was close to the Panaro River. We had water and grazing for our horses. I had commandeered a wagon within a day of our arrival and as the mercenary companies hired, no doubt, with Milanese gold approached, I was able to observe them. To swell their numbers they had men from both Ferrara and Modena. They would be feditore and their numbers meant nothing. I allowed them to approach to within

Legacy

half a mile of our camp and that was deliberate. It meant that they had a loop of the Panaro Rover behind them. It would constrict a retreat.

I placed my men in the five blocks that they were familiar with. Men were more comfortable fighting alongside men that they knew well. They were all mounted as were my archers. I sent the squires with the archers and they spread out before the mounted companies. The men we fought had not battled with us before. They knew my reputation but, perhaps, they thought me an old man. They had more men than we did and were confident. They had two wings of horsemen and, in the centre, the infantry. They had mixed feditore with provvisionati. Another advantage we had was that we had all fought together for many months. The men who were still with me knew my calls and my signals. Back, once more, on the back of a wagon, I was able to see the whole battlefield before me. Gaston de Foix and his squire had proved invaluable to me. I had used them to fight alongside my White Company but I also employed them more as messengers. Both were good warriors and rode good horses, captured from our enemies. I could use them to ride across any battlefield knowing that my messages would be delivered.

My captains and my archers knew my plan. We would let the archers thin the ranks of the advancing infantry and weaken their resolve. When I ordered the charge then the White Company, flanked by Captain von Landau and the Bolognese would charge the infantry. I knew that the enemy cavalry would then make their move and Sir Konrad, Carlo and Captain Coiser would react to that movement and charge. If the enemy did something that I did not expect then Gaston and his squire could change my commands quickly.

The men of Ferrara and Modena were confident and they moved towards us with purpose. The brightly coloured banners were held proudly aloft as half of the force facing us moved across the flood plain of the river. I had a good eye for such things and when the infantry were two hundred and fifty paces from us I said, "Zuzzo, sound arrows." The trumpet sounded and I heard the distant command. Sir Jack of Derby always used English. The majority of his men were English. It meant that any of the enemy who had never fought archers knew not what to expect. When the arrows descended then we could see which ones they were. They were the ones tardy in raising their shields. Little holes appeared in their lines and those holes were enlarged with each successive flight of goose-feathered death. I saw the line falter and then heard the enemy trumpets. They were reforming their lines and it was the perfect time.

"Zuzzo, sound the charge."

The enemy knew what the call meant but they still had to react and these men were slower than the Milanese had been. As my archers mounted and moved to the flanks the three companies hurtled towards their infantry. As I had expected the movement of archers to the flanks caused concern for their own cavalry which watched in anticipation. If my archers dismounted and prepared to loose at them then they would pounce on the archers. I had no intention of doing so. My archers would dismount behind Sir Konrad's company and Captain Coiser's men. The hesitation cost their infantry. In the process of reforming their lines, they were struck by three companies of lances. It was only then that the enemy cavalry belatedly charged. I did not need to give the command for my two captains led their companies to smash into the flanks of their cavalry. Men say that Castagnaro was my greatest victory. That may have been because of the numbers or the importance of the battle. That day at San Cesario sul Panaro I felt more than satisfied that I had fought an almost perfect battle. Not only were the infantry broken, the two companies of horsemen outnumbering mine were totally destroyed and driven from the field. We took their baggage and many prisoners. So great was the victory that by the end of the first week in September, the Este family begged for peace and this time provided hostages for their surety.

We left Bologna in triumph. Captain Coiser had been hired by Bologna and so I headed for Florence with just three companies as well as the Florentines and wagons laden with coins, armour, weapons and plunder.

Legacy

The Arno Valley 1391

Chapter 16

September 1391 The Arno River

So great was our victory that we were accorded, when we returned, that most rare of events, a victory parade through Florence. At a feast held in our honour, Captain von Landau was paid an annual pension of twelve hundred florins. I was also paid a bonus of one thousand florins in addition to the fee for my company and my annual stipend. We three captains also received various silver objects, including eight large chalices, twenty-two cups and two basins, all the work of the Florentine goldsmith Giacomo di ser Zelli. Carlos Cialdini, who despite his age was still, effectively, the podestà of Florence, sat on one side of me while Michael and his wife sat on the other.

It was hard to reconcile the man who had employed a spy in my household with the merchant who heaped effusive praise on me at the feast. "This has been a great victory, Giovanni Acuto, and you have shown that time has not diminished your skills, but I fear we cannot rest on our laurels. Word has come to us, while you were dealing with the threat of the Este snakes, of an army heading for Florence. It is commanded by Jacopo dal Verme. Your wife's uncle seeks vengeance for the hurts you caused him in Lombardy. We would have you and Captain Prospero stop him with your companies."

"And Captain von Landau?"

"We will keep him here in Florence. The council is worried that Visconti may send a second army and that dal Verme is there to draw you away. You have one thousand lances and you know the land around the Val d'Arno. We are confident that you will prevail and more rewards will come your way."

The contract was lucrative and I took it. We had confidence, especially after dealing with the Este family so easily. I also felt that I had the measure of Jacopo dal Verme. He had almost outwitted me twice but I had dealt with the threat.

Casa Donnina lay in the direction we were travelling and we headed directly there. I would have a couple of nights at home before I headed on campaign again.

Legacy

Donnina welcomed us warmly. She had not met Konrad Passberg before but she made him welcome. I knew we could talk later and she fussed in the kitchens ordering the food we would eat. My son had grown. At almost four years old, he was a bundle of energy but it was in my two elder daughters that I saw the greatest change. Ginnetta was thirteen and looked like a young lady and even Caterina, who was just twelve no longer had the body of a child. I could see the difference in Konrad's reaction. He saw, not the children I had left, but young women. I had missed the change from a child to a young woman.

During the meal, my two elder daughters and Konrad chattered as all young people do. John and Anna were ignored by all. I know I should have paid more attention to them but I had missed my wife. Ever the mind that thought of business, her first comments had to do with the coins we had accrued. I had not had the time to fully count them but my bodyguards had ensured that the chests were safely locked in my strong room. When I left to deal with Jacopo dal Verme, there would be time for her to count it.

While the others chattered about, I know not what, I spoke with Donnina, "I had thought to visit with Robin but there will be no time, I fear, I need more archers."

Her face darkened and her voice dropped, "Word has come to us from Montecchio Vesponi, my husband. In the time you were away, Robin's reports ceased to arrive as regularly. I sent Edgar and he reported that Robin is not in robust health. He has some serious ailment. He is no longer young and Edgar feared that his time on this earth is growing short."

Robin was younger than I was. Not by much but even so…, "I am no longer young but I do not see my death on the horizon."

"But you are still active and that keeps you young."

"Then I have all the more reason to deal with dal Verme quickly. Giovanni died and I had not seen him for a long time. I would not have the same for an even older friend."

I had even more reason to deal with the Milanese threat quickly. I wanted to be with my friend at the end of his time on this earth. The news that Robin was ill, perhaps even dying, upset me more than I would have expected. I had seen many comrades die. I was a warrior and death was always at my shoulder. How I had escaped death and lived to see more than seventy summers, I would never know. Perhaps God had a purpose for me although his priests might say the opposite.

When I rose, after a much-disturbed sleep, I summoned my leaders and my bodyguards. It was too early for my family to be awake and so I had Ned and Edgar prepare food and bring it to the dining hall. We would eat and begin our day before my wife and daughters had risen. "Our old foe, paid again by Visconti, is coming to pay back Florence for the financing of the war against him. We have to stop him. We need not actually bring him to battle, just keep him from Florentine land. Pisa can fend for itself and the Luccans have decided, so the podestà told me, to ally itself with Visconti. The question is, where will they attack first?"

Konrad was more focused without two pretty young girls to distract him and he said, "Do we have numbers of the enemy, Sir John?"

I shook my head, "Not exact numbers but we know who he has as his lieutenants: his brother, Taddeo, Gentile da Varano, and Vanni d'Appiano. I cannot see him having less than ten thousand men."

Captain Balzan shook his head, "And we have one thousand lances and less than four hundred archers. Can it be done, Sir John?"

I smiled and broke the still-warm bread in two so that I could smear butter upon it, "I am sure, Sir John, that he has more than ten thousand men. He comes to take Florence and he knows that I am the one to defend it. He will not fight us unless he is convinced that he can win and that means bringing the greatest number of soldiers he can."

I bit into the bread, Donnina had hired the best of bakers, and the melted butter allied to the fine white bread was a delight. I had missed such simple pleasures whilst on campaign. I gobbled it quickly.

Konrad said, "Then how will we do it, Sir John?"

I began to spread butter on the next piece of bread and spoke as I topped it with some of the fried ham that Edgar knew I loved, "All of you here are young men and I am old but when I first came to this land, to Tuscany, I fought for Pisa and I had to do what Jacopo dal Verme is attempting to do. I had to negotiate the Val d'Arno. It is narrow and there are many places where an army can be stopped. As we discovered in Lombardy, river crossings where there is no bridge are hazardous. He will have to use the bridges. Quite simply we bar his progress." I bit into the bread with fried ham and closed my eyes to enjoy its taste. Simple pleasures were the best. I knew my men were thinking about my words and I chewed slowly this time to allow them the time to think. I was training them and when I was gone my legacy would be young condottieri who could think as I had. They were soldiers. Konrad had the ability to think strategically but he was young and he still had much to learn. Michael had been more like me and studied maps. He would have understood what I planned but he was in Florence with Konrad Landau. Donnina's brother, Carlo, was still learning. That gave me more freedom. I knew that even if I failed to stop Jacopo dal Verme from reaching Florence those two captains, Michael and von Landau, would hold him. However, I knew that I would not fail. I had outwitted Captain General dal Verme at every turn and fighting in this land I knew so well I was not about to lose. For one thing, I did not want Casa Donnina to suffer at the hands of vengeful enemies.

Wiping my hands on my cloth, I said, "So, we move as swiftly as we can down the road towards San Minato. Carlo, you have Italians in your company who know this land," he nodded, "then they shall be our scouts. I need to know where we can find our foe."

Zuzzo and my bodyguards were dining with us and it was my trumpeter who asked, "Will you use a wagon again, Sir John?"

I shook my head, "While the road that runs to Pisa suits a wagon we may have to use mountain passes. I shall ride Ajax." I smiled, "Sorry, Robert, you will have to be mounted."

He shrugged, "I am becoming a better horseman although I can never be a lance. I will still dismount to use Bettina to protect you, my lord."

We left the next morning. I said my goodbyes to Donnina the night before and we slipped away before dawn. There were always spies and while we had rid ourselves of those within our walls, like Guccio, I knew that Visconti had allies in Florence and they would send word. By leaving before dawn, we gained half a day. In half a day we could disappear.

We headed down the Arno Valley and stopped at the fortress of Empoli. The bridge there was the only way that an army could cross the Arno until further upstream. Coming from the north the men sent by Visconti would have to cross the bridge and, if he did cross there, then I could hold him. While our Italian scouts scouted the land to the north, I put some of the infantry I had brought into the fortress while the rest camped at Pontorme, a hamlet a mile to the east of the bridge. I would not contest his crossing but I would make it hard for him to move up the valley towards Florence.

Even before the scouts returned, we were joined by five hundred crossbowmen and more lances led by Giovanni da Barbiano and Luigi da Capua. I split the crossbowmen and put half in the fortress. Carlo's scouts reported back a day later. Jacopo dal Verme was leading twelve thousand men towards us. I had my army dismounted and we spread out from the river to the foothills. If we were to be shifted then it would mean he had to endure an attack on his rear from the fortress. If he chose to attack the fortress then we would attack his rear. If he wanted to battle us, he would have to risk his whole army and fight on two fronts. Another arrival was John Beltoft and his company. I had not seen him since I had chased him from Florence and Siena. He had lied to me at Mondavio but I was a professional. If Florence hired him then I would accept him as a subordinate. Like the Germans, however, I would not trust him entirely. I would use his men but they would not be in a position to betray us.

Jacopo dal Verme sent a thousand lances across the river. Dismounted, with plate armour and shields, they were immune from my missile attacks. Even bodkins would fail. When they stood and faced my army, I knew he was tempting me to attack him. There was no point. After a couple of hours where we all watched each other, he reinforced the one thousand with another thousand so that he outnumbered my men in Pontorme. I turned to my captains, "Sir John, Sir Konrad, Carlo, he will attack us soon. Put our men at arms in the front rank and send the infantry to the rear."

Sure enough, after a short time of forming his ranks, his lances surged forward. They all had shields and that meant they could only use spears. My men were armed with lances and pole weapons. I smiled as I sensed the eagerness in Robert to join them. This was the sort of battle he relished. When the two forces met there was a cracking of wood on metal and the screech of spearhead on plate. Our longer lances kept them at bay. They tried to use their weight of both plate and numbers to push back my men but we had the houses and walls of Pontorme behind us and archers and crossbowmen on the tops of buildings were judiciously targeting any enemy who gave them the chance to cause a wound. After an hour, the enemy sounded the horn, and they pulled back across the bridge.

We had lost but two men and they had lost eighteen. We stripped the armour from their bodies and took their weapons while our dead were taken to the church to be buried. "Captain Balzan, have the corpses thrown in the river." I pointed upstream, "Do it up there so that they can watch the passage of their dead. I would anger them."

That night I made a decision. It was a bold one but I had confidence that I had the measure of my rival. "Giovanni da Barbiano and Luigi da Capua, I want the two of you to stay here with the crossbows and the men at arms you brought. I will slip away in the night. You need to make the enemy believe that my whole force is here. Have your men move around as much as they can. We will cross the bridge at Signa." Signa was ten miles closer to Florence. The road from Signa to Empoli on the other side of the river was not a good one, but my army was small enough to cope with it. "We will threaten his supply lines and make him withdraw north. Your task is to prevent his crossing."

"Yes, my lord."

"Sir Konrad, Sir John, and Carlo have the hooves of the horses muffled and we will walk beside them for the first four miles." I did not want my enemy to hear us moving. I wanted him fixed by the river and planning his next move while I outwitted him.

"Yes, my lord."

"Make sure that the men eat well."

Legacy

After we had eaten and I led my men back towards Florence, Zuzzo chuckled, "For an old man, my lord, you make some strange decisions."

"How so, Zuzzo?"

"You walk when you could ride."

"I want the army to know, Zuzzo, that I can endure the same hardships that they do. I will eat the same food and walk the same miles."

We headed upstream, crossed the river by the bridge and then headed for Jacopo dal Verme's supply lines. By dawn, we were almost three miles north of the enemy at the hamlet of Sant'Ansano. My men secreted themselves along the sides of the road that led into the village and rested. Their horses grazed the grass beneath the trees. I sat with my bodyguards outside one of the houses. I paid the owner and his wife cooked us food. We sat and ate.

Zuzzo said, "You eat but your men do not, Sir John."

"Zuzzo, do you not know me yet? We are bait. Jacopo dal Verme will need supplies and they will come down this road. I want the eyes of those who travel down this path to be on me. We have plate and mail and I do not fear men bringing food in wagons. Besides, my men can eat if they so choose. The difference is that I eat freshly prepared food."

Gianluca said, "Suppose he has sent for more men?"

"Excellent! Then we shall eliminate them here. Do you not trust Captain Prospero, Captain Carlo and Captain Balzan?"

Zuzzo shook his head, "You are still like the fox my lord. It is the grey hairs that give the illusion of slowness."

It was noon and I was dozing a little for the sun was warm. This was September and it was hotter than England in the middle of July. I was woken by Robert. "My lord, I hear horses."

I opened my eyes and said, "Fill my coistrel, Robert." He frowned, "We are gentlemen resting on the road. Act the part."

"Yes, my lord."

I looked up the road and sipped the wine. I wore no helmet but I had mail beneath my plate and my sword was close to hand. I saw that the soldiers were Milanese men at arms. There were twenty of them and behind them trundled the wagons bearing the

Legacy

food bound for Jacopo dal Verme. They reined in and one said, "You are Giovanni Acuto, Sir John Hawkwood."

I smiled, "That I am."

The knight, for he wore spurs laughed, "Then General dal Verme will reward me for I have caught his enemy."

I smiled, "If I might correct you, you have met his enemy but capture and reward are still beyond your grasp. Zuzzo, the horn."

Zuzzo had the horn ready and he sounded it as Robert and Gianluca held their weapons before me. The knight paled as a thousand men suddenly surrounded him and his wagons.

"Now, my friend, if you would dismount so that I might speak with you. I am getting a crick in my neck looking up at you."

He dismounted and handed me his sword, "You truly are a fox, no that does not do you justice. You are a wolf."

"Your men and your wagons are now mine but you…"

"Giacomo, Giacomo Castricani, my lord."

"You, Giacomo Castricani, are free. I would have you ride to your master and tell him that he is surrounded. I will give him just two days to quit Florentine land and if he has not departed then he will suffer my wrath." I paused to let that sink in. "Is that clear?"

"It is, my lord."

Looking ruefully at his lost command he mounted and headed down the road to the Arno and the army on its banks.

I stood, "Well done. Let us see what we have. Gaston, have these men at arms dismount. Take their plate and weapons. Give them a couple of loaves between them and let them follow Giacomo Castricani."

Gaston smiled, "Yes, my lord."

Konrad, Carlo and John had wandered over. Konrad said, as he watched the lances take off their mail and plate, "Is this wise, my lord? These nineteen men will be able to fight us again."

I nodded, "I remember a condottiero who was defeated at Rimini and came to me with neither horse nor sword. Do you remember him, Konrad?"

He smiled, "I do, my lord."

"And how did you feel?"

"Humiliated and eager for revenge."

"Just so. Now these men will not be as lucky as you. They will not be given horses, plate and weapons by Jacopo for he does not have them. They will be eager for vengeance and that will make them reckless. I welcome such wild attacks from men without decent plate and weapons. Robert, Zuzzo and Gianluca will whittle them down to size. Now, send your Italians down the road to follow these men and then have them secrete themselves. I would have a warning of the enemy's approach."

The food and wine we took not only benefitted us but I knew would hurt the enemy. Dal Verme would have counted on taking a town. The wagons had been a backup. When our scouts returned the next day, it was with the news that dal Verme had broken camp and was heading northwest. They had given up on their attempt to head up the Val d'Arno. They would find another way to get to Florence. I sent the scouts to bring Giovanni da Barbiano and Luigi da Capua and their troops to join me.

I held a council of war. When I was younger, I had not bothered with such matters. I now felt like a teacher. I was a master condottiero and I had a duty to teach the young. My legacy would be that the captains who served under me would be better for the time that they had spent learning from me.

"We have blocked one road and so he must take another. He will move into the Val di Nievole and then take the road through Pistoia and Prato. Sir Konrad, when we are done send our squires back to Florence to inform Captain Michael of my decision and what I believe are the intentions of these mercenaries. If we cannot stop them then he will have to do so."

Sir Konrad nodded, "So, Sir John, how do we stop them?"

"Until we get more men then we are somewhat hamstrung. However, I know this land and we have the advantage that we have no wagons and we know the quiet ways. We will use tracks and trails to fall upon him. We will defeat him with ambush and not open battle. As he showed at Empoli, he has no intention of fighting a major battle if he can avoid it. I would rather make him bleed to death. Do you all remember how, after the defeat of Count John," I saw Gaston flush; he was still angry about that, "we began to lose soldiers? I intend to make him suffer the same fate. When his smaller companies begin to die then others will desert, and he will be left with fewer men." They nodded. "We leave tomorrow and take the road to Pescia."

We could have reached the mountain village quickly but I was aware that if we lost horses in the mountains then we would be in trouble. It took two days to reach Montevettolini. When we did, I discovered that Michael had responded immediately to my riders. He had simply ordered the feditore who lived to the west of Florence to fulfil their feudal duties. We had numbers. He had sent another four hundred lances too and that gave me the chance to do something about the threat from Milan.

The Italian scouts reported that the Milanese were trying to cross the mountain range known as Monte Albano. Now that we had so many spearmen and crossbowmen, we could hold them at Montevettolini. Once more I held a hurried council of war.

"Sir Konrad, I will leave you here to command the feditore and the crossbowmen. Your company will follow me as will you, Captain Carlo along with your company. Captain John, you will take the White Company, the lances sent from Florence and those brought by da Barbiano and da Capua. Head through the mountains and take their rearguard. According to the scouts they are at Pescia. I want you to approach Uzzano from the northwest. We will then combine to attack their rear at Uzzano. Carlo and I will join you in the attack when you reach Uzzano. Captain Jack, bring a hundred of your archers and leave the rest with Konrad." He nodded, "Captain John, your attack will be at dawn and we will await your arrival." He nodded. I turned to Konrad, "While our enemy tries to break through our spears we will take him in the rear." I smiled at Gaston de Foix, "We can repay him for his victory at Alessandria."

"And I will be with you, my lord?"

"Of course."

My plans made, I changed into the darker clothes that would help to hide me. I would ride Blackie and Robert had to ride one of the horses we had taken from the supply wagons and escorts. He chose one of the fraught animals that was slower but could bear his mailed weight more easily.

We left at night with local men from Montevettolini. To avoid confusion in the dark, I gave Captain John a half-hour start. Donnina's brother had learned well from me and he too rode a black horse and was cloaked.

We had to move in a single file for we were following local trails. They were wide enough for more than one horse but in places that would have been dangerous and so we rode in single file. We passed through the land like ghosts. We stopped, before dawn, above Uzzano. Men ate, made water and prepared for the battle. I went with Carlo, Gaston and my bodyguards to view the small town and Milanese camp. I saw some standards and banners. In the moonlight, I saw the liveries. Taddeo dal Verme, Gentile da Varano, and Vanni d'Appiano were there but I did not see that of Jacopo. I deduced that he was with the main part of the army and approaching Montevettolini. We went back to the others. I took some dried meat from my saddle bag and chewed. It would not fill me but it would take away the pangs of hunger. I washed it down with ale. Robert had managed to find a woman who could brew ale. The first thing he had done when we had reached Casa Donnina was to broach a barrel. The two of us now drank ale. It was more refreshing than wine. To refresh with wine often meant that drunkenness followed.

Dawn had just broken when we heard the sounds of alarm from Pescia which lay half a mile away. As soon as the clash of weapons could be heard from the direction of Uzzano, the horns and trumpets of those in the town were sounded. I mounted Blackie and my men emulated me. My archers had tethered their horses and they now strung their bows. We filtered down through the trees towards the awakening town. It was clear that Sir John Balzan had succeeded for as we neared the town, we saw the survivors of his attack pouring into the town. Taddeo dal Verme, for I assumed that it was he who commanded, had ordered all his men to face the threat. He had no idea that I was about to launch my attack on his flank and his rear. He did not even know we were there. My archers were above us. They could release above our heads and we would then be free to charge. I was flanked by my bodyguards and Gaston. Robert had not been able to bring his beloved Bettina and so he had opted for a smaller war axe. Carlo and his men were on the other side.

"Now, Jack!"

Legacy

The arrows soared. When they landed it was into a mass of men, some of whom were mailed and some who were not. More importantly, even the ones with shields could not defend for the arrows came from their right where they had no shield. I allowed my archers five flights and then I ordered Zuzzo to sound the charge. I spurred Blackie and he raced down through the trees. I found myself laughing. It was as though I was a bold young warrior once more. Some may have thought it foolish or reckless but I was confident that I would not fall. I drew my sword when we neared the first body. Blackie leapt over the arrow-pocked body and as he landed, I swept my sword into the side of the head of a surprised man at arms. He had no helmet and my hand was jarred as my blade crashed through his skull. Robert's axe did the same but his victim did have a helmet. His axe cared not. We reached the main square as Captain John and his men galloped into the town.

My archers had raced down the mountain to follow us and as we reined in, I heard Sir Jack shout, "The archers are ready, my lord."

I took off my helmet and said, "Taddeo dal Verme, you have one chance to surrender. Spurn it and my archers will ensure that you die."

One of his men spat and raising his sword said, "There is no honour in that. Fight them."

"Jack!"

The arrow slammed into his face. I was close enough to see it buried to the fletch and the arrowhead was covered in blood and brains.

The example was enough for the condottiero. Taddeo dal Verme said, "We surrender, my lord."

I dismounted and went over to take his sword. He gave a sad smile, "You are still the fox, my lord. Is it not time for you to retire?"

I laughed, "I have never felt so alive, my friend. I should do this every morning. A chase through the forests has given me a mighty appetite. Zuzzo find food!"

Chapter 17

September 1391 Montecarlo
Hindsight is a wonderful thing. One always sees everything perfectly with absolute clarity. Looking back, I know what I should have done. I should have left the archers to watch our prisoners and ended the threat to Florence by pinning Jacopo dal Verme and his men between us and my infantry at the river. I did not. I confess that I was tired. A night without sleep was never a good thing and I had felt too weary to ride immediately. Montevettolini was only eight miles away and I thought that we could rest first and then ride. To be truthful we could not have moved quickly for we had the whole of the Milanese baggage. Looking back I could have used just my horsemen and left others to watch our prisoners and my booty. Hindsight!

We rested until early afternoon and then began to move down the road. We were slowed by the prisoners we had taken. They had to be guarded for although the leaders had given their words that they accepted that they were prisoners, I was not so sure about the men.

Dal Verme must have had scouts out or perhaps there were men watching the town for even as we approached, he and his army were slipping away from the trap. He was proving as wily an opponent as I was. By the time we reached Montevettolini, he had managed to disengage. Sir Konrad and his feditore had done well. They managed to hold the enemy and hurt him. I suspect that the plan had been to fix my army there while the five hundred lances we had captured and the others we had killed were intended to fall upon our rear. I had managed to thwart his plans. Inside I knew that a great deal of luck was involved but my men saw it as another example of Hawkwood genius. They did not see it as I did, a partial failure.

I sent messengers to Florence to tell them of the victory and had the leaders escorted back to Casa Donnina where they could wait until we had received their ransom. His lances suffered the same fate that Konrad had suffered at Rimini. Stripped of mail and weapons, they were sent back up the road to Uzzano with the threat that if they returned, they would die.

Legacy

I had the plate shared out amongst the victors, and those amongst the feditore that Konrad had identified as having shown the greatest courage were given the weapons. I knighted more men. There had been knights amongst the slain and the captured. The giving of spurs was a small but significant event. Half of those that I knighted were Englishmen. When they returned to England it would not be as simple swords for hire but knights, and with the money that they had accrued they would be able to buy lands. I promised those that I knighted a letter to King Richard. I believed he still held me in esteem and with so many domestic enemies, knights sent from Italy would be more than welcome.

I sent out the Italian scouts and we prepared to pursue. Carlo's men knew the area well and were keen to impress me. My fear was that my enemy might try the crossing of the Arno once more and this time, with the defenders there now with me, he might succeed. I was relieved when the scouts returned and told me that dal Verme had taken the road to Lucca. The Luccans would welcome him and he would be able to resupply. I had my sword in his back and having made one mistake I was not about to make another. Leaving the feditore and crossbows under the command of Roger Nottingham to guard the road to Florence, I took my lances and archers to pursue Jacopo dal Verme.

The area to the north of the road that leads from Lucca to Pistoia is called Montecarlo and it was there we found where he had camped. Our pursuit had not been in vain. So swift had been our chase that he had been forced to flee and leave his supplies and, more importantly, his bombards. They would have been able to batter the walls of Florence and that told me that the Milanese threat was almost over. I left one hundred lances to guard the supplies and I raced to Lucca. I rode with my bodyguards to the gates. The gates were not barred but they were guarded. I had fought for Lucca and, I think, that they liked me. Certainly, we were not showered with crossbow bolts but were greeted with words and respect.

"I seek the condottiero, Jacopo dal Verme. Does he take shelter in your fine city?"

Legacy

The Captain of the Guard who addressed me from the walls shook his head, "No, my lord. He and his men have fled to Ripafratta."

I nodded, "Thank you." Ripafratta was far enough away from Florence to show me that the threat had ended. Jacopo dal Verme had been defeated. He had lost his brother, most of his army and his bombards. For me, the campaign was almost over. He could still return to threaten Florence but that would take time and more men. I could go home.

As we headed back to the army Robert, who did not know Italy at all, asked, "Where is this Ripafratta, my lord?"

"To the north of Pisa and it is a place he can fortify. We will return to San Minato. If he is at Ripafratta, he is far enough away from Florence not to pose a threat. He will pay the ransom for his brother and then we can worry. San Minato allows us to watch all the roads that lead to Florence."

We headed back, first to the captured supplies and bombards, and then to Montevettolini. The bombards slowed us and I realised why he had abandoned them. I took my army to San Minato, releasing the feditore and sending the bombards to Florence as a gift. I would never use them and their capture had enhanced my reputation. The hills of Tuscany rang out with my name as the feditore cheered me prior to leaving. They had fought a battle and won. They had defeated men sent by Galeazzo Visconti, the Lord of Milan. and they had lost few men. The condottiere that they had killed had been robbed so they were all in profit. Best of all they had only served for a couple of weeks.

We had frequent messengers from Florence and I wrote reports for Carlos Cialdini.

On one such occasion, the messenger also brought a commission for Konrad. My young German condottiero was addressed by Carlos' man, "The podestà of Bologna has requested that Captain Corrado Prospero bring his company to Bologna. We have enemies there."

It was a huge compliment to the young condottiero. I was pleased for him but also saddened a little for I had enjoyed his company. I was just pleased that he had been one of the men I had knighted. I could see that he was upset too but excited at the

Legacy

same time. When he left with his company, there was a hole in the army. We had fought so long together that we felt like one company.

I sent my scouts to watch dal Verme and at the start of October, he moved south to Cascina. That confirmed my suspicions. He would try to attack along the Arno Valley. This time he would move south of the river to avoid having to cross it. We planted ourselves in San Minato. The castle was Florentine and I took rooms in the castle. There were other castles between San Minato and Castelfiorentino. As we patrolled the road, I sent my scouts to keep watch on the enemy. Gaston de Foix often accompanied them.

After one of his excursions, he came to see me privately, "My lord, the enemy now has a company of Breton condottiere."

"And?"

"And I know them. They were in the army of Count John. I believe that I can subvert them and make them allies."

"That would be useful. Firstly, it would tell us when they were coming and we could arrange signals to make them change sides at a crucial point. The question is, how do we arrange this?"

"Allow me and my squire to make contact with them. We can then arrange a meeting between you and their leader. I know these Bretons, they are fighting for Visconti not because they like him but because they are paid. If we were to offer them more then they would do as we wished."

Anything that would weaken my enemy was to be applauded, "Do so and I will find the money." The money was not a problem. We had taken a great deal at Uzzano and I would use that and account for it when I returned to Florence. "I want to meet the captain of this company and speak to him face to face."

"Of course, my lord."

I was aware that this could be a trap laid by my enemies. Gaston de Foix had reasons to believe that his countrymen would betray Visconti but I knew my wife's uncle well enough to see his snake-like fingers all over this. It was a tasty enough piece of bait to attract me. I prepared my bodyguards. Such a clandestine meeting would have to be private. I told them what I planned.

Legacy

Zuzzo said, "When we are to meet these men, my lord, Gianluca and I will hide in the dark to watch for assassins and you must wear your mail. The head of Sir John Hawkwood is a pretty prize that your enemies seek. Robert here can guard you against one man."

"Of course." I wondered how I had coped without these three men to watch my back. I felt totally safe in their presence.

A week later Gaston told me that we would meet at La Rotta. It was halfway between San Minato and Cascina. The Breton captain would come with his squire and meet us in the huddle of houses that made up La Rotta. The meeting was arranged for midnight. I deemed that losing one night of sleep to ensure we defeated Jacopo would be worth it. I told only John Beltoft and Sir John Balzan what I intended. Both were concerned that this might be a trap.

"Zuzzo and Gianluca are my guarantee against treachery. They will skirt La Rotta and if more than two men come from the direction of Cascina then they will sound the horn and we will return."

Konrad said, "But you do not believe that there will be treachery."

I shook my head, "I trust Gaston and his judgement."

Riding Blackie and with a black surcoat and cloak we were almost invisible. Zuzzo and Gianluca disappeared a mile after we left San Minato. The four of us rode close together. Robert and Gaston flanked me and Pierre, the squire, rode behind. It was both exciting and a little frightening to be riding in a land that was completely black, I would say silent but it was not. The snorts of our horses and the clip-clop of their hooves were augmented by the sounds of nature's life and death struggles. The screech of an owl as it took the life of a rodent; the calls of the foxes. All of them seemed louder in the black of night. I began to second-guess myself, what if this was a clever trap? Perhaps, even now Jacopo dal Verme had men doing what Zuzzo and Gianluca were doing and insinuating themselves behind us. The first we might know of their presence would be when Pierre died.

We reined in at the tiny hamlet on the banks of the Arno. The villagers wisely kept within their homes. The arrival of horsemen

Legacy

never boded well and all would have securely bolted doors. The sound of horses coming from the west made Robert take his axe in two hands. I did not go near my sword. There were clearly just a couple of horses and there were four of us.

The two men arrived and, as far as I could see, were alone. Zuzzo and Gianluca would remain, hidden, to watch the road.

The Breton who approached us was not young. His neatly trimmed beard was flecked with grey. Gaston made the introductions, "Sir John Hawkwood, this is Alan La Flèche, condottiero."

I took off my glove and held out my hand, "I am pleased to meet you."

"And I am honoured to meet the legend that is Giovanni Acuto."

"You are still determined to help our cause?"

"I am. After our captain was killed, I sought work but Visconti was the only paymaster for you had already left the north."

I nodded to Gaston who handed over the purse of florins. "How many men does Jacopo have?"

"Ten thousand. Another thousand arrived last week."

"And do you know his plans?"

"He intends to raid the Val di Calci and take Santa Maria a Monte."

"Good, then I can thwart that. Now what I need from you is the promise that when your army faces me in battle you will heed my horn signals. When you hear the horn sound four times is the moment that you will defect. Take the baggage."

It was dark but even in the moonlight I saw him smile, his teeth showing white, "And that is generous of you. For we will be able to escape and be rich men while you will have the hole in the enemy lines through which you can pour."

I nodded, "It matters not where you are placed for wherever that is will be our point of attack."

"Then we shall make it so." He held out his hand and I shook it, "Farewell, Sir John, it has been an honour."

We waited until the two had mounted and the sound of their hooves faded before we mounted. We were just a mile east of La

Rotta when Zuzzo and Gianluca appeared. "There was no treachery."

"And we now know the enemy's plans. I will send John Beltoft and Ugo di Monforte to Santa Maria a Monte. If Jacopo dal Verme thinks he can take it easily, he is mistaken."

My two condottieri took two hundred men at arms and a hundred archers to the fortress north of the Arno. They had been there a week when news came from the Milanese that the exchange of gold for the prisoners would take place. I sent to Florence for the three men. Jacopo dal Verme showed his cunning. He launched his sudden attack on Santa Maria a Monte. Had we not been forewarned and its walls reinforced then it might have fallen. By the time Taddeo dal Verme and his fellow prisoners arrived, we had word that the attack had failed and Jacopo was back in Cascina.

Taddeo dal Verme was just anxious to leave and he flattered me with compliments. When the ransom arrived, escorted by twenty lances, I made sure that it was counted before I allowed the hostages to move. The captain of the escort smiled as he said, "Captain dal Verme also sent another present for you, Sir John. This is not a fox although you may wish to allow it to escape." One of his men brought out a basket.

I nodded to Robert who opened it. I wondered if this time it was a reptile and that it was an attempt to assassinate me. He pulled, from the basket, the head of Alan La Flèche.

The captain said as he wheeled his horse, "If you want the heads of the other traitors, you will find them adorning Cascina's walls. The Captain General hopes you will try to recover them."

Gaston was far more upset than I was. I had not known the Breton. I was sorry that he had died but his fate was not something I could have stopped. As we rode back to San Minato, I reflected that when dal Verme had found the fortress fortified, it must have made him suspicious. Perhaps the Breton had a traitor in his own ranks. We would never know. At least his attack had been thwarted.

The campaign ended in early December. Michael himself brought the news. "I bring word from Florence, Sir John. The Doge of Genoa, Antoniotto Adorno, has intervened in the war. He has brokered a peace between Milan and Florence."

Legacy

I frowned, "Why?" I was curious as to why Genoa would wish the war to end. It was in their interests for there to be conflict in Italy. They always benefitted from the misery caused to their enemies.

He smiled, "It is money. Genoa has been contracted to take Henry Bolingbroke, the Earl of Derby, to the Holy Land on a crusade. He needs peace. The crusade is not until August but you know how long these things take. You are free to return to your home. Florence is grateful but she no longer needs to pay for your men." Florence was saving money.

Thanks to the ransoms the men were all well off and the march back to Florence was a happy one. We had not been defeated and we had prevented Florence from being raided. Many of my men had been knighted and some of them, hearing that many English knights would be joining Henry Bolingbroke on the crusade, saw the chance to go home to England. They realised that there might be an opportunity to buy manors cheaply. It also made me think, once more, of a return to England.

Michael also brought news of Konrad. He had learned from the master, it seemed. He had met the condottiere sent by Visconti at Reggio Emilia and ambushed them. He had taken many prisoners and the Milanese condottiere had been forced to leave Bolognese land. He had managed to complete his task in less than a month. Bologna was safe. Both Florence and Bologna were delighted and it was not only Konrad who was praised, I was seen as the architect of that victory for I had been Konrad's teacher.

A parade through Florence was held and I was accorded every honour from the city. The days of my exclusion were long gone. I was now the saviour of Florence and given the freedom of the city. My men having been paid off, they departed. Carlo and his men were given a contract to serve in the Neapolitan struggle for power. I had left John Beltoft in the Val d'Arno but my archers and half of my White Company went to my estate to the east of Florence. I would join them when I had seen my wife and family. I was anxious to see Robin.

That feast was also the opportunity to speak to Carlos Cialdini about the pension and the dowries. The podestà confirmed that they would be paid and paid happily. I had saved Florence from being ravaged. The condottiere had not managed to take one inch of Florentine land. No farm had been plundered and Florence was prosperous for it had not been raided. Pisa, Siena, even Lombardy had suffered the privations of war but Bologna and Florence, protected by Sir John Hawkwood had not.

"And you, Sir John, do you wish more work to be sent your way? I hear that you have not disbanded the White Company."

"If there is another commission, my lord, then we will take it but I will go no more to Lombardy. Il Novello can battle Visconti there. I have no intention of retiring but let us say that I will take things a little more slowly from now on."

With just my bodyguards for company, we rode the few miles to Casa Donnina, reaching it the week before Christmas.

Chapter 18

January 1392 Montecchio Vesponi
Once more it was a delight to be home. When I had been younger, I had almost regarded it as a punishment but now with young ladies for daughters and a son who could understand what I did and sought to hold my weapons, I could not be happier. My two elder daughters were disappointed that Konrad had not come with me and that there were no other handsome young warriors with me. I suspected that Konrad felt the same.

We were rich, once more. Donnina had plans to liquidate more of our lands and turn them into coins. She was happy that I was home but even happier that I had told her I would not retire. We were accruing money for the time when I did hang up my sword.

"I wish to travel to Montecchio Vesponi and see Robin." I paused, "He still lives?"

"He does, I sent Ned and Edgar with some gifts and they told him of your victories. When they returned, they were sad. He does not leave his bed but they said that he is well cared for. He has good people around him."

That made my decision for me and I left with just my bodyguards for the ride to my estate. It was sixty miles but by leaving well before dawn and with a change of horses, we did it in one day. I resolved to never do so again for every bone and muscle ached by the time we reached its walls. I yearned for my wagon.

The estate was the place where Robin trained archers. Since his illness, he had not trained any but Sir John Balzan and my White Company were now in residence. It was my captain who greeted me with a sombre face, "My lord, it is good that you have come. Sir Robin has not left his bed since we arrived and each day he seems weaker. When you see him be prepared for a shock. He is the shadow of the man we knew. He seems more like a wraith than what he was, a master archer. His skin is so thin that it is almost transparent."

That my condottiero was shocked prepared me somewhat for my meeting with him. I nodded. Edgar, Ned and Donnina had

Legacy

also prepared me. I was used to death. It was part of my world but death from sickness was another matter. I took off my cloak and composed myself before heading for the bed chamber. Robin liked women and the house was filled with them. I do not think he had a single male servant. I tapped on the door. The three ladies who bowed as they opened the door and allowed me to enter, were tearful. As soon as the door opened my nose was assaulted by the stink of decay. It was not the damp decay of a badly maintained house but the decay of a body that was rotting from within and seeps out through every pore. It was a smell with which I was familiar. I had spent most of my life on battlefields filled with corpses. Here, though, the body still lived.

The woman who addressed me was not young but neither was she old. She was attractive and had the kind of figure that I knew Robin admired. She was his consort. "My lord, I am Maria and I have been Sir Robin's companion these last five years. I will fetch you wine." She forced a smile, "He will want to drink with the man he most respects in the whole world."

"Thank you."

I walked next to the bed. The candles that burned gave the chamber an eerie glow. Even in that golden light, his face looked ghostly white. I could see his bones and both his hair and his beard were thinning. Had I not known that this was Robin I would not have recognised him. He was asleep and I was loath to wake him.

When he opened his eyes, he stared up at me in terror. When his eyes adjusted a smile appeared on his face. He had lost many teeth and his mouth looked like an ancient graveyard with tumbled headstones. I smiled, "Now then, Robin." He tried to rise. I put my hand on his shoulder, "You do not need to rise. Lie there."

He shook his head, "I am come to this. When I piss, they have to bring a pot. I cannot feed myself and now I cannot rise to greet the man who gave me everything. This is a living death."

I sat on the huge bed, "I gave you nothing. What you have you earned."

He tried to laugh but ended up coughing. When he stopped, he shook his head again, "Had I not followed you I would have died many years ago. Perhaps that would have been for the best.

That is the way for a warrior to die. Not like this, inch by inch. You let me live on this estate and live a life I could not have dreamed of back in Wakefield."

"What did the doctors say it was?"

"They know not what it is for certain." He snorted, "All that they can do is to bleed me. If I have a pint of blood left in this shell of a body, I will be surprised. I stopped them coming some time ago. If I want to be bled, I will just shave myself. My hands shake so much that they will do the job and it will be cheaper than paying those leeches."

Maria came in and put two goblets and a jug of wine on the bedside table, "Come, Sir Robin, let me sit you up so that you may talk to your friend and enjoy wine." As she put her arms around him to lift him, he kissed her. She laughed, "Sir Robin!"

"Time was, Sir John, that Maria could not enter my room without I tore off her clothes. Now a stolen kiss is all that I can manage."

I could see the love between them as Maria straightened his pillows and, as she turned, wiped a tear from her eye. She said quietly, "This is the best medicine for a dying man. He has yearned for your company, Sir John."

"If you will make up a couch for me in this room I will sleep here."

She looked shocked, "That is not necessary, my lord. One of us sleeps in here each night."

I smiled, "Good, then I shall not want for company."

She nodded. "You are a good man, Sir John. I know that from Sir Robin but now that I have met you, I see the truth of it."

The door closed and I went to the bed and put the goblet in Robin's hands. I lifted mine, "Here's to us, the survivors and the ones who perished." We drank. I did so deeply. Robin sipped as though even the wine slipping down his throat was painful. "Giovanni died, you know?"

"Ubaldini?" I nodded. "No one told me. When?"

"Two years ago. He was poisoned by the Florentines. He tried to foster rebellion."

"He was always too clever for his own good. Like me, Giovanni did best when he served you. He wanted to be a condottiero and a plotter. I knew I could never be like you." He held the goblet so that I could take it from him and place it on the table. "From the moment we first met I knew that you were destined for greatness. When we had to serve with Paer and those other condottieri I could see that you were head and shoulders better than they were and I was right. Men will remember you long after we are both in the ground. I will be there before you but I know that you, too, are getting old."

I laughed, "I rode here in one day, Robin Goodfellow, so less of the old."

He laughed and looked, in that laugh, a little healthier. "How is Michael?"

"Married, a father and under the thumb of his wife. He has children. He is no longer the thin little youth we rescued. He lives in a mansion and he could retire now. He has done well."

"And that is thanks to you." He settled back into the pillow, like my son when I was about to tell him a story, "Now tell me all about this last campaign. We heard parts but they were incomplete. It is said you almost took Milan."

I shook my head and finished the goblet of wine, "We were within sixteen miles of Milan but the French who were supposed to be our allies, were defeated. I had another retreat." I then went through all that had happened since I had last spoken to him. I had not finished when he drifted off to sleep. I went to the door and found Maria seated outside. "He is asleep."

"Your men are in the kitchen. They said they were more comfortable there than in the Great Hall. I can have your food brought to the main hall."

I said, "No, the kitchen is good enough for me." I took her hand and kissed the back of it, "Thank you for caring for my friend."

She suddenly burst into tears and throwing her arms around me buried her head in my chest, "My lord, this is not fair. Sir Robin is a good man and does not deserve this slow death."

I let her sob herself out and then held her away from me, "Then let us make his last days happy. I shall not leave until…" I found myself unable to speak. I did not want to unman myself.

She stood on tiptoe and kissed me on the lips, "We shall both be there at the end."

My bodyguards and Sir John were finishing off their food. When I entered, they stood, "Sit."

Robert said, "I will fetch you food, Sir John. You need to eat."

I sat, "Aye, I know I do but seeing Sir Robin has taken away my appetite."

Sir John's voice was filled with sadness, "The archers he trained cannot believe in the change that they see. The doctors do not know what it is. Their best guess is that it is some sort of worm or a canker that eats from within."

Robert put the food down and then poured me some ale.

"I intend to stay here until it is over."

John Balzan said, "Sir John, that will not be long. Each day he is worse and he is so thin I cannot see him lasting longer than a few more days."

Zuzzo said, "Where will I put your bags, my lord?"

"Maria is putting a couch in Sir Robin's bedroom and I shall sleep there. I am only here now because he is asleep. I was not there when Giovanni died. I do not intend for Robin to slip away, too. I will watch until he passes. I owe him that much and more."

After I had eaten, I returned to Robin's bed chamber. Maria had brought in a day bed and blankets. She smiled, "I will eat now, my lord. Should you need anything or anyone in the night there will be one of us on duty outside the door." She hesitated then sighed, "He has not eaten much for the last week but he has drunk, if he needs to make water…" She pointed to the porcelain pot.

I smiled, "He told me and do not worry, I can handle such matters. It is the least I can do for a man who followed loyally and for so long."

Left alone in the room, Maria had put fresh candles in the holders, I sat and watched him sleeping. It was a fitful sleep. Once, on one of the rare occasions I had been home, Caterina had endured a fever and Robin's sleep was like that one; not quite awake but never in a deep sleep. I must have dozed off for a short time. When I woke, it was like the times I had been a young archer on sentry duty. When you dozed off and woke, you did so fearfully. He was still asleep and I stood to stretch and pour myself some wine. I knew I should sleep. I needed to close my eyes but something made me stay awake.

I saw Robin's eyes slowly open, "Is Maria outside, Sir John?"

"She is but what do you need?"

"To make water, my lord."

"And you think me too old to manage. I will show you, Robin of Wakefield." I threw the covers back and gently put my arms beneath him. All that I could feel were bones. "Put your arm around my neck for balance."

When he had finished, I put him back in the bed and then went to the door with the pot. As soon as I opened it the young serving girl stood.

"He has made water."

She took the pot from me, "I will empty it my lord. You should have called me."

Back inside I saw that Robin had sat himself up, "Wine?"

"I might as well. It is one of the few pleasures left to me. I cannot eat and it has been so long since I pleasured a woman…"

I poured him some wine and laughed, "You old goat, you have spread, by your own admission, your seed far and wide. You have pleasured more women than I have met!"

He laughed and drank the wine, "While we are alone, my lord, and we can talk I need to ask you about my end." I swallowed and nodded. I owed it to him to listen, but this would be uncomfortable for me. "I would like to be buried in England. It does not have to be Wakefield, just so that my bones reside in the land of my birth. I was born an Englishman and while it is many years since I fought for her, like you I have never fought against her."

"I swear that your bones will be taken to England."

He nodded, "My heart can be buried here, for Maria's sake. In truth it belongs to her already."

"I will do all that you ask, my friend." I drank some wine. I did so to save having to say more for Robin's words were upsetting.

"I have written a will. It is in my gardyvyan. It is simple enough. I leave my bow and sword to your son and all my money goes to Maria. I have not spent much. She will have enough to buy a home and live comfortably."

Legacy

"The gift of the sword and the bow is a fine one but I cannot promise that I will take your bones back soon. I have a mind to return to England with my family but I first need to put my affairs in order."

The smile he gave me was the old Robin, "Would that I could come with you. 'Tis about time you did so, Sir John. You have given Italians too much of your life already. They are all a treacherous tangle of snakes."

"Aye, they are that but we have dealt with them, have we not, old friend?"

He smiled at the memory my words evoked, "When I was in my prime, Sir John, the two of us along with Giovanni, were unstoppable. I shall see him soon enough but you should know how much I enjoyed following your banner. I was honoured to be your lieutenant."

"It was our banner, Robin, and while I was the visible head, the rest of you made it a banner to be feared. Even now your spirits are in that banner for when it is unfurled men know who comes and they shake with fear. That is not just Sir John Hawkwood, Giovanni Acuto, it is the men who made the White Company the force it is now."

We talked, until almost dawn and then, when he was asleep, I went to the couch and covered myself with blankets. It was good that I had come. I slept.

Robin lingered for a week. Maria was sure that he lived longer than he might thanks to my presence but each day I saw him worsen. His sleep, whilst longer, was also more fitful. He was in pain and he was fighting it. That was what men like Robin did. Death was an enemy that you fought. We knew he was dying and that his death was imminent when he asked for a priest. That was not Robin's way. He had never been a churchgoer. He believed in God, I never knew a soldier who did not, but having seen what the church had done, especially at Cesena, he did not like priests.

The priest heard his confession and then Maria and I sat on his bed. She held his hand and stroked his brow. When she began to weep, he said, "None of that. We have enjoyed a good life together and now is the end. I am weary and eternal sleep will be a relief."

Legacy

She nodded and sniffed back the tears.

"Sir John, enjoy your life while you may. Donnina is a fine woman and your children are there to be cherished. You have lost one family, do not lose this second one. Embrace them. You need not prove yourself on the field of battle. Who else is there to conquer? The world is yours. Enjoy it."

I found tears springing to my eyes and heedful of his words nodded and said, "You are right, Robin. I had a fine Christmas and while January will never be the same for me again, I can return home and enjoy the green growth of spring. I do not think that I will be long in following you to Christ's muster."

"You are hale and healthy. Enjoy life, Sir John."

I smiled at him and squeezed his hand. He smiled back and then with a soft sigh, he died. Neither of us needed a doctor to tell us that he was dead. Maria leaned over and kissed him, "Farewell, there will never be a man such as you and I shall miss you."

I said nothing. I had spoken enough and Robin was at peace.

Maria folded his arms and stood, "I should prepare him for burial, my lord."

I shook my head, "Robin told me that he wished his bones to be taken to England for burial. His heart can be buried here."

She smiled, "I should like that."

"And what will you do?"

She waved a hand around the house, "I worked here before it was given to you Sir John, and I know little else."

"Sir Robin left all his gold to you. He told me he hoped you would buy a house somewhere and be happy."

She threw herself on Robin's body and began to weep again. Through her sobs, she said, "You were the best of men and I shall spend each day thinking of the times we enjoyed together."

Robin's request meant that we had to pay a doctor to remove his organs before his body was boiled to leave just the bones. Robert had never heard of this and after the body had been taken away, I explained it. "It is called mos Teutonicus, Robert. If a body is to be taken a long distance then it must either be mummified or the flesh removed. I was told, when I served in the English army, that when Henry of Almain was murdered here in Italy at Viterbo, he had the same done to him and his

Legacy

heart and bones were carried back to his father, the King of the Romans, for burial in England."

When the heart and the bones were returned, we buried the heart in a rosewood casket in the village church. The White Company and Robin's servants attended and the church was packed. I paid a stonemason to make a gravestone. It would say simply, 'Here lies Robin Goodfellow of Wakefield. He was an English archer and had no peer'. Maria said that Robin would have approved. I knew he would.

We held a wake in the hall. Robin would have wanted us to celebrate his passing. We sang old English songs and explained them to Maria and the servants, all of whom attended. We told stories of Robin and his idiosyncrasies but mostly we all reflected on the memory of a man who had been alive just a few days earlier and was now gone.

We spent another week there. I had the gardyvyan and sword and Maria the money but there were many other possessions that I distributed amongst the servants and those of the White Company who wished to have them. On the night before I left, I spoke with Maria and Sir John Balzan. "I intend to sell this estate. It was a home for Robin but my old friend was right. My time as a condottiero is coming to an end. John, I need you to bring what remains of the company to Casa Donnina. Maria, I will not evict you. Send word when you have a home and then I will have my agents sell the property. Take whatever sticks of furniture and other household items that you or the others wish. I care not if the house is a shell when I sell. Robin would like his people taken care of."

She smiled, "You have an ill-deserved reputation, Sir John. Your enemies speak of a cruel and venal man but I have seen nothing of that. I will learn to judge people by what I see and not what others say of them. You can put the sale in place, my lord, for I already have made an offer on a small house just outside the village. It overlooks the church and I shall be able to see Robin while I hang out the washing. It has a small vineyard and there is a vegetable plot. Christina and Caterina wish to live there with me." She laughed, "We can have cats. Robin could never abide cats but I was fond of them as a child. I can visit his grave and put flowers there. The stonemason said the stone will be ready in a week. By then, I shall be in my home."

We left the next day with Robin's bones and his gardyvyan on the back of a sumpter. I gave each of his servants and Maria, one ducat each as severance pay. Maria thought it too much but I now knew that my time on this earth was coming to an end and I wanted to reward those who had served me and my family well.

As we headed home, we would take two days at least, to make the journey, I spoke with my bodyguards, "I know not if I will go to war again. You are all young men and may wish to serve another. I will not stop you from seeking employment."

Zuzzo shook his head, "My lord, I have served you for many years and whilst I still have skills, I have no desire to serve another lord. When you retire, I shall take my chest and do as Maria is doing. I will buy a home and live peacefully. Perhaps I will emulate Sir Robin and take a woman."

Gianluca nodded, "Aye, and that is my plan too, my lord. I have a mind to buy an inn. Serving you has brought me much gold and I have spent little. I could serve wine and tell tales of the times I served Giovanni Acuto. Those stories alone would make the inn a success."

I smiled for I was flattered and, if nothing else, when I was gone my name would live on.

"And you, Robert? Have you tired of war?"

"No, my lord, just Italy. When you hang up your sword, I will take a ship and return to England. There may not be condottiere in England but there are lords who need Bettina and me."

I nodded, "Then all is well and if you would, Robert, when you do return to England, I would have you take Sir Robin's bones to Wakefield for burial. I will pay you."

"You will not, my lord. To carry back the bones of such a great Englishman as Sir Robin would be an honour for which I should pay."

By the time I rode into the yard at Casa Donnina, I had made all my decisions and my plans. After I had spoken to Donnina I would hang up my sword and place my baton on the wall.

Chapter 19

February 1392 Pisa

I did as Robin had suggested and when I returned home, I looked at my children and wife with new eyes. If I only had a short time left, and my age suggested that was likely, then I wanted to make the most of it. John was excited about the sword and the bow although I was not sure that he would ever be able to draw Robin's great war bow. I knew that even I would struggle. I suspected it would hang on his wall when he was a man grown with his own lands. The sword, too, was an archer's sword. It was well-made but functional. It was not as beautifully decorated as mine was. This would be a sword that John would use to learn how to be a swordsman. It would serve him well as a second sword. He was too young to begin to practise and by the time he was, Zuzzo would have left my service. Zuzzo could have taught him how to use two swords at once.

I spent more time talking to Donnina. Maria and Robin had spent more time together than Donnina and I. I wanted to make up for lost time and so we planned our future. I told her of my plans to sell Montecchio Vesponi and she approved. "Florence will buy it from you."

"How do you know?"

"Since your last victories, Lady Hawkwood is more than welcomed into the great houses of Florence. I am seen as a grand lady now and they tell me things. The Florentine merchants see the acquisition of property as a way to not only make more money but also to spread their influence. They think that warriors like you are useful to defend them but growth comes through money. Perhaps they are right."

"And England?"

She shook her head, "I do not rule out a move there someday but not yet. We have three daughters to marry off. They are Italian and will not welcome an English husband or a cold climate. I do not relish the move but I would follow you there for I know you wish for a return to England and you deserve it. Our daughters are different."

Legacy

I had hoped to return soon and take Robin's bones myself. I now saw that it would be Robert who took them.

"But our daughters, they are young. That could be years away."

She smiled, "Not so my husband. The di Porciglia family have a son who admires Ginnetta. It may be the dowry that has attracted them or, more likely, the chance to be connected to Giovanni Acuto but whatever the reason they have let me know that their son, Brezaglia, would not be averse to a marriage to our eldest daughter."

"And how does Ginnetta feel about this?"

Donnina snorted, "Did I have a choice in my husband? No. Brezaglia is a personable young man. He is a little dull, it is true, but dullards rarely transgress. Ginnetta will learn to, if not love him, then like him. I was lucky and I know it. My father picked a man for me and I fell in love with him. You have always been faithful. I do not doubt you had many chances to stray but you did not."

"How do you know?" I had never strayed but as I had often been on campaign I did not know how she could know that for certain.

She gave me an enigmatic smile, "I have ways."

"And when would Ginnetta be wed?"

"Oh, that is some way off. I have to sow the seeds and she is but fourteen this year. Perhaps in a year, when she is fifteen, eh?"

With that knowledge, I approached Robert and told him that he would be the bearer of the bones. "You have decided then, Sir John?"

"Not yet, Robert."

"Then I will continue to serve until you do."

We make plans but Fate is always there to interfere. The remains of my company had arrived and Sir John Balzan and I rode to Pisa to meet with William. He held the funds of the White Company and if I was to retire then those funds had to be paid. The five of us rode to Pisa. I was not as welcome as I had once been and William's wife showed her displeasure at our arrival by leaving to stay with her parents. It suited me as I did not like her sour face. William was a mouse around her.

Legacy

I insisted that my bodyguards dined with us. Knowing that our time together would be limited I wanted to enjoy as much time in their company as I could. The fact that their presence, especially Robert's with his scarred face, made William uncomfortable was a bonus.

I waited until we had dined, and the platters cleared before I spoke. The servants had been dismissed so that we could speak privately. There was wine, bread and cheese for us to enjoy and the detritus of the dinner could be cleared in the morning.

I came directly to the point, "William, it is time to disband the White Company."

He nodded, "You are retiring."

"Not yet but soon."

"And you, Sir John," he smiled at my captain, "you will take over the White Company?"

"I will."

"Then we can come to some arrangement, I am sure."

John was going to answer for we had talked of the future at Casa Donnina but I knew my accountant better than any and so I held my hand up in his direction, "You misunderstand, William, I am taking the White Company funds from Pisa. You may take your commission, of course, but I would have written accounts prepared so that Lady Hawkwood can cast her eye over them. Sir John will make other arrangements for the security of the funds."

His face paled and his voice sounded shocked. He had not foreseen this day. "But that money is not a small amount."

I leaned forward, "You have it safe and secure do you not?"

He could not meet my gaze and was shifty, "Not all of it. You must understand, Sir John, that it has grown because I have invested it. There are ships bringing cargo into Pisa that will add to the funds."

I smiled, "Then our earnings have grown. Well done, William."

"No, Sir John, I am saying that it will take some weeks to gather it all together."

"You have a month and tomorrow you and I will look at the accounts, along with Sir John, so that we can see how much there is. Sir John wishes to hire more lances with the money that belongs to the White Company."

214

Legacy

William was like a deer cornered by hunters. He looked from me to Sir John, "And where will you keep those funds, my lord? They are safely guarded here."

"I am not Sir John Hawkwood. I am not tied to either Florence or Pisa. There is employment all over Italy and I will keep the funds for the White Company with me. I do not think that bandits would risk taking them from the White Company."

William's shoulders sagged. He was defeated. I suspected that he had been using our funds fraudulently. I smiled. Long after we had gone to bed William Turner would be busy trying to create accounts that would pass my wife's scrutiny.

When we rose I saw, from the drawn face of the bookkeeper, that I had been right, he had not slept. After we had breakfasted I said to my bodyguards, "Sir John and I will be busy all day here. Enjoy the sights of Pisa; see the Leaning Tower. The bell chamber was added just twenty years ago. You shall see the completed tower."

The three were happy to enjoy some time in the city. All of them had full purses. They knew that their employment was coming to an end and this was the opportunity to prepare for a new life.

It became abundantly clear that William had been defrauding the White Company. That he had made us money whilst doing so mitigated it somewhat but the profits from his investments had not gone directly to the White Company but been shared between the Company and him. I saw that he had even bought a cog.

When he had read through them, I fixed him with a stare that made him wither. "When Lady Hawkwood sees these, what do you think she will say, William?"

William was defensive as he answered, "I have made money for the company."

"You have made more for yourself." I pointed to an entry, "The ship, we will jointly own, you and I." I looked at Sir John Balzan, "You have no objections?"

"No, my lord, I need no ship."

"As for the rest," I tapped the parchment, "You will repay us half of the money that you have made. Call it interest."

"That is usury!"

Legacy

"Call it what you will. If you wish I can simply bring the White Company here and we will take all of the gold for the vault belongs to the White Company. The guards all served in the White Company. Do you think that you could stop us?" I knew that his wife's family would be appalled at the thought of my mercenary company being in Pisa.

He shook his head. He was defeated. "That will take longer than a month. I have cargoes at sea and they will need to be sold."

"When then?"

"I can give you half now and the rest by September."

"August."

His eyes met mine and he nodded, "August."

"Then Sir John and I will leave you and enjoy Pisa. We leave in two days." I paused, "I presume you have a wagon for us?"

"Yes, Sir John."

Sir John Balzan shook his head and chuckled as we mounted our horses to ride into Pisa, "He is a slippery one."

"He was not always so. When he was first my bookkeeper he was loyal and honest. Marriage corrupted him. The cog though, that is a useful addition. It means that when I return to England I can sail and not endure the passage through France with all its attendant problems. I have many enemies in France for Avignon is where the anti-pope resides."

We found an inn and stabled our horses. It was a pleasant day for February and we sat outside to enjoy the wine and watch the world go by. My bodyguards found us. They had made purchases. I told them what had been decided. "Robert, when you leave my service, I will employ you for a further six months."

"I do not mind, my lord, but doing what?"

"You can travel to England on the cog I have just obtained a half interest in. You can take Robin's bones back and some of my gold to lodge with Sir William Coggeshall, my son-in-law."

"I would do both for nothing, my lord."

"I know but loyalty should be rewarded."

We left with a wagon laden with gold. More than half of it was mine and the rest belonged to the White Company. My bodyguards were part of the White Company and they would benefit. Sir John Balzan would give half of the money to the men who still remained in the White Company and use the rest to hire new lances.

When we reached Casa Donnina, the first thing I noticed was the presence of horses I did not recognise. We entered my hall and Ned said, "You have visitors from Bologna, my lord. Lady Hawkwood is entertaining them."

I frowned. I had been looking forward to time with my family and visitors meant I would have to smile and be polite. I took off my cloak, hat and gloves. The ride had not been a particularly long one but I was still dusty. I knocked as much dust from my clothes as I could.

The visitor was Ambrogio Bentivoglio and another Bolognese noble. He was no longer the diffident-looking young man who had first sought my help. He had grown and filled out. Clearly, the campaign had given him confidence and it looked as though he was now taking his role as captain seriously. He looked more muscled than before we had tweaked the Milanese nose. He had with him a younger version of himself.

"Sir John, it is good to see you again. Your wife has been keeping us entertained."

Donnina rose, "And now that the host is here the hostess will arrange food."

I sat and Ned, who was hovering nearby, poured me some wine. I saw that my two guests had goblets that had been filled already.

"This is my younger brother, Carlos. He is learning to be a warrior and acts as my squire."

"You have chosen a good career, Carlos." I hoped that Ambrogio did not wish me to train him.

"I must come directly to the point, my lord. Bologna has need of your services."

I shook my head, "I have just finished with Jacopo dal Verme and most of my company has left my service. I have less than two hundred lances and a hundred archers left. Sir John Balzan commands the company now."

"We have other men and condottiere, my lord, Ugo di Monforte has been hired."

Hugo of Montforte was a German who had fought with us in Lombardy and his men had been with me in the Val d'Arno. He was a good warrior.

"Then why do you need me? Hugo is a good man."

"There are three companies of condottiere who threaten us, my lord. Galeazzo Visconti has cut them loose and they seek to plunder both Bologna and Florence. They are Ceccolo Broglia's company, Brandolino Brandolini's company, and Biordo dei Michelotti's company."

They were all good companies and the condottiero who led each of them was a worthy opponent. There were few condottieri who were their equal. I was their superior and I could see why Bologna had come to me.

"I do not know and that is an honest answer. Dine with us and stay the night. I will consider your offer and sleep on it. I have just returned from Pisa and I am still fatigued from the journey."

"Of course, but time is pressing, my lord."

"When you are as old as me then every moment is precious. I promise that when we have breakfasted, you shall know my answer." I stood, "And now if you will excuse me, I must change. Ned, see to these gentlemen's needs and then send Edgar to me."

I went to my bed chamber and sat. I waited until Edgar knocked on the door and I said, "Come in, Edgar."

"Yes, my lord? You have need of me?"

"Find Sir John Balzan. Tell him that Bologna wishes to hire the White Company to rid their land of three companies of condottiere, Ceccolo Broglia's, Brandolino Brandolini's, and Biordo dei Michelotti's companies. Ask him to join us for breakfast in the morning."

"Yes, my lord."

John would know, after our recent conversations, that my heart was not in this. He would work out if it was advantageous or not.

Of course, Donnina was more interested in the news from Pisa than this contract. During the meal, I sensed her need for answers. For that reason, we retired early and once in our chamber I was able to satisfy her need for information. I gave her the accounts. She snorted, "But for our Bolognese visitors I could have read this already."

I sighed, "There is nothing urgent and the contract does not sound arduous. While these three companies are good ones and well-led, they are opportunists. They see a weak Bologna and would raid. It is a chevauchée."

"You would lead them?"

"I will hear their offer. If it is large enough and short enough in duration then I might accept. William needs until August to gather our money."

"I never trusted him!"

"He was an honest man once but gold not to mention power seduces and he has a greedy wife. By the end of summer, my sword will hang above our fireplace."

She nodded, "You may be right." She stroked my hand, "A few thousand extra florins would not go amiss. We have a dowry for Giannetta but weddings are expensive."

I smiled and put my arm around my wife. She wanted me to take the contract.

"And you need to speak to the girls before you leave. They need to be in no doubt about your intentions."

"Yes, my love."

I did not make it easy for the Bolognese. I feigned disinterest and so they raised their offer. I still did not agree but, instead, I said to Sir John Balzan, "You now lead the White Company, Sir John, what say you to this contract?"

John knew how to play the game and he shook his head, "I do know, Sir John, I would not wish to be campaigning in September or August."

Ambrogio added, quickly, "We can limit it to last until August, my lord. By then, we should have rid our lands of our enemies and the crops will be harvested." The grape harvest, as I well knew, was vital to Bologna and an interruption during the harvesting could prove disastrous.

I nodded, "And it goes without saying that we would only march under the banner of Sir John Hawkwood."

"And we would have it no other way." He looked at me eagerly.

Legacy

I nodded, "Very well, you have my services and the White Company until the last week in July," I smiled, "at my age, it takes a week to travel."

"Of course, my lord, and when will you arrive?"

"That is an easy one to answer, when we get there. Until then you will have to rely on Hugo and your nobles."

After they had gone, Sir John went to organise the men and I told my bodyguards of the change of plans. Surprisingly enough they were very happy about it. I think they had resigned themselves to never having the chance to draw a sword and now they did. It was, for Zuzzo and Gianluca, a last opportunity for glory.

Before we left Donnina brought my two eldest daughters to see me. Donnina had told me what I needed to say. The last thing she needed was a bluff old plain-speaking soldier to say the wrong thing. "Daughters, I will not call you girls for you are now young women. The time is coming when you will want to be wed." I smiled, "From what your mother has told me there is interest already." Ginnetta giggled but Caterina pouted. "While whoever seeks the hand of a daughter of Giovanni Acuto needs to have his approval, know you that a suitor must also win the approval of your mother. I do not think that anything will change in the next months but as I will not return until August you need to know this. Do you understand?"

"Yes, Father."

When they had been dismissed Donnina kissed my cheek, "Did your puppet perform as you hoped he would?"

She sighed, "You are not a puppet, my husband, but you sometimes need a nudge, that is all."

It took just three days for us to prepare. I decided to take a wagon once more and that pleased Robert who could use his beloved Bettina. For me it meant comfort. It was the smallest company that I had ever led but I knew every warrior who followed me. The campaign in Lombardy had made us all closer.

Chapter 20

March 1392 Bologna
I was grateful for the wagon as we headed to Bologna. The weather was like March in England. It was wet, unseasonably cold and windy. I was able to hunker down in the wagon bed, a piece of oilskin protecting both me and my belongings, and my body covered in furs. I was comfortable while my men and my bodyguards were both cold and wet not to mention uncomfortable.

The podestà allowed us into his city. We were a small company and if he could not trust us then he was in serious trouble. Ambrogio had new intelligence that told us that the three condottiere companies were raiding the Este lands around Modena. They would be bought off before they could move to Ferrara. That gave us just a few days to move north and west to meet them. I made sure that Hugo, who dined with us, understood that I would be in command and Sir John Balzan would be second in command. Hugo appeared quite happy with the arrangement. His company had benefitted from the recent campaign and men who had served in Lombardy had flocked to his banner. As this was one of the first times he had led so many men he was happy, I think, to have a mentor with him. He knew that I would happily give advice. I told him, privately, that I would go to war no more and he knew I was not a threat to his authority.

The rain finally stopped and the skies cleared. We moved to the borders of the land controlled by the Este family. I used the Bolognese nobles to scout and it was they who discovered the three groups of raiders. The enemy soldiers were scouting out the land to the south of Modena. Bolognese land. We moved the fifteen miles to Savignano sul Panaro. It was a small village close to a ford and a bridge over the River Panaro. With no castle there it would be an easy place to cross into Bologna. Ambrogio was worried that if we left the road to Bologna unguarded the enemy might simply raid closer to Bologna.

"You are right. What say we use you and your nobles to stay here and guard the main road? We are close enough to summon if you are in trouble."

He did not like my suggestion, but he was forced to accept it. I was always happier commanding just provvisionati. Whilst nobles were better than feditore, they could still be unpredictable and seek glory or honour. Many thought that they were better warriors than condottiere. They were not. With the two companies of condottiere we reached the village before dark and before the condottiere had arrived. One of the farmers told us that he had seen scouts who appeared to be Breton, scouting the crossing. It confirmed what I had thought. The men made hovels and slept in their positions. Hugo had some handguns and the eight were split between the ford and the bridge. I did not like the new-fangled invention. I believed that they scared horses and were unpredictable but as our horses were tethered more than half a mile to the east of the village, it would be enemy horses we affected and one advantage of handguns was that they could clear a space better than any other weapon. If the stones they sent went astray it would not matter overmuch.

I slept in comfort as did my bodyguards. We were warm and cosy; me within the wagon and they beneath it. We rose before dawn and enjoyed a hot breakfast. The villagers of Savignano sul Panaro, which was in Bolognese land, knew that whatever we ate that was freely given would be much less than what they would lose if three rapacious condottiere companies arrived. I told Hugo that we would fight beneath his banner. Hugo wondered about the wisdom of my decision, "But, my lord, yours would inspire more fear."

"True but we need to hurt these men before I reveal my presence. They think that I have retired and that I am in my bed in Casa Donnina, let us keep up that illusion for a while. Besides, when we win, you will have your reputation enhanced. That is good, is it not?"

I could see that I had confused him but as he had nothing to lose and everything to gain, he agreed. For that reason, I did not use my wagon but I rode Blackie and my bodyguard and I wore black cloaks and positioned ourselves thirty paces from the bridge which was guarded by Sir John Balzan and the White

Company. Hugo impressed me with the positioning of his troops. He hid his crossbows in the buildings. Perhaps he was emulating Sir John Balzan who had placed his archers where they could loose their arrows and yet remain unseen. It meant that the scouts who appeared counted less than a thousand lances. Our intelligence was that the three companies numbered more than three thousand soldiers in total. The three condottieri arrived with their men, by my estimate, an hour before noon. They had clearly expected the crossing to be unguarded or else they would have made a dawn attack. They planned, from their dispositions, to use dismounted lances to cross the bridge and the ford. The other half of their lances were mounted and on the bluff overlooking the river. They would exploit the breakthrough when it came. Their horns sounded and the lances marched forward. They were plated and marched in step. These were well-trained soldiers. The three condottieri had been employed by Visconti and well paid. That was reflected in the plate armour of their three companies. I wondered how many of the opposition had been in dal Verme's army in the north. Hugo looked nervously over his shoulder at me. I smiled encouragement and he nodded. One thing that condottieri who fought alongside me learned from me was timing. There is a moment when the judicious use of missiles can have a devastating effect. It is often when an enemy thinks you have none to use. So it was with Hugo. He waited until the enemy soldiers were on the other bank of the Panaro and just a hundred paces from us before he gave the command. He glanced again at me and I nodded my approval. The first lances had stepped both onto the bridge and into the river when he ordered his trumpeter to sound for missiles.

 I smiled as Zuzzo shook his head and said, "The man should have spit. There was but one clear note in that call!" He was a perfectionist.

 The arrows arched and the crossbows cracked as the handguns boomed their smoky discharge. The horses on the bluffs reacted badly and some reared while others fought their riders. Of course, that blast was the only one they would suffer. In my experience, handguns took far too long to reload. They took even longer than a crossbow. The arrows and bolts smacked into the lances. The plate on some and the bucklers on the back of their hands protected many but at least twenty men fell. Once they were in the water and on the bridge more missiles came at them. The ford slowed up those trying to cross the water but the bridge, narrow though it was, meant that those men moved quickly.

Hugo timed his next command well and showed that he was a leader. He led his lances to charge across the narrow bridge and smash into the advancing soldiers. The ones in the river were moving more slowly for the water was up to the waist of many and above it of some. The arrows began to take their toll. When Hugo and his charging lances drove the enemy from the bridge, many falling into the river where they would drown, the enemy horns sounded and those crossing the ford fell back. We had won and with virtually no losses. The men cheered as the three condottiere companies slunk away to lick their wounds and plan their strategy.

That night Hugo was beside himself with joy. I counselled him, "That is just the opening pass. This is like a tournament." When we had been in Bologna, we had heard the name of Corrado Prospero as the greatest warrior to take part in tournaments. My former condottiero, Konrad had won the tournament. Hugo had been a spectator and had told me of Konrad's success. "Just as your countryman Konrad was patient, so, if we want to emerge victorious so must we. We leave tomorrow and return to join Ambrogio."

"We leave this crossing unguarded?" There was surprise in his voice.

I sighed. I had to spell everything out, "No, we leave some of your light horsemen and squires. They can keep watch and fetch us in the unlikely situation of the enemy returning."

"You do not think that they will return?"

His men had recovered the plate and the weapons from the bridge and the river. I pointed at the river, "They have many horses. Here they cannot use them but closer to Bologna, they can. I am confident that they will do as Ambrogio feared and use the Modena road to advance on Bologna."

We marched back to Ambrogio. On the ride back I thought about the cunning Galeazzo Visconti, the Lord of Milan. He had cut loose these three companies knowing that they would have to raid and in that raiding he would profit. They were doing his work but they were not being paid. It was a clever strategy.

It took three days for the rogue companies to approach the border. They had returned for a desultory couple of days of raiding the land around Modena but the bird having been plucked already the pickings were scant. We had camped in battle formation so that when Ambrogio's scouts rode in to tell us of their approach, it did not take long for us to form lines. I had discussed my plans with Hugo, Ambrogio and Sir John Balzan. I had surprised them and that pleased me. If I could surprise these three then I might be able to do the same with the condottieri who approached. Hugo's and Ambrogio's men were in the front ranks and mine in the rear. Ambrogio and Hugo, with their bodyguards, had placed themselves before the dismounted lances. I rode Blackie and like my bodyguards, we were cloaked. I wished to remain hidden once more.

The enemy approached and I saw that they slightly outnumbered us. Ambrogio's men had kept their scouts from discovering our numbers and they halted to take stock of our dispositions. Hugo and Ambrogio rode forward and their trumpets sounded for a meeting. The two sets of leaders met just one hundred and fifty paces from our lances and my bodyguards and I nudged our way forward.

Ambrogio had Bolognese standards flying. He looked like a lord and he addressed the three condottieri. He spoke loudly so that both sets of soldiers could hear his words, "Provvisionati, this is Bolognese land you approach, and I command you to turn around and leave on pain of death." It sounded arrogant and dramatic. I knew that the three condottieri would think that they had the measure of this young Bolognese noble.

One of them, I recognised him as Ceccolo Broglia, took on the role of spokesman and it was he who answered. He seemed to know Hugo and addressed his words to him; it was intended to insult the Bolognese noble, "Ugo di Monforte, I do not know what Bologna is paying you but come and join us. There is no one who can dispute our progress. Let us take Bologna and then ride into the rich land that is Florence. There we can sup from the tit of that rich cow. What say you?"

Hugo answered, "I am a true condottiero, Ceccolo Broglia. I have given my word and taken florins from Bologna. I will not be foresworn. We will do our duty and dispute your passage. I was trained by Giovanni Acuto and I live by his principles."

Ceccolo laughed, "Acuto? He is now misnamed for Hawkwood is dulled by age. His time has gone and now that he has sheathed his sword and hung up his baton he will soon become a memory. He will be a tale told by old women to frighten their grandchildren."

I smiled and said, quietly to my bodyguards, "And now, the grand entrance, eh?" As I threw off my black cloak to reveal my white surcoat and shining armour, I thought that if this was my last time in the saddle then I had, indeed, left a lasting memory. Spurring Blackie and with my bodyguards also revealed, we rode to flank Ambrogio.

"Ceccolo, you use my name a little too freely and while I might be older than I once was, I can still take offence at your words."

The three looked visibly shocked. Ceccolo was clearly their leader for it was he who eventually found his voice, "Giovanni Acuto, we heard you had retired after defeating Jacopo dal Verme."

"I have not yet retired and I will confirm what my friend Lord Bentivoglio said, leave Bologna and return to the west for you are most unwelcome here."

Brandolino Brandolini jabbed his baton in my direction, "It was you who were at the river. You commanded the crossing at San Cesario Sul Panaro." I gave a theatrical half-bow. He turned to Ceccolo, "I told you that it was more than a Bolognese noble and a young condottiero who thwarted us."

"And now you will leave," I raised my hand, "If I drop this arm, and, as you say, I am an old man and tire easily that will be the signal for five hundred archers of the White Company to send five thousand bodkin arrows in your direction and your companies will all be killed."

As planned my archers, resplendent in white, all stepped before the lances. They did not draw their bows but the threat was clear. That there were nowhere near five hundred would be overlooked. They would just see the famed archers who had cleared battlefields up and down Italy.

The three condottieri looked at each other and nodded. Ceccolo said, "I am sorry for the insult Giovanni Acuto, we were told by Galeazzo Visconti that you had finished with war and Florence was a ripe plum ready to be plucked. We will head west."

"Farewell, but you will find that as you head to the Mediterranean you find you have a shadow, the white shadow of the White Company." I shouted, as the three turned and their horns sounded the retreat, "Captain Jack, stand down." I lowered my arm. It ached.

The three companies of condottiere took two hours to mount their horses and with their wagons laden with Modenese loot and plunder, trundle west. We dismounted to watch them.

"Ambrogio, we will follow them. You and your nobles need only come for the first day. After that, you can return to Bologna. This is work for provvisionati."

"You are sure?"

Hugo laughed, "Did you not see their faces, my lord? The mere presence of Sir John Hawkwood, Giovanni Acuto, was enough to make them quake in their boots. He defeated Jacopo dal Verme and destroyed Verona at Castagnaro. They will find easier victims."

I nodded, "My name and that of the White Company, Hugo, but I also see the clever mind of Galeazzo Visconti at work. He saves his gold and still has his dogs of war do his work. By letting loose the three companies in Florence he hoped to weaken the land. He will have more men ready to exploit their success."

The three companies had many routes that they could have chosen. When, at Rubiera, they took the road south and west we knew that they were not going to return to Milan. That made sense. Visconti would not welcome them. Ambrogio left us and we began our journey. The three companies left little in their wake. They plundered and raided every village and settlement along the way. They left the castles. Condottiere did not waste time reducing walls unless they could help it. It was at those castles that we were welcomed and given shelter.

When, after a month in the saddle, we neared the coast, then we were able to stop. "They are heading for Sarzana. That makes them Pisa's problem and we can return home."

There was a shorter route home for the White Company. We would head through Lucca to reach Casa Donnina. Hugo would retrace his steps to Bologna. "Have our gold sent to Casa Donnina, Hugo."

"I will, my lord, and I do not doubt that there will be a bonus."

I shook my head, "I do not think so."

"And will you reconsider your decision to retire, my lord?"

If nothing else, this campaign had shown me that keeping my plans secret benefitted me and I shrugged, "Who knows? It is now summer and a pleasant ride through Tuscany might change my mind. I have made gold and we have won. Not a member of the White Company died and our enemies fled at my name. We shall see."

With just my company and bodyguards we travelled to Casa Donnina and I enjoyed the ride in the wagon.

We did not reach home until August. The wagon, whilst comfortable was slow. In addition, the land through which we passed had heard of our almost bloodless victory and we were feted as we travelled. Every town wished to honour Giovanni Acuto. We were few enough in number to entertain and the White Company had a well-deserved reputation for professionalism.

My leaders and bodyguards knew my mind. I would retire. The last contract had made me financially secure. When I sold Montecchio Vesponi I could buy another estate, far from Florence. As I told my leaders, when we camped each night, "Visconti will come again for Florence. He hates me and while I do not think that Florence will let down its guard it will be prudent to have a home which is not threatened by him."

I already had a place in mind but I would keep those plans until I had spoken to Donnina. Sir John Balzan showed that he was ready to take the baton from me. On that eighty-mile ride through Tuscany, he let all the men of the White Company know that he would now be the paymaster. He told any who wished to leave the company that they would receive all their backpay once we reached Florence and they would part as friends. I was pleased for both him and the company when all chose to continue to serve. They would still wear white but it would no longer have my chevron and shells upon it. The sight of white on the battlefield would still inspire fear and men would look for the legend that was Giovanni Acuto but it would be up to Sir John Balzan to make his own name and reputation.

My wagon trundled into my yard, and I dismounted. I would no longer be a condottiero. I had ended my career as a warlord and a warrior with a victory, a very easy victory. The story of the three companies all departing at the mere mention of my name had spread like wildfire. The story had grown and become exaggerated. I knew that at some point it would be that Giovanni Acuto alone had made thousands of warriors flee. It was not true but no legend was wholly factual. I was content. I had made a good end.

Chapter 21

September 1392 Florence

Sir John and the White Company departed for Naples. The vicious struggle between Anjou and the Durazzo family meant that they had the prospect of employment for as long as they chose. They were following in the path of Carlo Visconti who was fighting in that bloody war. It was a sad parting for some of the archers and lances had been with me for more than ten years. I gave gifts of weapons to those. I had gathered quite a collection in my long career and they were touched by the gift. Once they had gone my estate seemed empty. The warrior hall would no longer be needed. There were now just my three bodyguards and soon, they would depart too. That they delayed their departure was not due to anything more than a reluctance to leave my side. We had been close. Even Robert Daring who had been there the shortest time had become more than a bodyguard but a friend. He had become so familiar that my daughters were no longer terrified by the scarred warrior. They had seen the gentler side of him.

They had been gone for a week or so when I was summoned to meet the council in Florence and my bodyguards came along with Donnina who had also been invited. There had been a time that I would have feared such a meeting for it might have meant a blade in the back. Those times had passed and I was now a hero in Florence.

Michael was now a member of the council. There was a rumour that he would be the podestà once his father-in-law retired. It was Carlos Cialdini who addressed me. "Sir John, now that you have hung up your sword, the Council of the city of Florence has decided to honour you. We have ordered a funerary monument for you in the Santa Maria del Fiore church. The tomb will be built of stone and adorned with marble statues." He smiled, "We hope that it will be many years until you need it for we have only just begun to build it. It will stand to show the world that Giovanni Acuto was Florence's greatest captain."

I accepted the gift with a bow, "I am touched and, as it is to be built of white marble, it will honour the White Company,

Legacy

many of whom died fighting Florence's enemies." I was thinking of Robin and Giovanni Ubaldini as well as those like Dai and Eoin who had long left the company. The feast was a splendid affair and Michael, a little drunk perhaps, told me of his prospective promotion.

"I owe it all to you, to Robin and Dai as well, of course, but mainly you. You found me and you made me. Whatever I have comes because of Sir John Hawkwood."

I nodded, "And I am happy that it is so. One of my sons serves the church, one died, so I heard, in England and John is a child. Who knows the man he will become. You are like a son to me and I am proud of you."

We parted as friends. I did not see much of him after that for he was busy learning not the trade of a warrior but a politician. His martial skills would stand him in good stead.

We returned to Casa Donnina. My wife and I had discussed a new estate and I had purchased one on the borders of Florence and the states ruled by the Pope. My service against the anti-pope had ensured that I was seen as a friend by the true Pope. The estate, at San Donato in Polverosa, was close enough to the papal states to give me an escape route should I need it. I sent Edgar to complete the purchase and to organise the servants. He would be the steward and Ned would continue to run Casa Donnina. We had sold Montecchio Vesponi to Carlos Cialdini and made more than the new estate cost. That was down to my wife's business skills. We were well in profit thanks to my last three contracts.

My bodyguards all left at the end of October. The four of us rode to Pisa with Robin's bones. Zuzzo and Gianluca had decided to travel with Robert and see England. I think it was also to honour Robin as well as ensuring that the gold I sent to my son-in-law would be safe. They would not spend long in England but the three were close and it would be a last adventure for them. I saw them board the ship, in which I now had a half interest, and waved them goodbye. I found it sad. That night I stayed with William. He had not sent my gold in August as I had requested. I had not needed it but that was not the point. I rode Ajax into his manor and dismounted. I was alone and had no bodyguards but I did not fear William. He had always been a mouse and as Jacopo dal Verme had said, I was a fox.

"Sir John, this is a pleasant surprise."

I knew it was not but I smiled, "I know that this is an imposition but I would stay here this night. I have just sent Robin's bones back to England."

"I was sad to hear of his death."

I believed him for his tone was sincere. That Robin had no time for him was immaterial. "I also came because, it seems, you have forgotten to send my gold."

He flushed, "I have it, but I heard that you campaigned in Bologna and…"

"And thought I would forget or perhaps that I might die?" Before he could deny either, I shook my head, "Do not insult me, Willliam. I have white hair but I am no dotard. I have been home for two months and well you know it."

He hung his head, "You can take it on the morrow."

"And I would go to see it now." I did not trust him and I wanted to see my chests of gold. We went to the secure building, guarded by the six former White Company soldiers. There had been more but death had taken the others. Their quarters were attached to what was, effectively, a bank.

The six of them gushed when I entered. I had not seen them for many years but we had been shield brothers and such bonds transcend time. "So, I see you have all grown, like me, a little older and a little fatter." I playfully patted Guiseppe Manzini's stomach.

He laughed, "Too little exercise."

"And what will you do now that I take my gold from this bank?"

Before they could answer William said, "That is another reason I did not send the gold, Sir John. With your share taken the bank is almost empty. I have no need of the guards. I was continuing to employ them as a favour." That was another lie.

Guiseppe glared at my bookkeeper, "We have been told, Sir John, that when your gold leaves the vault we are to vacate our rooms. We are to be thrown on the street."

"That is not true, Guiseppe." William's protestations were a little weak.

"That is what your wife told us!" The shamefaced look on William's face confirmed Guiseppe's words.

There was mutual animosity between William's wife and me. It was that animosity which prompted my offer, "Then what say you escort my gold back to Casa Donnina? I have an empty warrior hall which is yours for as long as you need it." I looked at William as I said, "And I will pay and house you until you no longer need such earthly things. I know how to reward loyalty."

Their faces gave me my answer. Guiseppe said, "Gladly, my lord, and would that we could leave this cheerless hall now."

I smiled, "First, we count the gold. I am sure that you six know its worth down to the last florin."

"Aye, we do."

William barely spoke while we ate. When we had counted the money I had discovered that he had tried to cheat me of one chest of gold. His treatment of the guards had come to haunt him. He was even less happy, the next day, when I commandeered a wagon and horses to take the gold and my guards back to Casa Donnina. I looked back once to see the man who had once helped me to build the White Company. Then I turned and looked ahead. That was the last time I ever saw William Turner.

Donnina fully approved of my decision. With Edgar in Polverosa and my bodyguards departed we needed some sort of guard and the six men were a perfect choice.

I had no time to enjoy my manor for we had a wedding to arrange. While I had been on campaign, Donnina had finished the negotiations with the di Porciglia family. They were happy with the dowry and their son Brezaglia would marry Giannetta in January. Some of the gold from Pisa would be spent by Christmas for the wedding would have to be a grand one. I told poor Caterina and Anna that when they wed their weddings would be smaller affairs.

In November we hosted a visit from Konrad. Captain Corrado Prospero, as he was known throughout Italy, was now not only a very successful condottiero but also a champion at the tourney. Florence hosted the tournament and Konrad asked if he could stay with me. I was delighted but I could see that he had an ulterior motive. He and Caterina flirted all the way through the meal. That night Donnina confirmed my impression.

"She has spoken often of the fine young soldier. It is a good match. He is successful and he is popular in Florence. If we ever go to England they could live here."

We had discussed my move to England at length. Once my daughters were married then it would be a real possibility.

Donnina and I were the guests of honour at the tournament. I noticed that Konrad had chosen red as his colour. His company was the Red Company. I took that as a compliment. He was copying me but choosing a different colour. If my daughter was not infatuated by him before that tournament his victory ensured that she was firmly his. He stayed with us just for one week. His company was hired to ride east and face Città di Castello. I could see that his star was rising and when he asked for permission to court Caterina, after discussing it with Donnina, I gave my permission.

Following the wedding of my eldest daughter and her departure from my hall Donnina and I could relax and enjoy each other's time. My wife, however, had a restless nature. When something was on her mind she worried at it like a cat with a ball of wool.

"I still have estates in Milan, my husband. We have no income from them thanks to my uncle and yet they belong to me."

I sighed, "I have no White Company to take what is owed. What do you suggest?"

"We appoint procurators to travel to Milan and to see the property."

I was not a man of business. I was a man of war. Until my wife mentioned them I did not know what a procurator was. "Then do so."

She smiled, "You should appoint some too."

"Me, why? I have no property in Milan."

"No, but Bologna owes you money. They have yet to pay you for your service last year and there is the matter of your annual pension which they have conveniently, it seems, forgotten."

I did as she suggested and was pleasantly surprised when, without recourse to force, the money arrived escorted by Lord

Bentivoglio's men. I was not going to war but our coffers were growing.

In the summer the gold grew even more. When Michael became the podestà he persuaded the Florentine council to reward me an extra five hundred florins a year and the right to keep twenty five lances. I did not need them at the time and the expense could not be justified but it was a useful gift to be given and both marked my high esteem.

The only blight in my life was the recurrence of the illness which had first manifested itself a few Christmases ago. I found it hard to rise for a few days. I did not let Donnina send for the doctors. They would just bleed me. Instead I slept a great deal and after a week rose. It was a warning for me.

Konrad returned to our hall in the spring when Florence hired him to oppose the Pope who had sent his own condottiere to claim land on the borders. We had been planning a move to our home there at Polverosa but the war being so close delayed it. It was on this visit that he proposed to my daughter and the wedding was arranged for the next year. They would be married in January.

It was in the autumn of that year that Zuzzo and Gianluca returned for a visit. Both had grown a little more portly. They had not practised the daily exercise they had when they were bodyguards and I think that they had enjoyed their time in England. Robert had secured a place in the household of my son-in-law, William Coggeshall. That was not a surprise but I was pleased for both of them. Robert would be happy and William and my daughter would have a bodyguard who would give his life for theirs. Robin had been buried in his hometown and the three of them had waited until the stone marker had been erected before they left.

"And now, what?"

Zuzzo said, "I am going back to Montecchio Vesponi."

"I sold that manor, Zuzzo."

He nodded, "I know but I think the village needs an inn. Before we left there, last year, I asked Maria to keep her eye open for such a place. She is a resourceful woman and I have no doubt that she will have found me one."

"Maria?" I smiled as I raised my eyebrows.

He laughed, "I am a man and not a eunuch and she is comely. She told me that Sir Robin had not been able to be as attentive in his last years. I would make her my wife." He shrugged, "I think she deserves that."

"She does. And you, Gianluca?"

"There is a small holding just five miles from here, my lord. It has been abandoned these last few years and I believe that I can pay a pittance. I would like to build something and, thanks to you, I have the coins in my purse to do so."

He had changed his mind, it seemed, about being an innkeeper, "And I would like to have you as a neighbour. This is all good."

Konrad returned to Florence, having been successful in his war. He went to the council who were more than pleased with his success. He asked for, and received, an advance of one thousand florins to pay for the wedding. Caterina would have a wedding as magnificent as her elder sister's. The measure of Konrad's rising reputation was marked by the attendance of Ugolino dei Preti di Montechiaro from Bologna and the famous condottieri Milano dei Rastrelli di Alessandria and Bartolomeo Boccanera at the wedding. They had not even been condottieri when I had hung up my baton but now they were seen as rising stars.

At the wedding feast I was flattered that there was as much attention on me as the bride and groom. Men rarely see how they are viewed by the world for the accolades and tributes are normally paid when they are dead. I was lucky. I enjoyed some of them while I lived.

With two daughters married then we could move to England. For Donnina this would be a visit only. Immediately after the wedding, I had felt unwell. I was dizzy and had a blinding headache. I put this down to too much wine and rich food but when a few weeks later I felt no better I knew it was serious. I knew that if I went to England I would not return. The planning for our departure kept us both busy. Donnina was too good a lady of the manor just to abandon everything. I kept my illness from my wife. She was so busy with the planning for our move that she did not see the signs. She had no need to know that I felt ill. I told Michael of my decision to travel to England and I asked the city to settle my life pensions and I received six thousand tax-exempt florins, with two thousand paid immediately and the remainder in several quarterly instalments. In addition to this amount, I was given one thousand florins as a farewell gift upon my departure. I was a truly rich man. Ironically a few days after the florins arrived, I became so unwell that I could not hide it and my wife discovered my illness. She found me collapsed on the floor writhing in pain. The pain came from my head. She confined me to bed and a doctor was summoned. He did what all doctors did and bled me. Donnina was told to confine me to bed. For a man used to being active, even at the age I was, this was hard to bear. I could not be ill.

When I found myself sleeping more than waking I knew that my end was coming. I was honest with Donnina and told her what I thought. I saw tears in her eyes as she nodded, "Perhaps, but let us heed the advice of the doctor and keep you abed. Perhaps he is wrong. I will tend to you. Your life has been spent away from me but you have ever been in my head and my heart, I could not have married a better man and you have been a faultless father. I was lucky that my father arranged this marriage." She kissed me and stood, "Now, rest and I will open a bottle of that dessert wine from Lusitania that you like so much. I know you are not hungry, you have eaten little this past week but I will find some olives and cheese that might tempt you."

"Thank you and know that you have been the best of wives and I believe I have been more fortunate than you in this marriage." She left.

I lay and looked at the ceiling. I knew that I should have had a priest for me to confess but as I had confessed a week ago and done little else I did not think I had committed enough sins. My next confession would be my last. I knew that I was dying. I had hoped to see Anna married but that was not to be. As I closed my eyes and dozed, I found myself reliving my life from my time as an archer in England and the plague through Crécy and Poitiers to Italy and the place I had found myself. I had enjoyed a good life and I had no regrets. I had done what every father and husband hopes to do, I was leaving my family well provided for and with a reputation that was almost flawless. Only I knew how close I had come to disaster. However, I had survived, and I drifted off to sleep.

Donnina

Epilogue

March 1394 Florence

As soon as I came back into the room, I knew that my husband, the finest man I had ever known, Giovanni Acuto, was dead. He looked at peace and that was good for he deserved peace. He had not enjoyed the last rites but I knew that God would welcome him for he had been, in the main, a good man. He was not perfect, no man is, but he was as close to perfection as I had ever known. I closed his eyes and folded his arms. I leaned over and kissed him, "Farewell, John, I shall never remarry and I will dedicate the rest of my life to your memory. People will know of your story and it will echo through time, as you deserve." When I was composed, and my tears were dried, I summoned Ned and told him. That huge warrior burst into tears. I found myself comforting him. "Send one of the guards to Gianluca and tell him. Have another ride to Florence to tell the podestà."

"Master John and Mistress Anna?" Ned was fond of my son and daughter.

"I will tell them. Then have the other guards take the body to the chapel and surround it with candles. I want it guarded day and night until the funeral."

"It will be done, my lady."

By the time I had told them all and comforted their tears I was exhausted but I had to be strong, John would have wanted it. I followed the men as they reverently carried his body to the chapel. They mounted a guard and would stand vigil over the man that they revered. That night, as I said my prayers I reflected that his tomb had been finished just in time, one month ago. I climbed into the bed I had shared with him. I put my arm into the depression where he had died. I could still smell him. It was in that moment that I broke. Rolling into the hollow I wept as I had never done before. My eyes had been dry for my father but for my husband, my eyes ran salty until, still weeping, I slept.

Legacy

The next morning, on the orders of Michael, the body was transported to San Giovanni where it stood on a platform set up around the baptismal font surrounded by candles. The corpse was covered with a golden cloth, and a sword was placed on his chest, while he held the commander's baton in his hand. The funeral took some days to organise. One does not simply slip a man like Sir John Hawkwood into the ground. Those days allowed word to reach others who flocked to Florence.

The funeral procession was led by his family followed by two hundred priests, three hundred monks and friars, and numerous knights. Sir Konrad and other condottieri, Roger Nottingham, John Balzan, Konrad von Landau, my brother Carlo and Gianluca, carried the coffin to place it in the newly finished tomb at Santa Maria del Fiore. The funeral had cost four hundred florins and was a mark of the respect of Florence. The city paid for the mourning clothes that I wore as well as his children. Florence had been his enemy in my husband's early years. How that had changed by the end of his life. Poor Zuzzo only reached Florence the day after the funeral. He was sad that he had not been able to pay his respects at the funeral of the man whom he and Gianluca had protected for so many years.

My tears had all been in the marital bed and the privacy of our home. Others wept at the funeral including men who had served with him: Michael, Gianluca and the White Company who were present. I daresay that those who did not know me well saw me as hard-hearted and uncaring. Nothing could be further from the truth, but I had control over my body, I would continue to grieve but it would be in private. The world would just see me as a strong woman, the extension of the man who had been called Giovanni Acuto. The world would never see his like again and I would spend my remaining years just remembering him. That the world would remember him was clear. His legacy was that the best condottieri who plied their trade had all been mentored by him. The exceptions, like Jacopo dal Verme and his brother had suffered at his hands and learned from his victories. The one who did not mourn was my uncle. He celebrated the death of his nemesis. I prayed for his death.

The End

Glossary

Battle - a military formation rather than an event
Bellinzona - Switzerland
Bevor - metal chin and mouth protector attached to a helmet
Brase - a strap on a shield for an arm to go through
Brigandine - a leather or padded tunic worn by soldiers; often studded with metal and sometimes called a jack
Canaglia - the bulk of Italian city-state armies. It translates as the rabble
Centenar - the commander of a hundred archers
Chevauchée - a raid on an enemy, usually by horsemen
Condottiere - Mercenaries
Condottiero - the captain of a mercenary company (pl. condottieri)
Cordwainer - shoemaker
Cuisse - metal protection for the thigh
Dodici - the council of 12 nobles who ruled Siena
Ducat - a gold coin minted in Venice
Ducato - the old name for Umbria
Faulds - a skirt of metal below the breastplate
Feditore - an Italian warrior
Florin - gold coin minted in Florence
Gardyvyan - Archer's haversack containing all his war-gear
Ghibellines - the faction supporting the Holy Roman Emperor against the Pope
Glaive - a long pole weapon with a concave blade
Greaves - protection for the lower legs
Guelphs - the faction supporting the Pope
Guige strap - a long leather strap that allowed a shield to hang from a knight's shoulder
Harbingers - the men who found accommodation and campsites for archers
Jupon - a shorter version of the surcoat
Mainward - the main body of an army
Mêlée - confused fight
Mos Teutonicus - the boiling of a body when the organs have been removed to facilitate the moving of the bones

Legacy

Noble - a gold coin worth about six shillings and eightpence
Oriflamme - the French standard which was normally kept in Saint-Denis
Pavesiers - men who carried man-sized shields to protect crossbowmen
Perpunto - soft padded tunic used as light armour during training
Pestis secunda - second outbreak of the Black Death in 1360-62
Podestà - ruler of a city-state/head of the council
Poleyn - knee protection
Provvisionati - professional soldiers
Rearward - the rearguard and baggage of an army
Rooking - overcharging
Soldo - a Milanese silver coin
Spaudler - shoulder protection
Shaffron - metal headpiece for a horse
Spanning hook - the hook a crossbowman had on his belt to help draw his weapon
Trapper - a cloth covering for a horse
Vanward - the leading element of an army, the scouts
Vintenar - commander of twenty (archers)
Vambrace - upper arm protection

Legacy

Canonical Hours

- Matins (nighttime)
- Lauds (early morning)
- Prime (first hour of daylight)
- Terce (third hour)
- Sext (noon)
- Nones (ninth hour)
- Vespers (sunset evening)
- Compline (end of the day)

Historical note

John Hawkwood was a real person but much of his life is still a mystery. At the end of his career, he was one of the most powerful men in Northern Italy where he commanded the White or English Company. He famously won the battle of Castagnaro in 1387. However, his early life is less well documented, and I have used an artistic licence to add details. He was born in Essex and his father was called Gilbert. I have made up the reason for his leaving his home but leave he did, and he became an apprentice tailor. It is rumoured that he fought at Crécy as a longbowman and I have used that to weave a tale. It is also alleged that he was knighted by Prince Edward at Poitiers.

The problem with researching this period is that most of the accounts are translations and the interpretation of the original documents leaves much to be desired. In one account the battle of Rubiera occurs in 1372 whilst in another in 1370. All I know is that von Landau was defeated and captured by Sir John and that the battle came about because he was still fighting for the Visconti family. As this was the last time he fought for the Visconti for some time and was employed by the Pope to fight against Milan and Florence in 1371, I have had to adjust what I know. The dates might be open for debate but the battles and the outcomes are not. Until I manage to get a time machine this will have to do.

The massacre at Cesena happened. Sir John was ordered by Robert de Genève to massacre the population. He was acting on the Pope's orders. Sir John saved many of the population. He was always, it seemed, trying to get payment for services and that explains his freebooting activities. There is no doubt that he acted like a warlord. He captured and kept castles in lieu of payment. There were many occasions when the employers of the White Company failed to pay them for their services. The White Company proved to be very loyal as it was Sir John Hawkwood who paid them from his own purse. That made him different from other condottieri.

I know that Hawkwood's marriage when he was in his fifties to a girl who was just 17 will make some people uncomfortable.

Legacy

However, it happened many times in the Middle Ages and to be fair to them they stayed together and appeared to love each other. Donnina bore him children and seemed an equal partner in the marriage. She was a strong woman and, unusually for the time, took charge of his finances.

Hawkwood's battles against Louis of Anjou and the Sienese were more skirmishes than battles. In both campaigns he used almost guerilla-like tactics. King Charles of Naples and Pope Urban were allies. I made up the visit of Sir John to Sorrento but the conspiracy of cardinals and King Charles did result in the ending of the alliance, the torture of the cardinals and the excommunication of King Charles.

Padua went from being an ally of Venice in her war with Genoa to a city to be gobbled up by the greedy Venetians. The Battle of Brentelle was Giovanni Ubaldini's victory and Sir John was not present. I had him present for the sake of continuity in the story. The conversation between il Vecchio and da Serego was documented as were the number of captives that were taken. Da Serego was held for ransom and languished for more than a year. When he was ransomed his freedom did not last long and he died soon after gaining his freedom.

Giovanni Ubaldini did hand over his baton to Sir John. Ubaldini was a good commander, but he knew that Sir John was a better one.

The emblem of the Visconti family.

There are many strange events around the Battle of Castagnaro. Firstly, it was the pinnacle of Sir John's career. He was an old man and yet he clearly outwitted his enemy. The chanting of 'carne' is documented as is the hurling away of the baton. Il Novello did refuse to retreat from the ditch and the battle for the ditch was paused when Buzzacarini was wounded.

The incident at Cerea with the poisoned wine and water is less easy to explain. The Veronese did poison both the water butts and the wine vats. As the Paduan army was on the point of mutiny Sir John had to do something. He produced the horn of a unicorn and grated it into the water and the wine. Clearly, he did not have the horn of a unicorn and the grating of an animal horn would not remove poison from either liquid. My theory is that not all the wine and the water were poisoned and he might have used a natural antidote. It was theatre and it did work but until we have a time machine to travel back and see the master performer at work we shall never know.

The Lords Appellant were English nobles who took charge of England after the defeat of Richard's supporters at Radcot Bridge. They were short-lived and when John of Gaunt returned to England Richard regained his power. Gloucester, Arundel and Warwick were the leaders of the opposition to King Richard. Henry Bolingbroke, the son of John of Gaunt became the next king after Richard. I used the material for a series of books called Struggle for a Crown. (See below.)

Konrad von Landau was wounded and as a result took his company to raid. That was the way the condottiere operated. The German treachery of Heinrich von Altinberg and the night attack all happened as did the predictions of the astrologer. Giovanni Ubaldini was murdered by a poisoned bowl of cherries. I have tried to be faithful to the events in Sir John's life after Castagnaro but I have changed the order of some of them to make a story that, I hopes, flows better.

I have used the words spoken whenever possible. I have also used exact numbers when possible. The funeral is one such example as is the pensions he received.

The ruses and tricks he employed were not made up by me. His retreats were legendary and he did ambush Jacopo dal Verme in a forest. The flooding of the river also happened as I said and it is typical of the man that John Hawkwood used that to his advantage. It was particularly satisfying to discover that his last act as a condottiero was to face three condottieri and defeat them by his mere presence. That is a true warlord.

Legacy

The incident with the Bretons was true as was the fortifying of the fortress that thwarted Jacop dal Verme. I have combined the two to make a better story. The Bretons were executed.

This book almost wrote itself. Castagnaro marked the high point of John Hawkwood's career and he could have retired but he did not. The campaigns against Jacopo dal Verme are as accurate as my research allowed and I found them to be more remarkable than his victory. He was knocking at Milan's door before he was forced, by another's defeat, to retreat. I found it almost unbelievable that he was in his early seventies and yet still capable of conducting such campaigns. The pensions he was paid and the dowries his daughters received are all well documented as is the account of his funeral.

His great enemy, Gian Galeazzo Visconti, the 1st Duke of Milan, outlived Sir John by eight years but he was a younger man. He had no sons who survived him and it was left to his daughter, Valentina, to carry on the family name. The year after Sir John's death, at the request of King Richard II of England, his body was transported to England and buried in the parish church of St. Peter in Hedingham Sible, where it rested for several centuries before his remains were dispersed and his tomb was destroyed.

I began this series intrigued by the story of an Englishman I had never heard of. It was the title of the Osprey book I used for my initial research that prompted the series. Castagnaro 1387 - Hawkwood's Great Victory - Devries, Capponi and Turner. I think he should be better known.

Griff Hosker
April 2024

The books I used for reference were:

- French Armies of the Hundred Years War- David Nicholle
- Castagnaro 1387 Hawkwood's Great Victory- Devries, Capponi and Turner
- Italian Medieval Armies 1300-1500- Gabriele Esposito
- Armies of the Medieval Italian Wars-1125-1325

Legacy

- Condottiere 1300-1500 Infamous Medieval Mercenaries- David Murphy
- The Armies of Crécy and Poitiers- Rothero
- The Scottish and Welsh Wars 1250-1400- Rothero
- English Longbowman 1330-1515- Bartlett and Embleton
- The Longbow- Mike Loades
- The Battle of Poitiers 1356- Nicholle and Turner
- The Tower of London- Lapper and Parnell
- The Tower of London- A L Rowse
- Sir John Hawkwood- John Temple Leader
- Medieval Mercenary: Sir John Hawkwood of Essex- Christopher Starr

Other books by Griff Hosker

If you enjoyed reading this book, then why not read another one by the author?

Ancient History

The Sword of Cartimandua Series
(Germania and Britannia 50 A.D. – 128 A.D.)
Ulpius Felix- Roman Warrior (prequel)
The Sword of Cartimandua
The Horse Warriors
Invasion Caledonia
Roman Retreat
Revolt of the Red Witch
Druid's Gold
Trajan's Hunters
The Last Frontier
Hero of Rome
Roman Hawk
Roman Treachery
Roman Wall
Roman Courage

The Wolf Warrior series
(Britain in the late 6th Century)
Saxon Dawn
Saxon Revenge
Saxon England
Saxon Blood
Saxon Slayer
Saxon Slaughter
Saxon Bane
Saxon Fall: Rise of the Warlord

Legacy

Saxon Throne
Saxon Sword

Medieval History

The Dragon Heart Series
Viking Slave *
Viking Warrior *
Viking Jarl *
Viking Kingdom *
Viking Wolf *
Viking War*
Viking Sword
Viking Wrath
Viking Raid
Viking Legend
Viking Vengeance
Viking Dragon
Viking Treasure
Viking Enemy
Viking Witch
Viking Blood
Viking Weregeld
Viking Storm
Viking Warband
Viking Shadow
Viking Legacy
Viking Clan
Viking Bravery

The Norman Genesis Series
Hrolf the Viking *
Horseman *
The Battle for a Home *
Revenge of the Franks *
The Land of the Northmen

Legacy

Ragnvald Hrolfsson
Brothers in Blood
Lord of Rouen
Drekar in the Seine
Duke of Normandy
The Duke and the King

Danelaw
(England and Denmark in the 11th Century)
Dragon Sword *
Oathsword *
Bloodsword *
Danish Sword*
The Sword of Cnut

New World Series
Blood on the Blade *
Across the Seas *
The Savage Wilderness *
The Bear and the Wolf *
Erik The Navigator *
Erik's Clan *
The Last Viking*

The Vengeance Trail *

The Conquest Series
(Normandy and England 1050-1100)
Hastings*
Conquest

The Aelfraed Series
(Britain and Byzantium 1050 A.D. - 1085 A.D.)
Housecarl *
Outlaw *
Varangian *

Legacy

The Reconquista Chronicles
Castilian Knight *
El Campeador *
The Lord of Valencia *

The Anarchy Series England 1120-1180
English Knight *
Knight of the Empress *
Northern Knight *
Baron of the North *
Earl *
King Henry's Champion *
The King is Dead *
Warlord of the North*
Enemy at the Gate*
The Fallen Crown*
Warlord's War
Kingmaker
Henry II
Crusader
The Welsh Marches
Irish War
Poisonous Plots
The Princes' Revolt
Earl Marshal
The Perfect Knight

Border Knight 1182-1300
Sword for Hire *
Return of the Knight *
Baron's War *
Magna Carta *
Welsh Wars *

Legacy

Henry III *
The Bloody Border *
Baron's Crusade*
Sentinel of the North*
War in the West*
Debt of Honour
The Blood of the Warlord
The Fettered King
de Montfort's Crown
Ripples of Rebellion

Sir John Hawkwood Series
France and Italy 1339- 1387
Crécy: The Age of the Archer *
Man At Arms *
The White Company *
Leader of Men *
Tuscan Warlord *
Condottiere*
Legacy

Lord Edward's Archer
Lord Edward's Archer *
King in Waiting *
An Archer's Crusade *
Targets of Treachery *
The Great Cause *
Wallace's War *
The Hunt*

Struggle for a Crown
1360- 1485
Blood on the Crown *
To Murder a King *
The Throne *
King Henry IV *

Legacy

The Road to Agincourt *
St Crispin's Day *
The Battle for France *
The Last Knight *
Queen's Knight *
The Knight's Tale

Tales from the Sword I
(Short stories from the Medieval period)

Tudor Warrior series
England and Scotland in the late 15th and early 16th century
Tudor Warrior *
Tudor Spy *
Flodden*

Conquistador
England and America in the 16th Century
Conquistador *
The English Adventurer *

English Mercenary
The 30 Years War and the English Civil War
Horse and Pistol*

Modern History

The Napoleonic Horseman Series
Chasseur à Cheval
Napoleon's Guard
British Light Dragoon
Soldier Spy
1808: The Road to Coruña
Talavera
The Lines of Torres Vedras

Legacy

Bloody Badajoz
The Road to France
Waterloo

The Lucky Jack American Civil War series
Rebel Raiders
Confederate Rangers
The Road to Gettysburg

Soldier of the Queen series
Soldier of the Queen*
Redcoat's Rifle*
Omdurman
Desert War

The British Ace Series
1914
1915 Fokker Scourge
1916 Angels over the Somme
1917 Eagles Fall
1918 We will remember them
From Arctic Snow to Desert Sand
Wings over Persia

Combined Operations series
1940-1945
Commando *
Raider *
Behind Enemy Lines
Dieppe
Toehold in Europe
Sword Beach
Breakout
The Battle for Antwerp
King Tiger
Beyond the Rhine

Legacy

Korea
Korean Winter

Tales from the Sword II
(Short stories from the Modern period)

Books marked thus *, are also available in the audio format.
For more information on all of the books then please visit the author's website at www.griffhosker.com where there is a link to contact him or visit his Facebook page: GriffHosker at Sword Books or follow him on Twitter: @HoskerGriff or Sword (@swordbooksltd)
If you wish to be on the mailing list then contact the author through his website.

Printed in Great Britain
by Amazon